Dear Reader,

Everyone seems to agree that spring is a special time for lovers—and that makes it a perfect time for Silhouette Books to celebrate with a new collection of short fiction by some of your favorite authors.

The title of this volume was inspired by an often quoted line from "Locksley Hall" by Alfred, Lord Tennyson: "In the Spring, a young man's fancy lightly turns to thoughts of love." Well, women of all ages have fancies, too, and when we asked authors Annette Broadrick, Lass Small and Kasey Michaels to create stories that captured those fancies, we got some wonderful results!

Sit back and let these men capture your fancy.... Succumb to spring fever with Silhouette! After all,

Spring has sprung
The sap has riz
We all know where
The cute men iz....

They're right here!

The Editors
Silhouette Books

SPRING
FANCY
COLLECTION 1993

ANNETTE BROADRICK
LASS SMALL
KASEY MICHAELS

Silhouette® Books

Published by Silhouette Books New York
America's Publisher of Contemporary Romance

SILHOUETTE BOOKS
300 E. 42nd St., New York, N.Y. 10017

First Silhouette Books printing March 1993

ISBN: 0-373-48262-0

CONTENTS

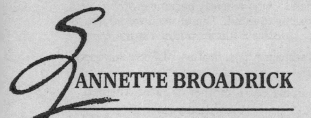

ANNETTE BROADRICK

Surprise, Surprise!

All the time I was writing this story, two friends, who recently became mothers, kept coming to mind. Therefore, I would like to dedicate this springtime story to:

Kathleen Abels, mother of Peter Anthony,
and
Paula Pearl, mother of Jason Michael,
. . . with my love.

Chapter One

Dane Ross studied the ceiling of the mountain cabin from his position in bed, his hands behind his head. Early morning light spilled through a nearby window, the splash of sunshine adding a decorative touch to the minimally furnished room.

After seven days and seven nights spent solely in his own company, Dane's only joy in the moment was the fact that he had two more days to go before he returned to San Francisco and the work he enjoyed.

Today was Saturday. He would go home sometime Monday.

At the moment he could think of nothing better to do with his time than to lie in bed, tracing the steps that had brought him to his present irritating predicament.

The truth of the matter was simple. He felt betrayed. Betrayed by his body and by his personality—his very nature—as well as by the two people closest to him: his best friend and his efficient administrative assistant. He felt like the victim of a conspiracy, even if the plot was for his own good...or so he had been told. After a week on his own, he still wasn't entirely convinced the enforced rest had been necessary. Reluctantly he might admit that there could be some basis of truth to their concerns, although he felt the arguments made were overstated.

So maybe he *was* a workaholic. There were much worse things in life, weren't there? He could be enamored of alcohol or drugs. Those were much worse addictions, weren't they?

What was wrong with his enjoying what he did to make a living?

The fact that he had presented this justification to his friend, Eric, a few weeks ago did not mean that it held any less truth today. Unfortunately his argument had carried no weight with Eric.

As a result of his having given in to the barrage of pressure, he had been isolated—no, jailed would be a better word for how he felt—in a cabin located somewhere in the Sierra Madre Mountain range a few hours' drive from everything of importance in his life: namely, his business.

Dane knew that he could have ignored Eric. No one had held a gun to his head, after all. He supposed that part of his problem was the fact that Dane respected Eric's opinion. Dane's respect was based on Eric's intelligence as well as his extensive knowledge of his chosen profession: medicine. Simply put,

Dane was at the cabin because he couldn't ignore Eric's stern warnings.

He replayed the scene in his mind....

"You're headed for a breakdown, buddy, if you don't get away for a vacation, and soon."

Dane and Eric, or Dr. J. Eric Lehman, as he was known to his colleagues and patients, had just finished a tough game of racquetball. They stood beneath the sharp spray of adjoining showers, allowing their sweat-soaked bodies to receive a well-earned wet massage.

"C'mon, Eric, just because I let you win once, you have me on the endangered species list. I was off my game today, that's all."

"*Let* me win? Ha! Besides, I'm talking about more than today, Dane. I've been watching the signs for months now. The years of constantly pushing yourself are rapidly catching up with you. Remember the old saying, 'The man who works for himself has a slave driver for a boss.'"

"I never heard such a saying. You're just making it up."

"Doesn't matter. Ask any self-employed person and you won't get an argument. You've been pushing yourself for so long that your routine feels natural to you. I doubt that you can visualize another way of life. Let's face it, Dane. Ross Enterprises *is* your life. Can't you see that you haven't taken any time to enjoy the fruits of your labor?''

''Nonsense. Look at all the traveling I do. I've been to Hawaii, Dallas, Chicago and New York all in the past six weeks. I'd call that getting away from things, wouldn't you?''

''Who are you kidding? You caught the late-night flights and on each trip put in eighteen-hour days after you arrived. Not once did you stop long enough to enjoy the local sights and just relax.''

Dane shook his head in disgust. ''How do you know? Have you taken to bugging my briefcase?''

He turned off the shower, grabbed a towel, and vigorously dried himself off. The strenuous workout had made him feel good, almost as good as a full night's sleep. Glancing at the wall clock, he was pleased to see he still had time enough for a quick lunch with Eric before his next appointment. He would—

''Kathryn told me,'' Eric said, opening the locker beside Dane's for his clothes.

Dane glanced around at Eric, puzzled by his comment. Caught up in his mental review of his afternoon schedule, he had already forgotten their present conversation. ''Who?''

''Kathryn Collier, your assistant,'' Eric prompted with precise diction, his voice wry.

Dane quickly recalled their previous discussion. "Oh! So Collier is your spy, is she?" He grinned. "I should have known she would enlist your help. She obviously doesn't feel she's making enough progress in her campaign to get me to slow down."

"She cares about you, Dane. More than you deserve, I'm sure."

"Is she complaining about her tyrant of a boss? Maybe I need to have a talk with her." They both knew he was kidding. Dane was the first to admit that Kathryn was invaluable to the smooth running of the company's operation.

Dane sat down to put on his socks and shoes.

"It's not a joke, Dane."

Dane glanced up and saw the serious expression on his friend's face. He was quiet for a moment before saying, "All right, so I'm making light of your concern," he admitted. "But as you said, I've found my work habits to be amazingly productive. Why should I want to change them?"

"To save your life, perhaps? You've got to give yourself a break. Spend some time without the phone and fax machine, without meetings over every meal you eat, without board meetings that stretch on into eternity. You haven't a clue how to relax. I bet you sleep with your jaw clenched."

"Don't tell me you've spoken to my dentist, as well!" Dane replied, grinning.

The men walked out of the private athletic club and headed toward a nearby restaurant.

"This is serious, Dane."

Dane didn't respond because he could think of nothing more to say. He knew that Eric spoke the truth. Dane had not admitted to anyone the number of headaches that had begun to plague him, their frequency, nor their increasing intensity. Despite his attempts to ignore them, they had not gone away.

After the two men were seated and had given their orders to the waiter, Dane finally said, "You're right, as usual, Doctor. So what do you prescribe?"

As though waiting for that question, Eric said, "I own a cabin only a few hours away from the Bay area, but the place could be halfway around the world from here, the mountains are so different. It has all the amenities. There's even a phone for emergencies. I want you to let me drive you up there. My professional advice is that you stay for two weeks without any business contact whatsoever. I'd like—"

"Two weeks! Don't be ridiculous. A weekend, maybe. I can't just walk away from the company like that. Why, the—"

"Are you such a poor C.E.O. that you can't delegate for a couple of weeks? Do you actually believe the place will fall into ruin if you aren't putting in those horrendous hours?"

Dane wanted to yell "Yes!" at the man seated across from him, but they both would know he was lying. The truth was that Dane had made a comfortable niche for himself in life. He felt challenged by his daily routine. He was forever being tested in the familiar arena of the business world and enjoyed knowing he could hold his own with the toughest adversaries.

The prospect of changing his routine, even temporarily, made him uncomfortable. What would he do up there all day? He didn't have any hobbies. He had no special interests outside of his profession. Dane had never understood the need for a vacation. He enjoyed what he did and had no desire to get away.

"A week," he finally muttered. "I'll go for a week, but no longer."

"When?" Eric's question bounced back as quickly as a racquet ball after a tough serve.

When? Dane asked himself, rubbing his temple thoughtfully. "Well, let's see. I couldn't go this month, my agenda is too heavy. Maybe by next month, if I rearrange—"

"Not good enough." Eric leaned back, allowing the waiter to place his lunch before him. After the waiter served Dane and left, Eric said, "You will always find an excuse to postpone taking time for yourself. I know you too well."

Dane took a bite of his sandwich and carefully chewed and swallowed before he answered. "Of course I'll go. I said I would, didn't I? It's just a matter of when, that's all."

"April is a beautiful time to be up in the mountains. Spring thaw has set in. The mountain meadows are blooming. You'll find it very peaceful this time of year."

"Peaceful, huh? What if I'm not looking for peaceful?"

"Don't worry. It will grow on you...."

In the end, Eric had negotiated a ten-day stay. Today would begin Dane's eighth day and as far as he was concerned, Dr. J. Eric Lehman had been wrong about Dane growing to enjoy being marooned in a lonely mountain cabin. Dane had been marking the days off the calendar much like a convict awaiting his release.

The problem was, he had so little with which to occupy his time. He had read a few of the books Eric had on the shelves, but Dane wasn't much interested in fiction. He had split several stacks of wood, taken long walks, and prepared some simple meals by opening cans and microwaving frozen dinners.

There was no television and the only clear radio station gave five-minute updates on the news once an hour, the rest of the time clogging the airwaves with dissonant music.

He had been unable to sleep the first two nights because of the lack of sounds—city sounds. By the third night, he had dropped off to sleep with no problem out of sheer, unadulterated boredom.

How did people stand to take vacations? Would he have enjoyed himself if he had invited company along? Perhaps, but somehow he doubted it. His female acquaintances would have been appalled by the suggestion. Not that he had many female friends from which to choose. The ones he knew graced his arm during important social functions, but for the most part went their own way once they discovered he was not interested in investing his time in developing a long-term relationship.

He didn't have time for entanglements.

As far as Dane was concerned, he also didn't have time to be wasting in a cabin in the mountains, either, but somehow he had been talked into the idea.

Never again.

He sat up on the side of the bed and stretched. Dane admitted to himself that he felt more rested than he had in years, which wasn't so surprising. After a few days of doing nothing more strenuous than chopping wood and hiking around the countryside, he found himself dozing off within minutes after he sat down to rest. His body had obviously taken command over his brain, which had overdosed on mountain air days before and shut down in rebellion.

In the bathroom he stared at himself in the mirror, rubbing his jaw. He had shaved each morning out of habit. Now he stared at his image, as though for the first time. Gray eyes stared back at him. He turned his head slightly, eyeing the strands of silver among his thick, black hair. Once again he touched his jawline, hearing the rasp of his twenty-four-hour beard. The lines around his mouth had eased somewhat.

He leaned a little closer, inspecting his eyes. Yes, he could see some changes. The strain lines were gone from around his eyes. He couldn't remember the last time he'd looked so relaxed and rested. No doubt Eric would be pleased with the results of his badgering.

Dane turned away, deciding not to shave. After all, he was on vacation. He might as well find some kind of enjoyment during these last few days.

He returned to the bedroom in a better mood. He pulled on a pair of jeans he should have thrown out a couple of years ago. The cabin had grown chilled overnight, which meant the fire in the other room had probably gone out. He shrugged into a plaid flannel shirt that he had found hanging in the closet and went into the main room that doubled as the living and dining rooms as well as kitchen and den.

First things first. He would start the coffee, then rebuild the fire. Halfway across the room he paused ... listening. Had he heard something at the front door or was his imagination playing tricks on him?

He thought he heard a cat mewing. What would a cat be doing up there? He had no neighbors. He had not seen or heard anyone since his arrival.

Dane strode across the room, unlatched the door and opened it. He stared down in bewilderment. There was no cat to be seen. Instead, two infants in an oversize basket were on the small front porch. They stared up at him without blinking.

Dane closed his eyes in an effort to clear the image of the impossible from his obviously hallucinating mind. As though to prove the reality of their existence, one of the babies let out a cry, its arms flailing, and Dane recognized the sound he had heard earlier.

He stepped out of the cabin and knelt beside the basket. "How in the world did you two get here?"

He hadn't heard anyone. There had been no sound of a car, nor had anyone knocked on the door. Bewildered, and still having difficulty adjusting to the reality of this new situation, Dane glanced around the clearing, absently seeking either an explanation or assistance.

As soon as he spoke, the infant who had cried out stared up at him with a wide blue-eyed gaze. The other one lay quietly, its lashes drooping. It yawned, closing its eyes.

Dane panicked. What was he going to do? He didn't know the first thing about babies. In a world filled with people who had some rudimentary skills in looking after small charges, why had fate picked him to find a pair of abandoned infants on his doorstep?

Obviously he needed to get them some help, but how? He had no transportation. He had no way of—

Wait a minute. He would call Collier. She was a woman; she would know what to do. With an overwhelming sense of relief from some nameless horror, Dane went back into the cabin to use the phone. Out of habit he started to close the door behind him when he remembered his visitors. He glanced down at the basket. He couldn't let the babies stay out in the brisk morning mountain air. Even he knew that much. He leaned down, grabbed the two handles of the basket and lifted his unexpected guests, carrying them inside.

The one who was awake never took its eyes off him.

"I wish you wouldn't look at me like that," he explained a little tersely. "I didn't do this to you, you know. I don't have a clue how to take care of you two.''

He spotted a pink sheet of paper folded and stuck along the side of the basket. As soon as he had placed the basket on the table near the fireplace, he reached for the note that hopefully held some kind of an explanation.

He read the neatly penned note with dismay, experiencing a sinking sensation in the pit of his stomach.

I've tried, but I can't take care of my babies. I love them too much to keep them. Please find them a good home.

Melinda and Melanie are two months old.

The note was unsigned.

Dane caught himself reading the note several times in the hope of discovering some pertinent information he might have overlooked during his hasty first reading. The note told him nothing. Who was this woman? Where had she come from and how had she managed to leave the babies without his hearing her? There was no sign of civilization in the vicinity—no other homes, no villages. Nothing.

Melinda—or was it Melanie?—ran out of patience and let out another cry, this time causing her sister to stir.

Dane reached the phone in three long strides. Collier was going to have to help him.

The phone rang at the other end several times before he heard someone pick it up. When no one answered right away, Dane said, "Collier? Is that you? This is Dane, and I—"

A sleepy voice responded, "I'm sorry, but Mr. Ross is out of the city at the moment. If you would like for him to call you, please—"

"Kathryn! Wake up, will you? This is Dane, and I need your help." He glanced over his shoulder as if half expecting the babies to have metamorphosed into monsters hissing fire.

There was a long pause before he heard Kathryn yawn and ask, "Dane? Is that you?"

"Of course it's me! How many people call you saying they're me!"

"But you aren't supposed to be calling. Eric made it very clear that—"

"I don't give a da—I don't care what Eric said, this is an emergency. I need you!"

He closed his eyes in frustration and embarrassment. He hadn't meant that in quite the way it came across. After all, their relationship was strictly professional. Somehow his plea seemed almost intimate.

Kathryn, sounding more alert, asked, "What's wrong?"

"I just found two-month-old twins on my front porch." His voice held a mixture of panic, frustration and indignation.

Waves of infectious laughter swept over the line. Dane stared at the phone in disbelief. Nothing he had said was in the slightest way amusing.

"Look, Collier, this is not a joking matter. I need you to—"

"Come on, Dane. I knew you would probably try some scheme in an effort to get me to come rescue you, but you only have two more days. I had no idea you had such a creative imagination! Twins, huh?"

He struggled to control his outrage at her cavalier attitude toward a very serious problem. He had to make her understand the urgency of the situation before she hung up on him.

In careful tones, he said, "Yes. I found twins on my doorstep. According to the note I found with them, their names are Melinda and Melanie."

Kathryn started laughing again, changed the laugh to a cough, cleared her throat, and said, "All right. I'll bite." Her obvious amusement bubbled through her questions. "What are they? Deer, squirrels, rabbits? Exactly what did you find on your front step this morning?"

"Infant baby girls," he said through clenched teeth.

After a brief pause, Kathryn breathed, "My God . . . you're serious, aren't you?"

As though in answer, one of the babies let out a wail and was quickly joined by the other one. No one had taught them pitch or harmony. The discordant sounds shivered through him like the scrape of chalk across a blackboard.

"You've got to help me!" he yelled over the noise.

"Me? What do you want from me?"

"I want you to come up here, that's what. The supplies left with them are sparse. We've got to find out who they belong to, we've got to notify the police or something. I need your help."

Melinda and Melanie were increasing the volume of their protest with every breath they took.

"Are they yours?" she asked.

Once again he glared at the phone as though holding the instrument responsible for what he was hearing. "Of course not! I've never seen them before in my life."

"That doesn't mean they aren't yours. Why else would their mother leave them with you?"

"How should I know! She didn't bother to explain that part in her note." He shoved his hand through his hair and tried to regain some semblance of calm, rational thinking. "Listen, Kathryn. Please get some formula, some disposable diapers and whatever else you think two-month-old babies might need, and get up here as soon as you can, will you? I can't handle this on my own.''

"I don't know if I could find the place, Dane. I've heard Eric mention it a few times but have no idea how to get there. Can you give me directions?''

He squeezed his eyes shut in an effort to recall the trip he had made with Eric last week. After a moment, he shook his head in defeat.

"No, darn it, I can't. Eric drove and it was after dark. I didn't pay that much attention.'' He could feel the beginnings of a headache coming on. "Call Eric and have him give you directions. Either that, or send him up here. I'm counting on you to get me some help.'' Dane could hear the panic in his voice while behind him the crying symphony continued.

"I'll do what I can,'' she replied. He could hear the doubt in her voice and his heart sank.

"Please, Kathryn,'' he pleaded. "You've got to help me.''

"Are you sure this is Dane Ross?''

"Damn it, Collier, you—''

"Yep, now I recognize you. Guess I've never heard you plead before. I'll see what I can do about rounding up Eric or a St. Bernard. Somebody will rescue you as soon as possible.''

He hung up the phone, muttering. Kathryn did not understand the seriousness of his predicament.

He returned to the crying infants. "Okay, okay, you made your point. Something's wrong, I can tell." The babies stopped crying at the first sound of his voice. Gingerly he picked up the loudest one, who he decided to call Melinda. As soon as he slid his hand beneath her bottom he understood her dilemma . . . as well as his own.

Two-month-old babies are not housebroken.

He had always known that on some intellectual level, but now was faced with the damp evidence.

"All right, all right," he muttered, looking into the basket for diapers. There were only a few disposable ones there, along with a couple of pajama-looking things.

Balancing the baby on one arm, he gathered the dry clothing with his other hand and placed the baby on the sofa. The other twin, left alone in the basket, began to whimper.

"I'm not deserting you," he called to her with exasperation. "I can only do one thing at a time, ladies." He began to unsnap Melinda's sleepers. She waved her arms and kicked her feet while she blew bubbles at him.

"Swell. Now you want to entertain me." She looked so tiny and so fragile, he was afraid to bend her arms for fear they might break. And how was he supposed to slip her legs out of the damp clothing without hurting her? He shook his head. How come changing a baby looked so simple in the movies and on television commercials?

After several anxiety-filled moments, he managed to get Melinda's damp clothes off. Now came the puzzling part: how to get the diaper strategically around her? The job wouldn't be quite so laborious if she'd just stay still. He'd no sooner get one side fastened and she would give a sudden froglike kick that would send the diaper flying. For some inexplicable reason, she was delighted with herself, chuckling and energetically waving her arms.

By the time he finally managed to get a dry diaper and pajamas on her, Dane felt as if he'd successfully wrestled a three-hundred-pound tiger.

Melanie, in the meantime, continued to cry. No doubt she was as wet as her sister.

He could have done without the reminder.

Dane scooped Melinda up and held her against his chest. "You two had better hope that somebody shows up here soon. Otherwise we're all in big trouble."

Chapter Two

Because of the severe downpour, Kathryn almost missed the road sign in time to turn. What was she doing out in this monsoonlike weather on her day off? she asked herself.

The answer came promptly. *Dane Ross needed her.* Maybe she should seriously consider therapy. Wasn't there supposed to be a limit to what a person would agree to do for someone?

Her joyously anticipated plans for the day had been simple. She had intended to sleep until noon, then spend the rest of the day doing as little as possible. Instead she had been up at an obscenely early hour for a day off, mindlessly responding to Dane's distress signals.

She had spent more than two hours in an attempt to reach Eric Lehman. She finally reached his answering service and was told he was not on call and would be unavailable for the weekend. Using skills she had honed over the past eight years, Kathryn eventually managed to contact one of Eric's staff members who knew the location and could give directions to the cabin in the mountains.

After obtaining the necessary instructions, she rushed to a grocery store for the requested supplies only to be overwhelmed by the aisle of baby products. She had never paid any attention to this aisle in the past, blithely sailing by with her list of groceries for a single, health-conscious adult.

She had stared in dismay, taken a deep breath and had proceeded to scrutinize every item offered. She had found the baby formula, bottle liners, extra nipples. She had decided to purchase extra bottles to be on the safe side. Amazed at the variety of diapers offered, she had tried to remember what Dane had told her. Babies. Young? Yes! Two-month-old girls.

After carefully reading all the labels, she'd found baby girl diapers from newborn to three months in age.

Feeling as though she had successfully negotiated a complex contract, Kathryn had continued down the row of products specifically designed for infants. By the time she'd left the supermarket, she had bought enough supplies to fill the back seat of her small sports car.

Now all she had to do was find the cabin before the way became impassable, an event that became more probable as she followed the twisting, climbing road while in the midst of a sudden storm that had developed since she'd left the Bay area.

The windshield wipers made a steady clacking sound as they swung back and forth in front of her. Once more Kathryn questioned her sanity and her continued illogical devotion to the man she had worked with for eight years.

She would never forget her nervousness the day he'd interviewed her. She smiled at her memories of the greener-than-grass, newly graduated young woman she had been, literally shaking at the thought of meeting Dane Ross, President and C.E.O. of Ross Enterprises, an environmentally sound and progressive property development company he had begun twelve years before.

Kathryn hadn't understood why the president himself was interviewing her. The personnel manager had not told her that Dane had decided to hire an assistant to help him wade through the mounds of paperwork necessary to efficiently guide the rapidly growing company to financial success. So, in her naiveté, Kathryn had thought the president personally screened every applicant who sought a position at his company.

He'd looked nothing like the man she had imagined the president to be. Somehow she'd pictured aging dignity with silver hair. Instead she'd found a man in his prime, built like a football player, who looked as if he would be as comfortable operating a crane or a bulldozer as he would be taking command of a directors' meeting or negotiating a substantial land purchase.

Later she'd discovered that at the time he'd hired her, Dane was thirty-two years old, ten years her senior.

He had begun his own company twelve years before, doing most of the work himself in an effort to put himself through college. Even then he'd had decided opinions on how construction sites should be cleared, the type of buildings that should be erected, and what needed to be done to protect the environment along the California coast.

Since his strong views on the subject of cleaning up and improving the ecological balance of the area had been one of the biggest reasons Kathryn had wanted to work for his company, she'd had no hesitancy in answering his questions regarding the subject, even adding her rather strong opinions to the conversation from time to time.

When the buzzer on his desk had interrupted them and his secretary announced the arrival of his next appointment, Kathryn felt that she had successfully handled herself with Dane Ross. What she hadn't expected was for him to hang up the phone and say, "All right, Ms. Collier. I think we could work together quite well. I recognize that you don't have actual experience as an administrative assistant, but with your background, distinguished grades and ob-

vious interest in the field, I believe you could contribute a great deal to the company.''

''You mean, you're offering me a position?''

''Yes. As my assistant.''

She remembered clutching her purse in a reflexive
grip. ''You mean, I'll be working with *you?*''

He'd lifted his brows, his gray eyes changing color
from a smoky hue to cold steel. ''Do you have a
problem with that?''

''Uh, no, sir, of course not. I just didn't realize
there was such a position open and available.''

''There wasn't. Now there is, and I want you to fill
it. When can you start?''

She had quickly learned that making rapid-fire
decisions—and generally being right—was one of
Dane Ross's strong character traits.

Over the years, she came to understand his thinking processes and was able to anticipate many of his
orders. Dane Ross demanded a great deal from others because he expected the same from himself. He
never asked another person to do something he
wouldn't do. Dane was generally the first person at
work in the morning and the last one to leave in the
evening . . . which was exactly the reason he was marooned on a mountaintop under doctor's orders.

Having him out of the office this past week had
seemed strange. Whenever Dane traveled on business, Kathryn accompanied him. The office func-

tioned efficiently, left in the capable hands of men and women carefully chosen for their particular skills.

Kathryn had done what she could this past week to deal with the various emergencies that invariably cropped up in a large corporation. Thankfully there had been no major crises.

She had her own work, of course, and she had handled her duties with a minimum of fuss, but the energy and the excitement of her job had left when Dane did. That knowledge had shaken her considerably. She had been forced to accept what she had been blindly denying for years: a good part of the reason she loved her job was because she was in love with her boss.

She found it humiliating to acknowledge, finally, the cliché she was living. Never one to date much prior to accepting the position with Ross Enterprises, once hired, Kathryn had immediately immersed herself in her work in an effort to prove to Dane he had made the right choice.

By the time she finished work each night, Kathryn could think of nothing more enticing than to have a quiet dinner at home, take a hot bath and curl up with a good book. Her social life consisted of meeting school chums from time to time, attending symphonies, an occasional play, or an even more occasional movie.

The years had slipped past while she was busy establishing her career. She had recently turned thirty without giving the matter much thought.

She could still remember her alarm when Eric first broached the subject of Dane's health to her. In her eyes, Dane was indefatigable. To think that something might happen to him had shocked her, once again bringing her feelings for him into sharper focus.

Now Dane had called her and—despite rain, a substance suspiciously like sleet, and predictions of possible snow in the upper elevations—Kathryn was determined to respond.

With that kind of dedication, she probably should have applied for work at the postal department.

Renewing her grip on the steering wheel, Kathryn peered through the misty rain and prayed the cabin wasn't much farther.

"C'mon, Collier," Dane muttered under his breath. "I need some help here."

Dane had managed to give each of the babies a bottle, carefully following the instructions on the label of the can of formula. From their greedy and slurping response, Melinda and Melanie had known without prompting what to do with the proffered nourishment.

Now they needed changing. Again. "Ladies, please. How about using some control here? I'm having trouble keeping up and I'm working as fast as I can."

Diaper changing would be a snap if the babies would lie still. Unfortunately, the more vocal they became, the harder they kicked and waved their arms. He thought Melanie's diaper change had been completed when she gave a sudden athletic roll, causing him to lose his grip on the diaper so that he had to start all over.

"Young lady! We're going to have to discuss your lack of manners. Please pay attention. When I am trying to make you comfortable, the very least you can do is lie still. Could we come to an agreement on this point of our relationship?"

Dane wondered how much longer the supply of diapers would last. He didn't know what he would do once they were gone.

The welcome sound of a vehicle coming up the steep grade that led to the cabin gave him renewed hope that help was on the way. He hurriedly secured Melanie's diaper and placed her inside the basket, then he headed for the front door.

Dane discovered when he stepped outside the cabin that the early morning sunshine had turned into a hard-driving rain mixed with slushy sleet. For the past few hours he had been too busy to notice the change in the weather.

He peered through the heavy rain toward the narrow roadway that led to the clearing in front of the cabin. He felt like cheering when he saw Kathryn's car. As soon as she stopped in front of the steps, Dane opened her car door.

"Thank God you're here! They're almost out of diapers, they seem to be hungry every two hours and—" Dane stopped in mid-speech and midstep, startled by the appearance of the woman getting out of the car.

He had never paid much attention to Kathryn's appearance before. She dressed with dignity, never calling attention to herself. He had grown accustomed to seeing her impeccably groomed in tailored suits and blouses.

The woman stepping out of the car wore a vibrantly red jumpsuit that displayed a trim waist, gently curving hips and long, shapely legs. Her dark hair—which she had always worn in a tidy chignon—fell in waves around her face and shoulders.

The unexpected change in her appearance startled him and he just stood there, staring at her transformation. Meanwhile, Kathryn leaned into the back seat of her car, displaying a view of her curvaceous backside.

"Here," she said, thrusting two full grocery bags into his arms. "I can get the rest."

Bemused, Dane turned absently and reentered the cabin.

Kathryn soon followed him, her arms full. She placed the bags on the floor, closed the door and immediately went over to inspect the contents of the oversized basket.

"Why, there you are! Aren't you something?" She leaned over and touched a waving arm, and was rewarded by having her finger grasped by a diminutive hand. Her delighted smile made Dane, watching nearby, catch his breath.

She was beautiful. Why hadn't he ever noticed? Her sea-green eyes sparkled when she glanced around at him. "What did you say their names are?"

"Melinda and Melanie," he replied hoarsely. "I don't know which is which. Guess it doesn't matter at this age."

"Well, you're beauties, both of you. Yes, you are," she said in a soothing voice.

"I, uh—I'm really sorry about all of this," he said, suddenly feeling a little embarrassed. "I realize that none of my present situation has anything to do with business, but I didn't know who else to call."

Kathryn straightened and turned to her boss. Now that she had a chance to look at him, she was surprised to see so many changes in a week's time. He looked much more rested, for one thing. For another, the impeccably groomed man in business attire was gone. In his place stood a tousle-haired, rugged-looking male, a little rough around the edges. He wore a pair of decrepit jeans, a plaid flannel shirt and aging sneakers.

Her heart did a quick somersault. Kathryn had never in her life seen anyone looking quite so attractive.

She pushed her hair back from her face, wishing she had taken the time to subdue it before she'd rushed away from home that morning. After washing it the night before, she'd gone to bed without styling it, so that it had dried naturally into detested waves and curls.

"I couldn't get in touch with Eric, I'm afraid," she said. "But one of his staff had been up here before and gave me directions."

"I'm just glad you came. I would have preferred to take on a roomful of angry board members than to deal with those two." He walked over to inspect the supplies. "The main thing we need to do is make certain we can keep them warm, fed and dry, otherwise they'll deafen us."

"I wasn't certain how much to buy. I made a guess, then doubled the amount."

He opened a box of diapers and handed her one. She looked at him in surprise. "What do you want me to do with this?"

He raised his brows. "Change them, of course. I managed the best I could, but I've never done anything like this before."

"And you think I have?"

Her incredulous tone stopped him. He impatiently shoved back the hair that had fallen across his forehead, ignoring the fact that it immediately returned to its former place. "I just thought that— Well, after all, you—" He came to a stumbling halt, suddenly aware of the yawning chasm that lay before him.

She crossed her arms and leaned against the table. "You thought that because I'm a woman, I'm automatically equipped with the knowledge needed for child care?"

Dane wearily massaged the back of his neck and sighed. "I just thought that...perhaps when you were a child...you played with dolls and maybe learned how to dress them...or something along those lines."

"I see. I'm afraid you're out of luck, then. I never liked baby dolls. My favorite doll happened to be a cloth one my grandmother made for me with long yellow yarn for hair."

Dane became distracted from their conversation by his view of Kathryn leaning against the table in her snug jumpsuit. Why had he never noticed how attractive she was? She looked sensational.

"Why haven't you ever worn red to the office?"

They were both startled by his question; its personal nature was out of character for him.

"Being a woman in a predominantly male environment, I've intentionally played down my appearance by wearing colors similar to those worn by the men with whom I associate."

"Oh." He could think of nothing more to say.

He was rescued from his tongue-tied predicament by the babies, who began to protest being ignored. He immediately went over and picked up Melanie and began to pat her awkwardly on the back. Kathryn followed his example by gingerly picking up Melinda.

"I think we should plan to leave as soon as possible," Dane said. "Once we get back to San Francisco, we'll have a better chance to find a place for these two."

Softly patting Melinda's back, Kathryn replied in the same crooning voice she was using to comfort the baby, "Have you looked outside lately?"

He glanced out the window. The storm had increased steadily in intensity since she had arrived.

Kathryn went on. "I had trouble getting up here. My car wasn't built for this kind of weather, I'm afraid. It has a tendency to slide all over the road when the pavement's wet. My heart was in my throat a couple of times on those winding, mountainous roads during the trip up here."

Dane felt like a prisoner whose reprieve had suddenly been revoked. "But we can't stay up here. We need help with the twins." He glanced around the cabin. Somehow the place had seemed to shrink with the addition of another adult and two babies.

"Frankly, I'd prefer to take my chances here where it's warm and dry than to find myself stranded halfway down the mountainside, or worse—going over an embankment!"

"Now there's a cheerful thought," he muttered.

Dane rocked Melanie in his arms until she dozed. He carefully put her to bed, then walked over to the window and peered outside, frowning. The trouble with spring weather was its unpredictability. Mother Nature couldn't seem to make up her mind whether to move toward summer or back toward winter.

He felt as though his life was in the midst of seasonal change, as well. He had been perfectly content with his routine. Since Eric's insistence that he take some time off, everything around him had seemed to change.

His reaction to Kathryn was a good example of his confusion at the moment. Was his sudden awareness of her the result of a week's solitude? Or had he allowed her manner of dress to influence how he perceived her?

Whatever the cause, Dane now found himself curious about her life away from work.

He looked across the cabin at her. She was in the process of placing a sleeping Melinda into bed. Dane was touched by her soft expression.

"You have a soothing effect on them," he said, forgetting to lower his voice. Both babies stirred at the sudden sound and he froze. Kathryn patted each tiny back until the twins settled into a deeper sleep.

When she went over to the kitchen area, he followed, tiptoeing.

In a low voice, she said, "I'm hungry. Do you mind if I make something to eat?"

Consciously keeping his voice soft, Dane replied, "You have no idea how much I would welcome someone else's cooking after spending a week eating my own."

"I'm surprised at the amount of food you have left," she said, opening the door to a well-stocked pantry.

He knew he looked sheepish. "That's because I've been eating the easy-to-prepare stuff first. I'm almost out of TV and microwaveable dinners." A little hesitantly, he asked, "Do you like to cook?"

She began to set out various ingredients. Without looking up from what she was doing, Kathryn replied, "Love to. Cooking has been a hobby of mine for years."

Content to lean against the cabinet out of her way, Dane folded his arms and watched. After a moment, he asked, "Have you always gone by the name Kathryn, or do you have a nickname?"

"My mother always calls me Kathryn. My brother called me Katie the Kid until I was old enough to hit him hard enough each time to make him stop." She cocked her head, remembering. "Dad has always called me Kathie. He's the only one who ever has."

"So you have a brother. Is he older or younger?"

"Alex is four years older."

Kathryn appeared to be comfortable with the silence, but after a few minutes Dane cleared his throat and said, "I've been thinking about the number of years we've worked together and how little I actually know about you."

She glanced up from her food preparation and smiled. "No reason why you should, is there?" she asked lightly.

He flushed. "I guess not."

"What would you like to know about me?"

He thought about that for a moment, then shrugged. "I don't know. I guess the general things you ask when you first meet someone. I know you've been living in the Bay area for years. Do you have family nearby?"

"My mom and dad are retired. They live in Santa Barbara. My brother is based in Atlanta but travels around the world. He works for a cable news service."

Dane straightened. "Alex Collier is your brother?"

"That's right."

"My God. I had no idea. He made quite a name for himself during the Gulf War."

"I know. We were all quite proud of him."

He shook his head in wonderment. "I can't believe it. You never mentioned a word and you must have been worried about his being over there during all of the turmoil."

"Yes, we were. It was a scary time for many people."

Dane nodded and after a moment turned away. He wandered into the bedroom, seeking a moment of solitude in an attempt to adjust to this new insight he had gained about himself.

Was he so absorbed in his business that he could exist side by side on a daily basis with someone for years and not know the simplest things about her?

How could he be so wrapped up in his own goals and desires and so oblivious to others around him? For years he had taken Kathryn's presence for granted, occasionally indulging in self-congratulations on his brilliant choice for an assistant without really seeing her as a person.

He absently smoothed the covers on the bed. He felt like a blind man who had been given sight.

Now his mind was flooded with dozens of questions about Kathryn. Their present marooned circumstances would give him some time to get to know her better.

Dane rubbed his jaw thoughtfully, suddenly reminded of his decision not to shave today. He went into the bathroom to remedy the situation.

When he looked at his mirrored image, he was surprised to see he was smiling.

Chapter Three

Hours later Kathryn sat before the fire and looked around the cozy cabin, amazed to find herself enjoying her day off in a way she hadn't enjoyed herself in years. She felt as though she had been playing house. After preparing a meal that Dane had complimented profusely, helping himself to several servings, she had spent most of the afternoon playing with and looking after the babies.

She still couldn't understand how anyone could have gone off and left them. What would have happened if Dane hadn't been in the cabin? With the weather turning bad so suddenly, they would have had no chance to survive the elements. The thought of what could have happened made her shiver.

She was glad she had bought some warm sleepers for them, even though the new clothes were a little large. They had such a pitifully small supply of shirts and gowns.

She had looked at the note several times, staring at the childlike handwriting as she tried to picture the mother of the twins. Was she a young girl bewildered by life? Had she herself been abandoned? The babies seemed healthy enough, which meant that the mother had done a good job of caring for them while she'd had them. Was she alone? Without finances? Kathryn shook her head, weighing the possibilities.

She stared into the multicolored flames, thinking about how different the day had been from what she had envisioned, even after Dane had contacted her. She had assumed she would arrive at the cabin, load the babies into the car and take them and Dane back to the city. She hadn't thought to pack a change of clothing for herself. Thank goodness she always carried a small cosmetic bag in her purse with a toothbrush, hairbrush and a small supply of makeup.

She didn't relish the idea of having to sleep in the jumpsuit, then wear it tomorrow, as well, but at the moment she didn't have very many options.

What if the weather didn't clear by morning? She had no way of knowing how long she would be isolated on top of a mountain with only Dane Ross and two babies for company. She smiled to herself, thinking about Dane and how quickly he had grown accustomed to handling the infants. He probably hadn't given his progress much thought as he fed, powdered and diapered his charges, even remembering to keep his deep voice soft enough not to startle them whenever he spoke.

If his board of directors could only see him now! She wasn't certain why she found the situation so amusing, but she did. No matter what project Dane tackled, he focused his wholehearted attention to it and mastered it.

Would he be the same kind of husband?

She blinked, startled out of her reverie. Now where had that last thought come from?

"Is something the matter?" Dane asked. He sat on the other side of the fireplace in a matching chair to hers. She thought he had been absorbed in the book he was reading and was embarrassed to discover that he must have been watching her.

"Why do you ask?" She forced herself to meet his gaze calmly.

"I've never before realized what an expressive face you have. You seemed to be startled just now. I suppose I was curious about what had provoked such a look."

She could feel her cheeks heating. "Oh, I, uh—I couldn't help but compare the way I usually spend my weekends to the way this one is going." Now that was thinking fast on her feet. She felt pleased with her response.

"How do you usually spend your weekends?"

"Oh, you know, doing the usual weekly chores like everyone else."

"Such as?"

"Cleaning my condo, doing the grocery shopping, taking clothes to and from the cleaner, making certain my washable clothes are done."

"What about your social life?"

She grinned. "Social life? What's that?"

"Isn't there—I don't mean to pry, but don't you have a—" He shifted his shoulders as though uncomfortable.

"A man in my life?" she offered dryly.

Dane nodded in his most dignified manner.

"Somehow I don't manage to meet too many eligible men. I don't believe in getting involved with people with whom I have business connections. The few others I meet soon become disenchanted with my work schedule, my sudden trips out of town, and the fact that when I do have a free evening, I generally fight not to fall asleep over my dinner salad. Therefore they never seem to hang around for long."

Although she had kept her voice light and gave him a smile to assure him that she had long since accepted her situation, his grave expression did not change. He continued to study her for several minutes before he spoke again.

"I'd never before considered the consequences of the demands I make on your time."

"I've never complained, you know. I enjoy what I do."

He rested his head against the back of the chair. "I can relate to that sentiment. However, as much as I dislike to admit that Eric may have been right, I've spent the past few days reviewing my choices and recognizing how narrow my life seems to be. Now I realize that, because you work with me so closely, by necessity your life has become as narrow as mine.''

Once again Kathryn allowed her gaze to sweep the cabin. ''If you're suggesting that I take a week off to spend here alone, you won't get an argument out of me.''

He looked startled. ''You like it here?''

''I think it's lovely. If I were planning to spend much time here I'd bring the stack of books I've been wanting to read that has steadily grown on my bedside table for months...I'd bring a needlepoint project I started who knows how long ago and never seem to work on... Then I would probably spend the biggest part of my time sleeping!''

''You wouldn't be bored?''

''Not in the slightest.''

''You prefer being alone?''

She eyed him a little warily. ''Not necessarily. If you think I'm going to suggest you leave me up here with these babies while you go for help or something, you can forget it.''

He grinned and Kathryn was once again made aware of how very attractive this man was. ''You have a very devious, suspicious nature, Ms. Collier.''

''Coming from you, I'll consider that to be a compliment,'' she responded wryly.

He laughed, then glanced to see if he had disturbed the sleeping babies. "I've never intimidated you, have I?"

Her brows met briefly in a small frown. "Have you wanted to?"

"Not at all, but sometimes I may come across a little aggressively."

"Sometimes? That's one way of looking at it, I suppose," she said, her tongue lodged firmly in her cheek. "Perhaps I'm used to being around strong-willed, highly motivated males. Both my dad and brother have that same push to succeed that you do, so I grew up with it. It's not a bad trait to have, you know."

"Perhaps not. I had never bothered to see myself as others see me. Now I'm trying to imagine how you've managed to work for me all these years without wanting to strangle me at times."

"My, my, my. Eric is not going to believe what a few days cooped up alone in a cabin can do to a person. You're sounding downright apologetic."

The smile and gaze they exchanged was filled with humor, understanding and something not quite so easily defined. Kathryn shivered.

"Are you cold?"

"Not as long as I'm tucked up here in front of the fire. I'm afraid I didn't dress for the mountains and a sudden spring storm when I left the condo this morning.''

''You certainly didn't expect to stay the night, either, did you?''

She shook her head, suddenly uncomfortable.

''Well, don't worry about it. We'll manage. Eric has extra clothing up here.'' He glanced down at his shirt. ''This is one of his, as a matter of fact. You can have the bedroom and I'll sleep out here on the sofa.''

''Wouldn't it be better if I stayed out here where I can look after the girls?''

He widened his eyes in mock disbelief. ''Is that why you think I asked you to come?''

Now she felt really confused. ''Well, yes, of course it is.'' When he didn't say anything, she added, ''What other reason could you have?'' As soon as she said it, she could have bitten off her tongue. She closed her eyes, not wanting to see his expression.

''I don't think I was doing any thought-out reasoning,'' he said slowly. When she heard the seriousness in his voice, she opened her eyes to watch him. ''I'm discovering that somewhere over the last few years I've gotten into the habit of calling you whenever I need help. I don't think it occurred to me that this time my call had nothing to do with the business.''

''But I came, anyway.''

His eyes remained steady. "Yes, you came anyway," he repeated. "I'm not certain that I understand why."

"Like you, I'm probably a creature of habit. Besides, hearing the panic in your voice and knowing how out of character that was, I couldn't resist rushing up here to witness the situation first-hand."

"I'm very lucky to have you in my life," he murmured.

Kathryn looked away, directing her gaze to the fire. Seeing that the flames were dwindling, she jumped up and began to add more logs, doing anything rather than face him or respond to not only his words but the unaccustomed huskiness she heard in his voice.

What was going on here? she wondered. She could feel the tension building between them, as though another presence had entered the room and joined them. All right. Perhaps they had never been in this type of situation before, but that didn't mean that they had to allow the unusual circumstances to make a difference in their behavior toward each other.

Regardless of her personal feelings for this man, she was not going to do or say anything that might jeopardize their professional relationship. Her career was too important to her.

She heard the babies stirring, making soft sounds stretching and yawning—whispery sounds that tugged at her heart. Kathryn stood and started toward them, only to find Dane ahead of her. He was already picking up Melinda and talking to her.

"Did you enjoy your nap? You look so wide-eyed. Are you ready to investigate the world again? I bet you're hungry, aren't you, sugar? Well, have I got a deal for you. We'll start with a little soup, some salad, a nice entrée and follow up with a sumptuous dessert. Doesn't that sound like a treat?" His voice came out as a soft rumble.

Kathryn smiled at his nonsense.

She picked up Melanie and began to change her. She had already made up bottles for them. Now all she needed to do was warm the milk. She glanced over at Dane. "I must admit that it's easier to have help when it comes to feeding these two. They can be noisy when they're hungry."

"Here you go, little one," Dane said to his tiny charge. "Let's go see about that dinner now." Kathryn watched Dane carry the baby over to the kitchen and start heating the bottles.

Once again they worked companionably side by side to see that Dane's unexpected guests were suitably cared for. By the time the twins had been fed, dressed for the night, and had drifted off to sleep, Kathryn was ready to get some sleep herself.

"Where are those extra clothes you were talking about earlier?" she asked Dane.

He went into the small bedroom and Kathryn followed, watching him search through drawers and the closet. "Why don't you use this flannel shirt to sleep in?" he suggested. "Here's some long socks that should help to keep your legs warm." He eyed the items a little doubtfully. "Not much of a fashion statement, I'll admit, but I think they'll work."

With a murmured thanks, Kathryn took them into the bathroom and closed the door. After a quick shower, she donned her borrowed finery, looked into the mirror and burst out laughing.

The shirt came to her knees, as did the socks. All she needed was a couple of pigtails and she could be a replica of the little girl who had confiscated her dad's old shirts. Instead of braids, she brushed her hair vigorously and left it loose to fall around her shoulders.

She found Dane kneeling in front of the fire, rearranging the logs she had placed there earlier. "Are you sure I can't sleep out here?" she asked, pointing to the sofa that already had a pillow and blankets arranged on it.

He glanced over his shoulder at her, then came to his feet, staring. "You look about ten years old."

She grinned and shrugged. "That's what I thought, but it can't be helped. This will be much more comfortable than my jumpsuit for sleeping."

She glanced at the sofa again. "There's no reason for you to give up your bed, you know."

"You'll sleep better in there," he said, nodding toward the bedroom. "Don't worry about me." He paused, as though unsure of how to word his next suggestion. "You might prefer to leave the door open so that the warmer air can circulate through the bedroom, as well."

"Good idea." She stood there for a moment, feeling awkward. "Well, I guess I'll see you in the morning. If the girls wake up during the night, let me know."

"Are they old enough to sleep through the night?" he asked.

"I haven't a clue. This is all just as new to me as it is to you."

"We really make a pair. Good thing we aren't parents," he said with a crooked grin.

That same mysterious tension seemed to whirl around them at his words.

Unable to think of a reply, Kathryn returned to the bedroom.

"Kathryn?"

She looked around. He still stood by the fire. "Thank you," he said softly. "For everything. I couldn't have handled this without you."

She smiled. "Glad I could help." As she crawled under the covers, Kathryn recognized the truth in her words. She wouldn't have missed this opportunity for the world. Spending the day with Dane in an unbusinesslike setting had made her love and appreciate the man even more. She sighed, closing her eyes, feeling her weariness as her body relaxed against the soft, springy mattress.

She knew that this weekend would linger in her memory for a long time.

Kathryn floated in warmth and comfort, not wanting to move, but someone needed her. Slight sounds, unfamiliar and without identification, pinged lightly against her consciousness, causing her to slowly surface from a very relaxing sleep.

She realized that she was not in her own bed at the same time she identified the sounds that had awakened her. The babies were awake and hungry. Shoving the warm blankets aside, she swung her legs off the bed and sat up.

From her new position she could see into the other room. Dane had also been awakened. He had paused long enough to replenish the fire and was now leaning over the basket, murmuring soothing phrases to the infants.

Kathryn couldn't take her eyes off of him. He had pulled on his jeans but hadn't bothered to do more than zip them. Now he stood barefoot and barechested, the light from the fireplace caressing the muscled planes of his chest, shoulders and arms. She felt a pain in her own chest and realized that she was holding her breath at the sight of Dane Ross in a semi-undressed state.

Now she had to decide whether to intrude or to let him take care of the babies. One of them let out a quavering "wah" very pitifully, which decided her course. The most efficient way to care for the little tykes' needs was for her and Dane to work together. They had learned that during the course of the previous day.

Kathryn slid off the bed and padded into the other room.

"It's all right, darlin'," Dane crooned, "I'm going to feed you, don't worry. But let's get some dry clothes on, okay? We'll get you all warm and cozy, then I'll warm your bottle and..." He forgot what he was saying when he caught a movement out of the corner of his eye and glanced up.

Kathryn was coming toward him from the bedroom. Her hair was tousled and tumbled around her shoulders in charming disarray. She gave him a sleepy smile that did something strange to his insides.

"Need some help?" she whispered.

Trying to wipe away the alluring image she made, Dane looked down at the squirming infant in front of him. "Maybe you could heat their bottles," he suggested, his voice sounding a little ragged.

Without another word, she went into the kitchen area.

Dane reached for the other baby and changed her. By the time Kathryn returned with their warmed meals, the twins were more than ready to eat. Dane and Kathryn each took one of the babies and a bottle, then sat down in front of the fireplace.

At first the only sounds in the cabin were the whuffling, sucking, air-gasping noises of the two hungry babies as they greedily attacked their nourishment. Dane glanced up and shared a smile with Kathryn at the girls' enthusiasm.

"The survival instinct is strong, isn't it?" he said in a low voice. "It's amazing to me to see these tiny little humans, weighing just a few pounds, fight to survive."

"I've had the same thoughts," she responded softly. "I've never been around a baby before. I had no idea they showed such decided personalities so young. The one you're calling Melinda is very outgoing, quick to let her needs be known, what I would call strong-willed, while Melanie is content to be quiet and let her sister get most of the attention."

Dane lifted his hand slightly, enough to show Kathryn that Melanie had a firm grip on his little finger. "I suppose what surprises me the most is how individualistic they look. I always thought all babies were the same, looked the same, like little blobs of humanity that hadn't completely formed. That isn't true at all, even with these two who are twins. Their expression or something is different. I'm not certain what it is. Another thing that astounds me is that even though they're so tiny, their hands are perfectly formed, even down to the barely visible fingernails.'' He paused, touching the tip of the baby's nose. ''Those long lashes are going to catch a guy's heart someday,'' he added.

Kathryn had a hunch they already had.

Eventually the babies fell asleep, their lips slightly puckered as though they still had the nippled bottle in their mouths. Once the infants were settled back into their bed, Kathryn felt a sudden and inexplicable awkwardness about the moment. It was almost four o'clock in the morning, a strange time for her to be awake. She had no experience with this time other than to sleep through it.

She felt very vulnerable at the moment and with good reason. For the past half hour she had watched Dane through veiled lashes as he fed, patted, then continued to feed his small charge. The baby had looked even more delicate in his large, capable hands and lying against his broad, bare chest. She had yearned to reach out and touch him, to glide her hand across the bare expanse of flesh to where the baby rested her little head. Kathryn had a strong yearning to place her own head on his shoulder. Irrational, maddening thoughts, each one, but recognizing the inappropriateness in no way lessened her desire to experience the feel of his skin beneath her fingertips and cheek.

She took a ragged breath and released it before saying, "Maybe we can get a few more hours of sleep before their internal dinner bells go off again." She tried to keep her voice light but she could hear the huskiness . . . the need . . . just beneath the surface.

The night shed its own enchantment on the moment. Dane moved silently toward her until he stood only inches away, so close she was aware of the heat radiating from his body. She could feel the tension spiraling into a whirling, sensuous haze, binding them together.

"Kathryn?" he whispered, cupping his hand lightly along her cheek, his thumb brushing across the surface.

She sighed, her eyelids heavy with longing. "Yes?" She thought she was responding to his question with another question but wasn't entirely certain. She could just as easily been answering his unspoken one.

Chapter Four

As though magnetized, their bodies drifted closer. She went up on her toes, her hands resting lightly on his chest, as he lowered his head so that their lips could meet.

The swirling energy surrounding them seemed to edge them closer. Kathryn felt perfectly natural sliding her hands around his waist, filling her arms with his presence. Dane engulfed and consumed her full attention. Now that they were in each other's arms, she felt as though she had waited a lifetime for his lips to touch hers. At last she could savor their intimate contact and feel the shimmering arousal deep inside her surfacing in waves of longing to prolong the moment.

His touch, both with his lips and his hands, was so tentative and light that she felt like a fragile figurine that must not be grasped and given rough treatment. She tightened her hold, running her hands along the smooth expanse of his back. She could feel his muscles ripple beneath her touch and heard a slight catch in his breath. She found his sensitive reaction intoxicating.

With a heady sense of purpose she traced the slight indentation of his spine with her finger—from his neck to the top of his jeans—and was rewarded by a low moan.

He increased the pressure of their kiss...but slowly, oh so slowly, as though to give her the opportunity to pull away if she wanted. Instead she opened her mouth beneath his, inviting him to enter.

Dane picked her up and with a lithe stride carried her into the other room to the bed, where the covers were still cast aside. With obvious reluctance he released her, but only long enough to tuck her beneath the covers. Straightening, he unfastened and dropped his jeans on the floor before crawling beneath the inviting cocoon of blankets beside her.

Kathryn eagerly reached for him. She ran her fingers through his hair, cupping his head while she offered him her mouth once more. Dane covered her lips as though he had been long deprived of the pleasure. The difference in their height was no longer a problem now. He could savor and explore at a slow, mind-drugging pace without discomfort to either of them.

Dane teased her with his tongue, his darting exploration causing her to shift restlessly. So lightly did he caress her that her first intimation that he had unbuttoned her shirt was when she felt his fingers cupping and surrounding her breast. She could feel the tip harden in his palm.

When he lowered his head, she arched toward him, enjoying his touch. She felt a rush of pleasure surge through her when his tongue flicked across the top of her breast and his mouth tugged lightly on the quivering peak. She shifted, entwining her legs with his. She could feel his hair-roughened thigh between hers and she tightened her grip slightly, rocking against him in simulated love play.

Her provocative enticement was immediately rewarded and he eased himself between her legs. Aching with desire, she lifted her hips to him in supplication.

With a deliberateness that teased her eagerness, Dane allowed the weight of his body to slowly ease him inside.

The moment stretched as if captured by infinity while she held him, feeling his heart thundering in his chest, hearing his ragged breathing, which matched her own. Even her vivid imagination had failed to anticipate the all-encompassing joy she felt loving Dane. How could she have possibly known such boundless completion without having experienced this moment?

Dane raised his head where he had rested it on the pillow and looked down at her. Deep shadows filled the area, the only light coming from the fireplace in the other room. But there was enough light for her to see his heated gaze. He hid nothing from her in that look. She could see his yearning, his deep desire, his hesitancy and his recognition of the inevitability of what was happening between them.

She smiled up at him, her love for this man welling up within her with a suddenness that shook her body with its intensity. With new understanding of the phrase ''making love'' she recognized that by offering her body to him she could show Dane the unending love she felt for him.

He ignored the strong urge for completion. Instead he paused, holding her tightly, and placed a series of kisses along her cheek and brow and across her jaw, arriving at her mouth, which he took with a sigh.

Their bodies moved together in a slow, rocking motion, each movement triggering yet another strong response.

No longer two separate identities, they became something more, something very special . . . almost magical.

Gradually, inevitably, the pace quickened, their bodies begging for release. Reluctant to have the moment end, they both fought for restraint, fought to prolong the pleasure and excitement. Kathryn bit her lower lip, but she could no longer control the sudden convulsive movements deep inside that seemed to seize him with her contractions, triggering his release.

They clung to each other for long minutes afterward, shaken to their very souls by what they had shared. Eventually sleep claimed them while they were still wrapped in each other's arms.

The strident noise of someone pounding nearby jarred Dane out of a drifting, dreaming slumber. He muttered something, the sound of his own voice waking him.

Where was he? Who was making that racket? Why was his arm numb? He forced himself to open his eyes. Several pieces of knowledge simultaneously flooded his consciousness.

He was in the bedroom of the cabin.

Someone was pounding at the front door.

He was not in bed alone.

He forced his eyes open and discovered Kathryn asleep on his shoulder. Her presence there explained the numbness in his arm. He blinked in an effort to get awake. Kathryn was in bed with him? Why?

Sudden and very explicit images of the previous night swamped him. Dane swore under his breath. What had he done?

The sound of heavy pounding repeated itself. Dane raised his head, glancing toward the other room, and heard a familiar voice.

"Dane? Dane, it's me, Eric. Let me in, will you? It's cold out here."

The sound of his friend's voice brought him completely awake. A bolt of adrenaline shot through him. Eric was here! He had to let him in before he barged inside and found Dane in bed with Kathryn.

Moving carefully, he eased away from Kathryn in an effort not to disturb her, tucking the covers around her shoulders once he had gotten out of bed. He grabbed his jeans, unpleasantly icy after hours on the floor, and tugged them on, fumbling with the zipper in his hurry. Remembering to pull the bedroom door closed behind him, he hurried across the room.

He turned the bolt of the lock and jerked the door open. Keeping his voice low, he said, "If you don't stop making all that noise you're going to wake up the babies!"

Eric had been looking around the clearing. The sound of the lock caught his attention. He had his shoulders hunched against the cold, the collar of his ski jacket turned up and his hands in his pants pockets. His sharp gaze met Dane's, and he grinned, shaking his head.

"Well, aren't you a ray of sunshine this morning! I can see that a week's rest hasn't improved your disposition any."

Waiting until Eric had come inside before he closed the door, Dane asked, "What are you doing here? I thought you were coming up to get me tomorrow?"

Eric raised his brows. "You certainly don't sound like a man who needs rescuing. I must have gotten the wrong message."

Dane, still feeling the effects of his heavy sleep, ran his hand through his hair. "What are you talking about?"

"Your esteemed and long-suffering assistant left an emergency message with my service yesterday morning that you were the unexpected recipient of twins and were screaming for help. As soon as I got back into town and heard the news I came hotfooting it up here, racing to your rescue."

Dane's brain was too sluggish to think up an immediate response.

Eric stretched and yawned. "Man, could I use some coffee. Hope you've got some made." He dropped his arms and walked over to the basket sitting on the table near the fireplace. "So these are your visitors. I figured as much," he said, rearranging one of the blankets without disturbing the occupants.

"You mean, you know who they are?" Dane asked in a whisper, following him over to the table.

Eric sighed and Dane saw the strain that Eric's light manner hadn't managed to camouflage. "Oh, yeah. I know all about them."

Dane turned away and began to make a pot of coffee. "Don't tell me I've inadvertently stumbled onto something unsavory in your personal life, Eric. I'm not certain I'm ready to have all my illusions about you completely dashed and destroyed."

After silently studying the infants for a few minutes and reading the note lying nearby, Eric joined Dane in the small kitchen area.

"Thanks for the vote of confidence, pal. You seem to have a lot of faith in my integrity."

"Well, Kathryn immediately thought the twins were *mine.*"

"Ah, yes. Kathryn. I figured that must be her car outside." He glanced around, saw the makeshift bed on the sofa and said, "I take it she's asleep in the other room."

"I can't imagine how she could sleep through all the noise you were making earlier."

"You must have really been out not to hear me. I was beginning to think I was going to have to break into the place. I gave you the only key I have."

Dane flipped the switch of the coffeepot to brew, then leaned against the counter, folding his arms across his bare chest. "Are you aware that babies get hungry in the middle of the night? We were feeding them at four o'clock this morning." He glanced at his watch. It was a little after seven. "They'll probably be awake before much longer, demanding more food. Gluttonous little creatures, aren't they?"

Eric reached into the cabinet and grabbed two coffee mugs. "So. You really didn't need rescuing after all. I guess I should have called first. It might have saved me a trip up here."

"No, I'm glad you came. I'm way over my head when it comes to nurturing and nourishing the young."

"You seem to be doing all right so far. They appear to be content."

"So what's the scoop? How do you know about them?"

Eric filled each mug with coffee and walked over to one of the chairs in front of the fire. Dane set his cup beside the other chair, then knelt to rebuild the fire. When he was finished, he picked up the shirt lying nearby that he'd worn the day before and pulled it on. It still retained the warmth of the fire and felt good to his chilled body.

Eric waited until Dane sat down and picked up his coffee before he spoke.

"There's a fella that lives about five miles up the road. Raymond is a hunting and fishing guide. He's a loner. Doesn't have much to do with people unless they pay him. His wife left him with an eight-year-old daughter several years back." He nodded to the twins. "Those babies belong to Patty, Raymond's daughter. She came to me when she was ready to give birth, even though delivering babies is not my specialty. I asked her at the time they were born if she wanted to place them for adoption. She isn't married, and the father has long since disappeared. At the time she said no, she wanted to keep them. Obviously, she's changed her mind."

"How can she treat them like unwanted puppies, for God's sake! They're human beings."

"I know. I think she really wanted to try to be a good mother to them, but she's so young. Raymond wouldn't be much help with them although he had agreed that she could continue to live there with him."

"I never heard her bring them. The first thing I knew was when I heard one of them whimpering outside the door."

"She probably brought them along the trail between our places, which is considerably shorter than by road. No doubt when she saw the smoke coming out of the chimney she thought it was me staying here. She probably didn't want to talk to me again. After all, we had already had a full discussion on the subject. No doubt, in her mind, leaving the babies and a note was enough of an explanation."

"Well, it was quite a shock for me, let me tell you."

Eric chuckled. "I can imagine."

"So what do we do now?"

Eric leaned his head back. "I'd like to just sit here and relax with a good cup of coffee for a while and admire the fire, if it's all the same to you. I've had a long, rough week."

Dane grinned. "I didn't mean this very minute. I meant what do we do with Melinda and Melanie?"

"Who?"

"The twins . . . Melinda and Melanie."

"Oh! I must be more tired than I thought I was. For a minute there I was sure you'd switched subjects on me and were talking about a couple of your female friends."

"I was wondering what's going to happen to the babies."

"I'll take them to Social Services, who will have to start the proceedings to make them wards of the court. They'll probably be placed with foster parents until all the paperwork is done. Eventually I hope they will be adopted."

"Together?"

"Perhaps."

"You mean there's a chance they will be split up?"

"There's always that chance, Dane. Social Services does what it can, but not everyone is prepared to take on two babies at once. I'm sure they'll go to good homes, regardless of what happens.''

As though the rumble of voices had finally disturbed them, the babies began to make their little wake-up sounds accompanied by a great deal of squirming and stretching.

Dane was on his feet like a shot, talking to them, soothing them, promising them exotic breakfasts and unimagined pleasures for their newly developed taste buds while he changed them into dry diapers.

Eric watched in stunned wonder at the change in his friend.

''Here. Hold Melinda while I warm their bottles. She's much more impatient than Melanie. I'll be back in a minute.'' He placed the baby in the crook of Eric's arm and hurried over to the stove.

''But—'' was the only protest Eric managed to make before he found himself holding a baby who gazed at him with a disconcertingly wise and mature-looking stare. Before long, Dane returned, thrusting a bottle into Eric's hand. The baby spotted the bottle and immediately made her wants known.

Kathryn woke to the sound of men's voices in the other room. Recognizing her cowardness for what it was, she was glad that she didn't have to face Dane first thing this morning. She wasn't ready for whatever might happen next between them. She wasn't certain she would ever be ready.

Last night—or this morning, rather—had been one of the most unprofessional, the most stupid things she had done in her entire life. How could she have been so caught up in the undeniable pleasures of the moment to have allowed herself to succumb to temptation?

Dane was her employer. Going to bed with her employer was professional suicide. How could she have done such a dumb, irreversible thing?

The worst part, she admitted to herself, was the knowledge that given the chance to relive those hours, she wasn't convinced she wouldn't make the same choice again.

So where did she go from here?

She loved her job. She had already admitted to herself that she loved being a part of Dane's life, enjoyed the opportunity to see him every day, to work alongside of him. She was good at what she did, and she knew it. She and Dane made a strong working team. Now, in one weekend, she had jeopardized everything in her life she treasured.

She slipped out of bed and went into the bathroom. Her dark thoughts had in no way lessened the glow of fulfillment that radiated around her. Anyone looking at her would immediately know that she had been well and truly loved.

She showered and dressed, then spent an inordinate amount of time taming her unruly hair until she had managed to recreate the subdued hairdo that she wore in the office. After smoothing on a minimum of makeup, she mentally braced herself and opened the door between the bedroom and the rest of the cabin.

She couldn't hide her amusement nor the feeling of tenderness that swept over her at the scene before her. The two men were a contrast in color: Eric's blondness complementing Dane's dark good looks. But both men were similar in size . . . big men, making the babies in their arms appear very tiny. All four were engrossed in one another, gazing with solemn scrutiny, totally absorbed.

Thank God Eric had arrived. She liked Eric. She appreciated the depth of the friendship that existed between the two men. She was glad that Eric was a doctor. He could advise them about the care of their little visitors.

More importantly, Kathryn was thankful that Eric was there to provide a buffer between her and Dane. She needed some breathing space before facing Dane alone again.

"Since you're seeing to the girls' breakfast, how would you like me to prepare something for you two?" she asked, leaving the relative haven of the doorway.

Both men looked up at the same time. She avoided looking at Dane, choosing the coward's way out by smiling at Eric.

"Hi, Kathryn. Sorry I wasn't available when you called yesterday. I got here as soon as I could but it doesn't look as though my help was needed. You've done fine with them."

"We seemed to have managed somehow. But I'm sure that Dane is just as relieved as I am to see you."

She forced herself to look at Dane and saw that his expression was carefully masked. She had seen that look many times before in business surroundings. He gave nothing of his thoughts away. He probably made a killing playing poker.

She envied him his ability to disguise his feelings. Despite everything she could do, Kathryn knew her cheeks had flooded with color as soon as their eyes met. How could she forget that only a few hours ago she had been clinging to this man, encouraging him to make love to her? "Did you sleep well?" he asked, his voice modulated in order not to startle the baby in his arms.

She nodded, feeling very unsure of herself. "Quite well, thank you," she replied. Was that her sounding so formal? "And you?" She forced herself to hold his level gaze. He paused, causing her heart to race in anticipation of his answer.

"Well enough," he finally admitted with a lop-sided grin that did strange things to her insides. "That is, until Eric decided to come banging on the door at dawn."

"You know, Dane," Eric drawled, "I didn't expect you to throw yourself around my neck in an exuberant show of gratitude for my dramatic rescue efforts, but damn if I don't feel downright unwanted. I can always leave, you know."

Dane shifted his gaze to his friend. "Not on your life. Not unless you intend to take these babies back with you."

"I should probably take everyone with me," Eric replied, sounding more serious. "I wouldn't recommend the trip out of the mountains for a few days without a four-wheel-drive vehicle."

"But I can't just leave my car here!"

"Sure you can. I'll have someone bring it to you when the weather clears in a day or two."

"Sounds like a workable plan to me," Dane said. "I can always give you a ride to the office until your wheels are returned."

"Oh, but—"

"See?" Eric pointed out. "No problem. Now if you were serious about that meal, I'll certainly take you up on it. I didn't take time to eat before I came charging up the mountain on my trusty steed. My stomach has been protesting vigorously for several hours now.''

Kathryn went to the kitchen and started preparing breakfast. The most important thing for her to do was to get away from the intimacy of the cabin and its inevitable reminder of what had happened the night before. She could deal with her need for transportation later.

Tears filled her eyes. She turned her back to the men and impatiently dashed the moisture away. She would concentrate on getting through the next few hours while she worked on emotionally distancing herself from their recent intimacy. The most sensible course was to forget what happened and to regain a semblance of normality. Making love to Dane wasn't the end of the world, after all.

She just knew that she couldn't afford to allow herself to make the same mistake again.

Chapter Five

Over breakfast Kathryn plied Eric with questions about the babies—including queries about their origin and their future. Since Dane had already gotten most of the answers from Eric earlier, he took pity on Eric's hungry state and fielded most of the questions.

"But how can we just turn them over to strangers like that?" she asked after he had explained. "How do we know they'll understand their personalities and moods?"

With a crooked grin, Dane said, "We were strangers a day ago—" He paused, a dull red blush suddenly appearing along his high cheekbones. "To the babies," he added. He looked down at his plate. "It won't take long for others to get attached to them, as well."

Eric picked up his coffee cup. Before taking a sip, he said, "I'll do what I can to keep tabs on them for you, if you'd like."

"Oh, could you? I'd like that," Kathryn replied. "Maybe I could visit them once in a while."

"I can't make any promises, you understand." Eric glanced at his watch and frowned. "I hate to break this up, people, but we need to get on the road. We've had a brief lull in the weather, but more moisture is supposed to move in. That's another reason I decided to come up as quickly as I could."

With three of them helping, they rapidly straight-ened the cabin, cleaned and stored the dishes, thor-oughly doused the fire and loaded the car.

Kathryn rode in the back seat so that she could keep an eye on the twins, while Eric drove and Dane sat up front with him. She was pleased to be sitting directly behind Dane, out of his line of vision while still able to gaze at him without fear of discovery.

She listened to the men's conversation without feeling a need to contribute.

Eric said, "I have to say that, even with getting up at all hours to care for the twins, you seem to be much more relaxed and rested than you were a week ago, Dane." He glanced over his shoulder. "What do you think, Kathryn? Do you think the vacation helped him?"

"Yes, I do," was all she could think to say.

Dane turned his head toward Eric so that she could see his profile. "All right. So you want me to tell you that your idea worked. Okay. I'll admit it... I *did* need to get away. It took me a couple of days and nights to be able to sleep for any length of time. Then all I seemed to do *was* sleep. Other than that, I chopped wood and took a few walks. Guess I didn't realize how tired I was until I was forced to slow down.''

''That happens to a lot of people. We get on a treadmill without being aware of it until we fall off, reeling, wondering what hit us.'' Eric smiled. ''Did you learn anything?''

''Yeah,'' Dane drawled, and Kathryn froze at the amusement in his voice. When she realized he wasn't saying anything personal, she began to relax once again. ''I do hereby vow to adjust my work schedule so that I have some built-in time away from the office on a regular basis. Not a week at a time, of course, but a day here and there.''

''That's a start, anyway.''

The men lapsed into silence and watched the road and scenery. Kathryn forced herself to relax. She was being silly, tensing every time she thought Dane might say something about them. Why should he? He was a grown man. These things probably happened to him on a regular basis. There was no need for her to read more into his behavior than what had actually happened. Their actions were based on the mood of the moment. By now he had probably forgotten all about those few hours they had spent together.

Wasn't that what she wanted? To go on as if nothing had happened?

Of course it was. The entire weekend had been strange and unexpected, that's all. Once she returned home she would be fine. Everything would be back to normal.

When they crossed the Bay bridge she gave Eric directions to her home. As soon as they arrived, Dane got out and opened the car door for her.

"Thanks," she said, hearing her breathlessness and hoping he hadn't noticed. "Guess I'll see you in the morning?" She forced herself to look up at him, then wished she hadn't. The intimacy of the heated look he gave her immediately recalled some very erotic memories, effectively destroying her hard-earned peace of mind.

He had forgotten nothing.

His voice sounded casual, very much at odds with the lingering look in his eyes. "Why don't I pick you up at seven? That will give us time to get some breakfast and you can catch me up on what's been happening at the office all week."

She bobbed her head. "Fine. I'll, uh, see you then." She gave a quick wave to Eric, stole a last peek at the babies, then turned away.

Eric didn't pull away from the curb until she had let herself into her condo. After another wave to the waiting men, she closed the door and leaned against its reassuring bulk. She was home. Home represented safety for the moment. She felt safe finally to allow herself to experience the swirling emotions she had been suppressing.

The silence that greeted her seemed to resonate all around her. Kathryn had lived alone ever since she had graduated from college. She enjoyed being alone. She treasured her privacy. So why did she find herself listening for the soft stirring of one of the babies, when the babies were now gone from her life as quickly as they had appeared?

With a sob that caught her totally unprepared, she burst into tears.

Dane stood at the large plate-glass window of his office, staring out at the view. Today was Friday. He had been at work for a week. By now he should be comfortably back into the routine he had followed for years. Instead he felt like a stranger observing his life through new eyes.

Nothing seemed familiar.

Why did he feel as though everyone else around him had changed? Where had this sense of detachment come from? Ross Enterprises was his baby. He had conceived the company, nurtured and encouraged its growth, and now could step back and applaud all of its accomplishments.

Of course he was pleased with the way the organization had functioned when he wasn't there. What surprised him...no, it was more than surprise. What had *shocked* him was his lack of interest in all that used to consume his every waking moment.

He had met with each department head, listening to their reports, observing how seriously they were involved with their work. Is that the way he had behaved, singularly focused on the business of planning, negotiating, and financing the empire he had built?

Why did none of that seem so important to him now that he had returned?

He watched as a young couple strolled in the park across the street from his office building. They were holding hands, talking and laughing, obviously enjoying the day and each other's company. Splashes of color from blooming flowers and shrubs lined the pathways of the park.

Two women pushed baby strollers. Their young passengers leaned forward with animation, pointing at nature's natural bouquets.

Spring had arrived. He wondered when that had happened? He had gotten glimpses of the season in the mountains—hours of sunshine and warm breezes before a sudden shift would chill the air.

Had the flowers been blooming before he left? Had the trees shown the hazy green look that preceded full foliage?

He wondered if any of his employees had noticed that spring had arrived? For the first time since he had hired them, Dane speculated about the various members of his staff, wondering what they did when they left his office for the day.

Did they return to a quiet home alone, or was there a noisy family awaiting them? Did they study business reports at night, or help with a child's homework, or bath time, or read a story to a child at bedtime?

His thoughts returned to Kathryn, as they had for most of the past week.

Why couldn't he get her out of his mind? If he asked, would she take his hand and stroll along park paths, sharing her laughter with him? What would she do if he were to take her in his arms again and kiss her? Would she flow against him, returning his kiss, would she look at him with the heat of passion burning in her eyes? Would she—

Stop it! He had to stop fantasizing about his administrative assistant.

So they had made love. So what? They had known each other for years. They worked closely together. Without his realizing it, they had become friends, even if she knew him much better than he knew her.

The weekend in the mountains had opened his eyes to how little he knew her and how much he wanted to learn about her. From the time he had looked up to see her standing in the bedroom doorway on Sunday morning speaking to Eric, he knew that he didn't want to give up on the new direction their relationship had taken.

He had seen her embarrassment and her shyness with him and understood. He felt awkward, as well. What could he say? Eric's presence had been a mixed blessing. Having him there gave them an opportunity to retreat from the new situation without acknowledging their reactions. Would the weekend have ended differently if they had been given time to discuss what had happened between them?

Dane realized that he wanted the time they had spent together to mean something to her. What if it hadn't? If he pursued a physical relationship between them would she feel compelled to agree because of the working relationship?

He recalled last Monday morning when he had shown up at her door to give her a ride to work. Because of traffic, he had given himself plenty of time to get there and had made excellent time. Consequently he'd been more than twenty minutes early....

He rang the doorbell twice before Kathryn answered, looking flustered. She had on a dark skirt and a rose-colored blouse. Her hair tumbled around her shoulders. When she saw him, her face flushed a similar color to her blouse....

"I know I'm early," he said in an effort to put her at ease. "I was hoping for a cup of coffee. I didn't take time to make any before I left home." He held his breath, waiting for her response. Either his smile or his explanation seemed to reassure her because she stepped back, motioning for him to come in.

"I'm afraid I overslept this morning." Looking away, she admitted, "I've been having trouble getting to sleep at night." Clearing her throat, she added, "I shouldn't be much longer."

Dane followed her through her condo, looking around with interest. The rooms were large with high ceilings, built in a much earlier era. Her furnishings reflected an eclectic taste he found enormously appealing and restful.

She paused at the archway into the kitchen. "Coffee's made and the cups are in the cabinet, if you don't mind helping yourself."

"There's no rush, you know," he pointed out with amusement. "We don't have to punch a time card."

Her look of surprise made him realize how out of character his words sounded.

"I know how you like to get to the office early," she said slowly. "I didn't want to delay you."

"Actually, we'll get more accomplished by discussing business over breakfast than we would at the office where the phone will be constantly ringing."

"You have a point there," she conceded, looking a little more relaxed.

Dane went into the light and airy kitchen, found her cups in the first cabinet he opened and poured himself some coffee.

Being in Kathryn's home had a decided effect on him, one he wouldn't have believed possible. He had spent the past day and night struggling to push away the memories of them together at the cabin.

He had been less than successful. Being in her home now brought everything back to him in a rush.

He remembered her seated before the fireplace holding a baby... feeding, soothing, murmuring to first one infant, then the other.

He remembered her laughing at his stories regarding his week-long stay in the mountains.

He remembered her lying beneath him, her face upturned so that his lips could touch each feature.

Dane fought the groan that threatened to surface from deep inside of him at those memories. He took a sip of coffee and wandered over to the kitchen window. The early morning fog swirled in from the bay, dissipating as he watched.

He was at the window when he heard her behind him. "I'm ready whenever you are."

He turned and saw his very efficient administrative assistant standing in the archway. She had completed her office uniform with a jacket that matched her skirt and sensible-looking shoes. Once again her hair was pulled away from her face in a chignon. Her business smile was in place. He could read nothing in the expression of her eyes.

His memories of the weekend jostled with the picture she now presented. The woman standing before him was the woman he had known for eight years— intelligent, competent, efficient, businesslike. He had accepted her on those levels, unaware of the warm, loving human being that lurked beneath the calm exterior.

He reached out and took her hand, obviously startling her. "I never did get the opportunity to truly thank you for coming to my rescue over the weekend. I couldn't have gotten through it without you."

Her cheeks glowed with an endearing blush. "I'm glad you did. I enjoyed getting to know Melinda and Melanie." She picked up her briefcase and started down the hallway toward the door. "Where did Eric take them?"

He followed her, waiting until she locked the door before he escorted her to his car. "He took them to a small private hospital until he could contact the necessary authorities today."

"I feel so sorry for their mother, having to give them up."

"Yeah, that's got to be a tough decision."

"I kept waking up in the night thinking I had heard one of them, before I remembered they weren't there."

After helping her into the car, he climbed in beside her and started the engine. "It didn't take long to get attached to them, that's for sure."

"Yes."

They lapsed into silence, a silence that seemed to be filled with swirling images of hours past.

Dane felt that he should say something about what had happened between the two of them, but for the life of him, he didn't know what he could say. How could he apologize for something that had been so splendid? How could he pretend that he was sorry they had made love when all he could think about was how much he wanted to repeat what they had shared?

He knew to even consider the possibility was absurd. An office romance would be filled with anxiety. He wanted her, but he knew that changing their relationship now would endanger what they had already established. Kathryn had become invaluable to him over the years. He needed her too much to risk losing her entirely.

On the other hand, how could he continue to be around her on a daily basis without the constant reminder of their newfound intimacy? Just a whiff of her perfume with its light floral fragrance sent messages to every part of his body, and those messages had nothing to do with business.

He cleared his throat. "So tell me what's been going on in my absence."

The business conversation accompanied them for the rest of the drive and through their meal.

Through unspoken agreement they did not bring up the subject of what had happened between them, either then, or in the following days. Perhaps the only sensible way to handle the matter, Dane decided during one of his many restless nights, was not to handle the matter at all....

His buzzer sounded, bringing him back to the present. Dane blinked, realizing that once again he had been daydreaming, an affliction he had acquired during his week back at the office.

He pressed the button on his phone. "Yes?"

"Are you ready for me?"

His heart gave a double thump in his chest at the sound of Kathryn's husky voice and her provocative question. The fact that the question was a routine one and had never caused him to react in such a physical manner before this week was beside the point.

"Sure. Come in."

Dane sat down, relieved that he could hide his physical reaction behind his massive desk while he waited for Kathryn to enter his office and walk toward him.

Until now he had never noticed how gracefully she walked. Although there was never a sense of rush about her, she moved with a deceptive speed, her legs flashing in long strides, those very same legs that—

"Dane?"

He blinked, staring at Kathryn seated across from him.

"Mmm?" was the only response he could muster.

"You seem preoccupied about something."

He took a deep breath and exhaled, leaning back in his chair. "Yeah," he muttered, almost to himself.

"If this isn't a convenient time, I can always come back," she said, picking up the files she had just put down.

"No. That's all right. I'm just a little distracted." He glanced out the window.

She laughed. "Maybe you've caught a touch of the fever. I've always figured you were immune."

He returned his gaze to her. She appeared relaxed and at ease with him. Why couldn't he feel relaxed around her? Why couldn't— "What fever? Is the flu going around?"

She shook her head, chuckling. "No. I'm talking about spring fever." She motioned to the window. "It's this kind of weather that makes coming to work tough, knowing you're going to be indoors all day."

"Is that what it's called? Spring fever?"

She tilted her head and smiled. "I believe the dictionary defines spring fever as 'a listless, lazy or restless feeling commonly associated with the beginning of spring.' I think that definition certainly describes what most of us are feeling these days."

Today she wore a lemon-yellow blouse with a royal blue suit. She made him think of flowers, spring flowers, like the ones blooming in the park across the street.

"Dane?"

"Hmm?"

She laughed. "You've really got it bad, haven't you?" She snapped her fingers in a teasing gesture and said, "Do you want these figures or not?"

He stared at her for a long moment before saying, "Not."

His answer obviously startled her. "Oh. Well." She looked around with confusion. "I thought—"

"I have an idea," he said as images began to race through his mind. "Why don't we see if we can visit the twins? Maybe take them for a short outing? We could visit one of the parks, see—"

"On a Friday?" She stared at him in shock.

"Today's Friday, isn't it?"

"Yes."

"Then we'll do it on a Friday."

"But what about—" She stared down at the files spread in front of her.

"Is there anything there that wouldn't keep until Monday?"

"Well, no, but you seemed eager to find out as much as possible on that new site you were looking to buy. Everyone's been working as fast as possible to compile the data so that you could study the results before making a final decision."

He stood and came around the desk. "Don't you want to see Melinda and Melanie?" he asked, his voice coaxing.

He watched as several expressions chased across her face. "Of course. I just—I, uh—"

He held out his hand. "Then let's go. Business will keep for a few days. Who knows when we'll have such a beautiful day again?" He continued to hold out his hand to her until she hesitantly grasped it. He gave her a reassuring smile. "It's really okay, you know."

"If you say so."

He grinned. "I say so."

Dane hurried to the door, paused only long enough to give his secretary instructions for the rest of the day, then led Kathryn to the elevator.

"Will you please let go of my hand?" she hissed. "Carla couldn't stop staring!"

"Let her stare. I enjoy holding your hand." He squeezed gently in confirmation.

"I'm not sure this is a very good idea," she muttered.

They reached the parking garage and he led her to his car. Her car, which had been delivered to her earlier in the week, was parked beside his. "Should I follow you?" she asked.

"No. We can come back and get your car later."

Dane felt like a kid playing hooky as they left the garage and pulled onto the street. He flipped the locks on the convertible cover, pushed the button and let the cloth roof of the car lower itself, leaving them open to the sunshine. The breeze immediately tugged at Kathryn's sedate hairdo. When he saw her lift her hand to her hair, he said, "Take it down, why don't you?"

She stared at him suspiciously. "Dane, have you been drinking? Are you taking something? Did Eric prescribe—"

Dane threw his head back and laughed. "I'm sober as a judge, I promise. I'm in my right mind and Eric would be the first one to applaud what we're doing." He checked his watch. "The babies should be awake about now. They—"

"How do you know their schedule so well?"

He shrugged. "Oh, I've gotten into the habit of calling the place and checking on them. I've stopped in a couple of times to make sure they were adjusting and to play with them."

He kept his eyes on the traffic, refusing to look at her. All right, so he was embarrassed that those two had completely captured his heart. But then, who could be surprised? How could anyone be around them and not find them adorable?

When they walked into the small, privately owned institution, everyone there recognized Dane and greeted him by name. He caught Kathryn grinning and gave her a level look. Although she mouthed the words "A *couple* of times" she said nothing out loud.

They spent the day as he had envisioned. Kathryn kept exclaiming on how much the twins had grown in just a few days. Dane felt as proud as if he had helped them grow.

Once again the staid demeanor of Ms. Collier had been shed along with her jacket and shoes. They spread a blanket out on a grassy hill of one of the city parks and enjoyed the sunshine.

Dane couldn't remember a time in his life when everything seemed to come together so perfectly. The years of working during the day, attending school and studying at night, the years of putting in eighty-hour weeks all seemed to have slipped into his past without a struggle. Today was a new day. Today was a perfect day. Today he was with Kathryn, Melinda and Melanie . . . the women in his life.

He froze, conscious of where his thoughts had led him.

He must have a really bad case of spring fever.

After returning the twins, Dane and Kathryn ended up having dinner at one of the restaurants along Fisherman's Wharf. They had stayed at the small institution to feed and cuddle the babies, and to tuck them into bed before leaving with promises to come again soon.

Now Dane relaxed in his comfortable chair across from Kathryn, enjoying the view of her sun-kissed face, her hair that she had finally combed out and allowed to hang loose, and her contented expression.

"It's been a good day, hasn't it?" he asked.

Her gaze flicked to his, then away. She seemed to be absorbed in studying the candle-lit globe that made up part of the table's centerpiece. "It's been a wonderful day," she admitted softly.

"We'll have to do it again sometime."

She didn't say anything.

"Are you feeling guilty that we didn't spend the day at the office diligently working?"

She waited several moments before she replied, "I don't think this is a good idea."

"Playing hooky? Don't you think we've earned some time off?"

She raised her eyes to meet his. "When the twins are around I forget for a little while that you and I work together—that our relationship is a professional one." She lifted her glass of wine and sipped. "We've allowed the parameters of our relationship to blur considerably this past week. I don't think that's a very wise decision."

He reached over and took her hand. "Do you have any idea how much I value you in my life?" He could feel her racing pulse beneath his fingertips. She closed her eyes but did not pull away from him. Dane continued. "I'm not proud to admit that I've taken you for granted for years, depending on you in ways I wasn't fully conscious of. And yet, I feel that I only started to get to know you during the past week. Instead of blurring, our relationship seems to have come into clearer focus as far as I'm concerned."

"My career is very important to me," she said in a low voice. "I don't want to jeopardize what I have worked so hard to achieve."

"Do you feel that seeing me away from the office will jeopardize your career?"

Her level gaze met his. "Yes."

Dane forced himself to let go of her hand. "I see." They maintained eye contact and Dane could see the regret, the confusion and the pain she felt.

Despite his need to disprove her beliefs, he knew he had to respect her decision. She felt that she had too much to lose to get any more involved with him than she already was. Given the choice of having him as her boss or her lover, she had chosen the former.

The choice was logical, perhaps even wise, but at the moment, all Dane could feel was the desolate pang of rejection. Weighed against the company he had struggled to build over the years, the company had won. The irony of competing against his own life's work did not escape him.

"Well." He forced himself to smile. "Guess we need to get you back to your car."

"Yes." She looked down, but not before he saw the tears that had sprung into her eyes. He felt a large lump forming in his throat. There was nothing more to say. Silently Dane assisted Kathryn with her chair and accompanied her out of the restaurant.

Chapter Six

Dane pushed the intercom button without looking up from the sheet of print-out figures in front of him. "Kathryn, could you come in, please?"

He continued to make notations beside some of the numbers. When the intercom remained silent, he glanced at his watch. It was after nine, a good half hour after she normally arrived.

"Kathryn?" he repeated, but there was no answer. He pushed another button.

"Carla?"

"Yes?"

"Is Kathryn here."

"No, sir."

"Have you spoken to her?"

"No, not since she left here last Friday."

"Try her home, will you? See if there's a problem."

In the past two months since that fateful Friday when he and Kathryn had spent the day together, he had carefully maintained a professional front with her. Whatever he did, he didn't want to place any pressure on her to believe that he expected anything more from her than she willingly wanted to give.

In that two months, however, seeing her day after day had poignantly revealed to him how much he loved her. He had probably always loved her on some unconscious level. It had taken that unusual weekend in the mountains to trigger all of his feelings and desires, bringing them rushing to the surface, clamoring for relief.

He had no idea how she felt about him. What she had made quite clear was she did not want to risk losing her job by getting involved with him.

He respected her too much not to honor her wishes.

His actions had taken their toll, however. He had trouble sleeping. His mind kept wandering during long meetings and telephone conferences. He no longer mentioned the twins to her, feeling that the subject served only to remind them both of the weekend she so obviously wanted to forget.

His buzzer rang.

"Yes?"

"I managed to reach Kathryn. She sounded awful. Thinks she may be coming down with the flu. Said she'd try to be in later this morning, but I told her not to bring anything to the office."

"You've got a point."

"She seemed to agree. Said she'd call when she was feeling better."

Dane leaned back in his chair, remembering that Kathryn's parents lived in Santa Barbara. As far as he knew, she had no family in the area, no one who might be available to check on her.

Within minutes he was leaving the office.

He stopped off at a grocery store, filling the basket with soups, juices and easily prepared light meals. Then he headed to Kathryn's home, waiting on the front steps while he repeatedly pressed the doorbell.

He could hear her grumbling as she unlatched the chain and turned the bolt lock. "Please stop ringing the bell. What do you— Oh! Dane!" She stared at him blankly, her eyes glazed with fever.

Without waiting for an invitation, he stepped through the doorway, his arms full of groceries. Silently he continued to the kitchen, noting a small stack of dirty dishes in the sink and the non-prescription pain remedies sitting nearby. He turned to her. "How long have you been feeling this way?"

"I don't know. Yesterday, I think. I don't remember."

He put his hand to her face. She was hot to the touch.

"Why didn't you call?" He turned and found a clean glass, poured some juice and took a couple of caplets from one of the remedy bottles.

She took the caplets and swallowed them, then sipped the juice. "I thought I would feel better by this morning. I must have overslept. The first thing I knew was hearing the phone when Carla called."

"When was the last time you ate?"

She shuddered. "That's the last thing I want to do."

"You can't let yourself get dehydrated. Get back into bed. I'll warm you some soup."

She looked as if she was having trouble focusing. She shook her head slowly, muttering, "Am I dreaming?"

He grinned. "No. You're not dreaming. Now go to bed. I'll be in there in a few minutes to check on you." He turned her by the shoulders. "Now go."

She disappeared toward the bedroom.

Dane felt lighter than he had in weeks. She wasn't putting up a fuss about his coming to her home and taking charge. She must feel worse than he thought. It felt good to be able to do something for her, even though he knew his being there was just an excuse to see her.

Weekends were the toughest time for him, even though he stayed busy. But that's when he missed her the most. At least during the week they spent most of the day in each other's company. He had convinced himself that a business relationship was enough for him. It was better than nothing. But he dreaded Friday afternoons when he had to steal himself for the two-day separation.

He washed up the few dishes in the sink, put on some water for tea, and began to heat the soup he had purchased in the deli department of the supermarket. Once he had the steaming food on a tray, he headed in the same direction Kathryn had taken earlier.

He found the bedroom easily enough. The shades were still drawn, the only light coming from an adjoining bathroom.

"Here you go," he said, setting the tray beside the bed.

"Go 'way," was the muffled response. She had her head half under the pillow, turned away from him.

"I will, as soon as you eat."

Slowly she turned so that she was facing him. Her face was definitely flushed, her eyes feverish. "I don't want you to catch this," she muttered.

"I might already have it, who knows? Now eat your soup."

She eyed the tray uncharitably.

"It's good for you," he coaxed.

"A lot of things are good for me that I detest."

Dane fought to stifle his grin. The fever had certainly exposed an aspect of her personality he had never seen before . . . a very human, endearing side.

"You'll like this. Chicken soup is a must. My mom used to give it to me every time I was sick. The tea will be soothing, as well."

"You had a mother?" she croaked, reaching for the tea.

"Of course I had a mother! What kind of a question is that?"

"You never talk about her. I've never heard you talk about your family in all the years I've known you." She took a sip of the tea, made a face and set it down. He handed her the soup and watched as she carefully spooned the hot liquid into her mouth.

"No reason to, I guess. My dad was killed in Korea the year I was born. My mother raised me. She died several years ago. Not much to talk about."

She peered at him like a wise owl...a drunken wise owl. "Did you have any brothers or sisters?"

"No."

"So you're all alone in the world."

The way she said it sounded very pitiful, indeed.

"Are you feeling sorry for me?" he asked with interest.

She nodded very solemnly. "It's very, very sad to be all alone, with nobody to love you, and nobody to hold you, and nobody to..." She paused, obviously trying to remember other deprivations. "—And all that," she concluded, with a wave of her hand that almost spilled the soup.

He took the spoon and bowl away from her and began to feed her. She obligingly opened her mouth for him.

"Have you been feeling all alone with nobody to love you and nobody to hold you?" he asked quietly.

She nodded her head emphatically.

"I'm here," he offered after a few more bites.

"Because I'm sick," she replied.

"Because I was worried about you."

"You were?"

"Yes."

She gave him a beautiful smile. "That's nice."

He set the empty bowl back on the tray and wrapped her fingers around the cup. "Try to drink all of that."

"It tastes funny."

"It's chamomile. It will help settle your stomach."

"Did your mother give it to you?"

"No. I learned about the tea later."

"Oh." She stared at it in disgust, but drank it anyway.

When she was through, he coaxed her to lie down after he fluffed her pillows, then he pulled the covers up to her neck. She sighed and closed her eyes. He was almost to the door with her tray when she said, "'Bye."

He paused, looking back at her. Her eyes were still closed. His lips twitched. "I'm not going anywhere."

Her eyes flew open. "You aren't?"

He shook his head. "I brought some work to do. I can work here just fine."

She smiled her delightfully inebriated smile, and he left the room.

Dane continued to dose her with medicine to keep her fever down and kept her supplied with liquids for the rest of the day. He talked with Eric to be sure he was doing enough and Eric offered to drop by. Grateful for his friend's concern, Dane waited in the living room while Eric checked her over.

"How is she?" were the first words when Eric joined him.

Eric was laughing. "Actually, she's doing quite well. She's just very susceptible to drugs, I would say."

Dane grinned. "Yeah. I figured that out right away."

"I never thought the prim and dignified Ms. Collier could be such a chatterbox. She's going to hate herself when she remembers what she's been telling us."

"Will she remember?"

"Probably. She hasn't taken anything strong enough to harm her. Just enough to remove some of her inhibitions."

"I don't like the idea of her being here alone. I've arranged to stay here. If anyone needs to reach me, they can call me here."

"Are you this solicitous of all your employees?" Eric asked. Dane scowled, causing Eric to laugh. "Sorry. I couldn't resist. Does the lady in there have any idea how you feel about her?"

"She knows that I value her as an administrative assistant."

"Uh-huh."

"You don't believe me?"

"Of course I believe you. And what else you might feel for her is absolutely none of my business." He picked up his bag. "Call me if you feel anxious about anything. This is a pretty bad strain of flu going around. But she should be feeling much better by tomorrow."

"Well, that's good to hear." He held out his hand and Eric shook it. "Thanks again for dropping by."

"No problem. I'll see you at the club Wednesday for our racquetball game."

"I'll let you know. I may not want to leave Kathryn."

Eric left, shaking his head and grinning. As soon as he was gone, Dane went in to check on Kathryn. She was sound asleep.

He was dozing on her living room sofa sometime during the night when he heard her moving around. He slipped into his trousers and went back to check on her. She was just coming out of the bathroom.

"Are you okay?"

She let out a little yelp and grabbed the door facing. "Dane! You scared me to death. I didn't know you were still here."

She stood between him and the bathroom light, her figure outlined through her gown. He walked over to her. "Do you need help getting back to bed?"

Kathryn pushed her hair off her face with a frustrated gesture. "I hate feeling so weak. I can't seem to—"

He picked her up and carried her over to the bed.

"What time is it?"

"A little after two."

"What are you doing here?"

"Napping on the sofa."

"The sofa! But it's too short to sleep on."

"Which is why I'm napping."

"Oh, Dane, you can't put yourself through that."

"I don't mind."

"Why don't you sleep in here?" She patted the king-size bed. "There's plenty of room."

"I didn't want to disturb you."

"You won't."

"Sure you don't mind?"

She yawned and shook her head, closing her eyes.

He knew he shouldn't even consider her offer but she was right. The sofa was much too short to be comfortable and there *was* plenty of room in her bed. Besides, he would hear her more quickly from here should she need anything.

He walked around to the other side of the bed, slipped off his trousers and, wearing only his briefs, crawled in beside her, trying not to remember the last time they had shared a bed. The bed was a considerable improvement over the sofa and within minutes he was asleep.

Dane was awakened some time later by Kathryn's muttering. Half asleep, he used the name of his secret fantasies about her. "Kathie?" he whispered, reaching for her. "What's wrong, honey?"

"Oh, Daddy, I love him so much. It's awful. I don't know what to do. The weekends crawl by when I'm not with him, and the weeks fly by because I get to see him every day. It's like some kind of torture. How could I have done something so stupid as to fall in love with my boss!"

Dane had leaned up on his elbow to check on her. When she began to talk, he felt as though a light-ning bolt had hit him, setting every nerve end to quivering.

He touched her forehead, feeling the fever. Moving carefully so as not to disturb her, he went into the kitchen and found the medication for fever Eric had recommended, poured a glass of water and took them back to the bedroom. He sat on the side of the bed.

"Kathryn?"

She stirred restlessly, but didn't open her eyes.

"You need to take something to bring your fever down," he told her in a soothing voice. "Here. I have something for you to take."

When she opened her eyes, she blinked up at him in surprise. "Dane?"

"I'm right here."

She looked around the room. "But I thought—"

"You've probably been dreaming. Here you go." He handed her the medicine, which she took.

"Try to rest now."

She smiled at him and closed her eyes. He waited until she was quiet before he crawled into the other side of the bed. His mind was racing with new revelations. Was it fair to take advantage of something told you in confidence, particularly when the person was sick and thought she was talking to someone else?

Fair or not, he wasn't going to be able to forget what she had said. Knowing how she felt made all the difference in the world. They would work something out. He was good at finding solutions to all kinds of problems. All he had to do was convince Ms. Kathryn Collier that they could be a team, both professionally and personally.

Early one Friday morning, two weeks later, Kathryn had just stepped out of the shower when the phone rang. Grabbing a towel, she wrapped it around herself and dashed for the phone.

"H'lo?"

"Did I interrupt something?" Dane asked. "You sound out of breath."

"I was just finishing my shower."

"Oh!" After a brief silence he said, "Sorry to bother you so early, but I wanted to alert you that something's come up. We're going to fly upstate later today to inspect some property. Thought you might want to bring some extra clothes to work with you in case we need to stay overnight."

She was used to traveling with Dane at a moment's notice and found nothing unusual about his call. "Thanks for warning me," she replied. "I'll be at the office within the hour."

"Fine. See you then."

She heard the phone click on the other end and knew that Dane's mind was already racing off in new directions, their conversation checked off a mental list he had. She sighed and hung up the phone, then sank down on the side of her bed.

Ever since she had been sick, Kathryn had been fighting a bone-deep listlessness, almost a depression. Eric had told her that the flu strain presently running rampant in society was a particularly virulent one, difficult to shake, and had advised that she take it easy for a few weeks.

Dane hadn't wanted her to come back to work so soon, but after a week of lying around watching daytime television, she had known she had to get back to a sane work schedule or go mad. She had shortened her work day, which had helped, but by the time she got home each evening she felt like a rag that had been soaked in boiling water, then wrung out and hung to dry.

She was surprised he hadn't decided to make the trip alone, but had to admit that she was glad for a change of scenery.

Her illness had given her too much time to think, to remember, to miss. Her first few days were only a vague blur in her memory. Dane had been there. He'd seemed to be there every time she'd awakened, giving her something to drink or eat or medicine to choke down. Unless she dreamed it, even Eric had stopped by to check on her. She couldn't remember the last time she had been so sick. Kathryn sincerely hoped she never had to go through anything like that again anytime soon.

She finished drying herself off and went to the closet, choosing a couple of suits, one to wear and one to pack, with an extra set of underwear and a couple of blouses.

She knew one reason she was depressed . . . the twins were gone. She had gone to see them the weekend before she became ill and was told that they had been placed in the home of adoptive parents.

She hadn't even had a chance to tell them goodbye.

Kathryn wasn't sure why she had taken the news so hard. She had always known that they would end up being adopted. She had asked if the same family took them or whether they had been split up, but no one would answer any of her questions. Melinda and Melanie were out of her life permanently. She wouldn't get to see them when they could finally sit alone, when they cut their first teeth or took their first step.

Until the babies had come into her life, Kathryn had never given a thought to having a family of her own. Now she felt as if she had been deprived of one, which was absolutely ridiculous.

She was grieving over a loss that had never been hers to lose. Rational or not, the grief was real.

Glancing at the clock, she realized that if she didn't hurry she would be late. She knew Dane wouldn't say anything. He had been very considerate of her these past two weeks. Almost too solicitous. His concern and compassion had merely made her feelings for him grow stronger.

She checked her bag to make certain she had everything she would need, found her briefcase and left for work, following a routine she had established years ago.

"Lake Tahoe! Why would you be looking for property in Lake Tahoe?"

Kathryn and Dane were in the plane Dane had chartered just after take off. Only now had Kathryn thought to ask where they were going.

"I got a lead on a place up there I wanted to check out."

"But Ross Enterprises does commercial development. Surely you don't intend to—"

"No. This won't be for Ross Enterprises."

Kathryn stared at him in confusion.

"Ever since that week I spent at Eric's cabin I've been thinking about getting a place of my own. The rest made a big difference in my physical well-being and in my perspective about several things in my life.

If I decide to buy up here, I'll be able to come up on long weekends, take an occasional week off, enjoy life a little more. After all, isn't that the reason I've worked so hard all these years?"

Kathryn's confusion wasn't diminished by his lengthy explanation. "If this isn't a business trip, then why am I along?"

He smiled. "For company?"

"You don't need my company."

"Well, maybe I don't *need* it, exactly. Let's just say, having you along makes the trip more pleasant."

Her eyes narrowed. "Does this have something to do with my having been sick?"

Warily he asked, "What do you mean?"

"Are you trying to get me to rest more?"

"If I am, do you have a problem with that?"

She sighed. "Oh, Dane. You've been hovering over me lately like a mother hen with only one baby chick. Honestly, I'm fine. Eric said it would take a while to be completely over it."

"So humor me, will you? We'll look at this property, have some dinner, maybe see a show at one of the casinos and fly back home tomorrow. What's wrong with a schedule like that?"

She studied him for a moment in silence. Why did she feel that he wasn't telling her everything? Well, that was easy enough to answer . . . because he probably wasn't. She hadn't worked closely with this man for the past eight years without being able to read him fairly accurately. He was nervous about something. On edge. She had seen him like this before, when he had an important presentation, or when he determinedly was going after a contract he wanted.

He must want this Tahoe property badly to be so tense. She was touched that he wanted her with him when he went to look at it. Smiling to herself, she picked up a magazine and began to read.

Hours later Kathryn felt as though she was dreaming. If this was a dream, she didn't want to wake up. Instead, she would be content to circle the dance floor in Dane's arms for the rest of her life.

When they had reached Lake Tahoe that afternoon, they had rented a car at the airport. With the directions Dane had been given, they found the property he wanted to see.

What they had found was no primitive mountain cabin. With more than five thousand square feet, four bedrooms and five bathrooms, the home Dane wanted to view could accommodate a large family.

When Kathryn saw the size of the place, she was speechless. Why would a bachelor want a home that size? Was he intending to do a great deal of entertaining? Perhaps he planned to have clients visit him there.

The house was beautiful, built entirely of pine, with a massive fireplace in the great room whose ceiling towered two stories high. There was another fireplace in the master bedroom, as well.

After viewing the house, they had returned to the hotel. While Kathryn rested, Dane made reservations for one of the shows. Since she hadn't brought anything festive to wear, Kathryn went downstairs after her nap and bought a dress in one of the boutiques in the hotel.

The show had been splashy, colorful and vibrating with sound. Dinner had been deliciously intimate and quiet. And now... Dane had asked her to dance with him.

They had never danced together before. She'd had no idea how much she was missing. Nothing had ever felt so good to Kathryn as having Dane's arms wrapped around her.

"Kathryn?"

"Mmm?"

"Are you tired?"

"Not really," she replied.

"I was thinking—"

When he didn't say anything more, she said, "About?"

"Well, there's an oversized Jacuzzi in my room and I was thinking how nice it would be to share it with you."

She brought her head away from his shoulder so she could see his face. His voice had sounded very light, but his expression was anything but casual.

"Are you trying to seduce me?"

"If I am, how am I doing?"

She dropped her head against his shoulder with a sigh. "Oh, Dane. I don't know. I can't seem to think straight any more. I mean, I know what I'm supposed to do...what I need to do...I just—"

He placed a whispering kiss beneath her ear. "How about, just for tonight, you do what you *want* to do? If you don't want to do something, all you have to do is say no. You're as safe as you want to be."

Once again she looked into his eyes and recognized that heated expression. She remembered...she remembered so much. How could she say no when she wanted him so badly, when she loved him so much?

Without saying anything, she took a step back from him and turned, leading him off the dance floor and out of the nightclub toward the elevators and his room.

Chapter Seven

"Ooo-oh," she murmured. "That feels so good." She slid farther into the water that was churning all around her. "What a marvelous idea."

Kathryn had dropped her towel as she lowered herself into the tub. She leaned her head against the side with her eyes closed.

She didn't want to watch Dane step into the tub. She didn't want to be reminded of the way she felt when she saw him wearing nothing more than that lopsided grin of his. She had lost her mind, she had thrown discretion out the window, and for the moment . . . she didn't care.

Ever since that night almost three months ago when she and Dane had first made love, their relationship had been steadily changing. How could it not, given their circumstances? They would be working and she would glance up to see him watching her in such a way that she knew he was remembering what they had shared.

She was tired of fighting her own feelings. Tonight she discovered that she was ready to risk everything she had thought she wanted for the possibility of having more.

The water swirled and eddied around her and she knew that Dane must have joined her in the tub. She opened her eyes and saw that he had sat down across from her. "This is a wonderful idea. I'm glad you thought of it."

He rubbed his foot along her ankle and calf. "Actually, I've had several ideas lately that I wanted to toss your way, to see what you thought of them."

Leave it to Dane to choose such an intimate moment to discuss business, she thought, concealing a smile. "All right," she said, prepared to take mental notes.

"Ever since my week in Eric's cabin I've been doing a great deal of thinking about my life and where it's going. Eric was right. I really needed to improve the quality of my life and not be so one-dimensional."

She smiled. "Therefore, you're holding your business meetings in a hot tub. Great idea."

"Well, uh, this isn't exactly a business meeting. I mean— Well, I guess, basically, business is all I know. I don't have many social graces. It's just that..."

When he seemed to be at a loss for words, Kathryn said, "I was teasing you, Dane. Go ahead, pitch me some of these ideas of yours."

He stared at her for a moment of tension-filled silence, then muttered, "I would rather show you."

With a slight tug on her hand, he pulled her toward him until she was sitting on his knees, facing him, her legs on either side of him.

"Dane, I—"

His kiss silenced her, distracting her, as well. By the time he lifted his mouth from hers, they were both breathless. "I love you, Kathryn," he muttered hoarsely. "I don't know how to tell you any other way. I don't have any practiced delivery or smooth, experienced moves because I've never felt like this before." He held her fiercely, as though afraid to relax his grip in case she pulled away. Kathryn had no intention of pulling away from this man, not ever. She began to place tiny kisses along his jaw and cheek, slowly moving closer to his mouth.

"You're doing just fine, Dane," she whispered. "Just fine." She wrapped her arms around his neck so that her body was pressed against his, then kissed him with enough passion to cause the water around them to boil.

Still holding her, he stood and stepped out of the Jacuzzi. He snagged a towel and rubbed it across her back on the way to the bedroom. Once he lowered her to the bed, there was no more need for words when their actions spoke so much louder. Kathryn had thought her memories had exaggerated the depth of pleasure she had experienced the first time they had made love. Now she realized his impassioned lovemaking was better than she had remembered.

A long time later they lay amid the tangled sheets of Dane's bed, Kathryn's head resting on his shoulder.

"I want to marry you, Kathryn," he whispered in the quiet of the room.

She raised her head, her eyes meeting his. He looked so relaxed, as relaxed as she felt, and as contented. "Are you sure?"

He grinned. "Oh, I'm sure all right. I've known for months. I just didn't know how to broach the subject. I was afraid you'd be insulted and resign."

She brushed her hand across his chest. "Never that. I've loved you for so many years. I can't imagine not having you in my life."

"Does that mean that you will?"

"Marry you?"

"Yes."

She leaned over so that her lips could rest lightly against his. "I can think of nothing I'd like more." The kiss became the sealing of a vow.

Several minutes passed before Dane spoke again. "This doesn't have to interfere with your job in any way. We can still work together, although I intend to train Ralph to take over the daily management of the business."

She returned her head to his shoulder. "I would like to continue to work, for a while, anyway, but I would also like to plan a family. Ever since I got to know Melinda and Melanie, I've wanted a family of my own." She looked at him. "How do you feel about having children?"

"Exactly the way you do. Why do you think I want to buy such a large home?"

"Oh! Well, I suppose the size is appropriate if you plan to have a large family." She eyed him uncertainly. "How many did you have in mind?"

His glance veered away from hers. "Oh, I don't know, exactly. I just thought that with twins we might need more space than—"

"Twins? Are you telling me that twins run in your family?"

"Well, no, not yet. They're not quite six months old. That's too young to be running anywhere. But give them time and I'm sure—"

"Dane! What are you talking about? Who's six months old?"

"Melinda and Melanie." His gaze met hers a little sheepishly.

"Oh, Dane! Didn't you know? The twins have already been adopted. I was heartbroken when I found out. The Social Services are so secretive they wouldn't tell me anything about them—where they are, how they're doing, if they were adopted together. I didn't mention it to you because I figured you would be as upset as I was."

"Kathie, honey, I have a confession to make. I'm in the process of adopting the twins. They were moved to my place pending all the red tape a person has to go through. I already have the mother's written permission, I have a full-time certified nanny staying with them and I spend every available moment I have with them. But they need you, too, love."

Her eyes had grown steadily larger with every word. "You mean they could be ours?"

He nodded. "Looks that way. Of course, being married will help our case considerably—"

"Oh, Dane!" She hugged him to her, tears running down her cheeks. "I had no idea that—I thought I'd never get to see them— When *can* I see them? Couldn't we—"

"How about tomorrow? I thought we might fly back, pick them up, then fly down to Santa Barbara to tell your folks, if you'd like. I figured we might have a wedding to plan."

She chuckled through her tears. "You've got everything all worked out, don't you?"

"Subject to your approval, of course. These were just some ideas I've been kicking around in an effort to—"

"You don't have to convince me, Boss. I've always thought you had an excellent head for brilliant ideas."

Dane decided that his loyal and lovely administrative assistant also had an abundance of excellent suggestions and ideas as she physically demonstrated them during the next several hours.

He also realized that he hadn't been suffering from spring fever after all. He just hadn't recognized the symptoms of falling in love.

*   *   *   *   *

SPRING

There's just something about spring that is pure magic. How else can we explain a dormant tree suddenly wearing tiny green shoots? Or in the case of my favorite—the dogwood tree—intricately shaped flowers appear.

And how does grass know it's time to turn green?

Spring air seems to sparkle, somehow, with a gold and bubbly light, scented with those wonderful smells that only occur in spring.

Magic. That's the only possible explanation.

Love is filled with magic, as well. Even though there are no words that can explain what love is, we all know what love feels like . . . all warm and bubbly with golden light and . . . why, it's similar to the feelings we get each spring.

Is it any wonder that people fall in love in the springtime? Spring is a perfect time to fall in love with life, with nature, with ourselves and with those who share our lives.

The earth is never too old to celebrate spring.

None of us is ever too old to celebrate falling in love.

Annette Broadrick

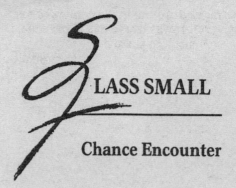

LASS SMALL

Chance Encounter

This story has niggled around in the corners of my mind for ten years. It was marvelous to have the "chance" to share it.

Lass Small

Chapter One

That spring—from Tampa, Florida—Jack phoned Darwin Moore who was being as stubborn as he always managed to be. Jack said, "It won't hurt you to come and take a look at her." Jack said that to Darwin with some impatience. "You can't close women out of your life just because you lost such a good one. There are other women."

"No."

"We've talked about this for over two years and I'm getting tired of going over and over the same thing. Judy would be irritated with you acting this way. If she'd'a been the one left behind, she would have looked around."

"No."

"I find you're not only limited in conversation, but your intellect is minimal at best. It isn't logical for a man only thirty-seven to give up on women."

"No."

"And you could do something about communicating. A 'no' is not enough. Are you impotent?"

"I wish."

"There, you see? You *can* get past a 'no' and that's a good sign."

Almost in a snarl, Darwin told Jack, "There's nothing left for me. I'll live out my interminable life."

With sarcasm, Jack exclaimed quite heartlessly, "Wow! Man, that's really poignant. You ought to write a story about your grief. Everybody who read it would be bawling and carrying on. But how would that help anything? What good would it do you? Every woman between sixteen and sixty would feel she could cure you, and you'd be neck deep in women. Meeting Phyllis's friend will be a whole lot easier."

"Jack, if we didn't go back all those years and if you hadn't found Judy for me, I'd never be a part of this."

"Your conscience bothers you. Right? Judy's been talking to you nights in your sleep and telling you what a stupid jerk you are."

"Don't push it."

"So you'll come down?" Jack held his breath.

"Let me think about it."

"No!"

Darwin growled, " 'No' is my word."

"If you hang up, you could slip off somewhere, and I'd never find you again. Promise. Now."

"Well, hell." Darwin took a deep breath and let it out impatiently. "When?"

"Let's say in a week? Come down early if you like and we can talk and go out fishing and get you in the mood for being congenial. You can't meet a woman when you have such a chip on your shoulder—you have to be cordial. The woman Phyllis's asked to join us is blond and—"

"I'm not interested in any woman. I'm doing this strictly to get you off my back."

"Okay, okay, okay! It's the middle of March and the water's getting reasonable. Come down in another week and then you can go back up to Minneapolis and freeze your—"

"I said I'd be there and I will." Then Darwin hung up the phone. He paced a while feeling impatient with himself for hanging up on Jack. Without Jack he'd probably have— He admitted it. He had been seriously tempted to follow Judy. But even then he'd known she would have been as irritated with him doing that as Jack. Maybe more. She had told him, "Live for us both."

Hell.

It was almost four years now. The worst possible thing was that her face was fading. He couldn't just close his eyes and find Judy there. He had to concentrate. He no longer saw the turn of her blond head in a crowd and for microseconds he forgot her death. He knew that she was gone. She'd been gone from him too long.

It was with bitterness that Darwin arranged to be away from Minneapolis. It was a long trip down to Florida and he didn't want to go there in order to meet some woman. But he appreciated Jack's friendship, most of the time, so he would go. Damn.

With a week to make the trip, Darwin got out of the snow and on down through the eastern part of the United States. He went through Dubuque, Peoria and Springfield to Cairo, then Birmingham, down to Montgomery and on to Tallahassee, driving from winter to spring. It was like watching another year vanish.

With the passing years, the time would go, and he would grow old and finally, finally he would be with Judy. He just needed to use up the time. This was one way.

He drove along, unduly aware of the change of seasons. The grass greened, then the forsythia was out and lower down the tulips and spring flowers were in evidence.

How long had it been since Darwin had noticed spring? Four long years. Now the colors caught his eye, forcing him to take notice.

Just below Tallahassee he took a small road over to the coast. The track was rough, his car went carefully, and he saw the Gulf. What was it about saltwater that lured people? It beckoned to Darwin.

Being the loner he had become, he had a bedroll and camping equipment in his car. For some time he hadn't had any fear for his welfare. It hadn't mattered. He was careless.

He found a place near Alligator Point. There were pines forty to fifty feet tall and harsh grasses and the tides kept the sandy shoreline cleared . . . enough.

He walked a long way along the curves of the irregular beach. There were fancy places, modest ones, and there was an isolated filling station that had never seen good times, but there was a pier in fair repair and two old tourist cabins.

The grouped buildings weren't on the beaten track. But gas was in the tanks, which had to be hand pumped. No one was anywhere around. The tools were left in plain sight and there were used tires on a rack. Careless. He didn't investigate the cabins. They were back a way and one had a door-wide bolt bar. The dirty windows looked crowded by junk.

Darwin's dad still talked about times when people could trust one another. Whoever ran that scraggly outfit was a leftover.

Darwin jogged back to his car, took a fishing pole out of the trunk and put it together. He went out on the beach of white sand and fine shells. He investigated how friendly the fish might be. And they could hardly wait for him to rebait the hook.

When he had several nice-sized fish, he built a beach fire and ate a supper that tasted as if it had been meant for the inhabitants of Mount Olympus. He lay back on his bedroll and looked at the sky, listening to the sounds of gulls, the lap of the waves, contemplating the motion of the universe.

He'd been a long time finding such peace. Was it possible that he could again find a reason to live and to take pleasure in his life?

He slept. He wakened in the night and took off his damp shoes before he slid into his bedroll. He slept again.

Darwin's eyes opened just before dawn. There were sky streaks that promised a spectacular sunrise. He stripped and went down to the water to see how swimmable it was. And he found a place that was just right. He swam far out, unmindful of the currents that carried him.

He came onto the beach with the morning sun just barely below the horizon, changing the colors of the clouds. With his flesh cooled by the chilled water, the warmer air was gentle on his nakedness. He jogged along and found he was on the other side of the old gas station with the two obsolete cabins. All was still.

He was naked and it was somewhat later than he'd expected it to be. He came closer to the gas station and its pier and he saw the dog.

It was a huge animal. It wore a collar. It looked fed. Being in a strange place, Darwin was leery of dogs, especially since he was naked. He jogged more slowly, looking for a rock or, better, a stick to protect himself if the dog was hostile.

Then he saw her.

She was in a long, translucent gown. Her dark hair was loose and covered her shoulders. Her back was to him. The lapping waves obscured the sounds of his steps. She didn't know he was there. She was facing the rising sun.

She looked like a goddess. One that had to greet the morning so that the sun would rise. Without her, the day would refuse to come. The sun wouldn't show its face. And the world would be bleak.

He glanced at the place on the rim of the world where the sun would rise. It was ready. Did she have to say specific words to greet it? He became fascinated and watched her.

As he came along to where she was, his steps slowed and he stopped. She was between him and where the sun would rise.

The dog watched him, but the dog was sitting, its mouth was closed and it was not at all hostile... yet. It was a big black dog with short hair and a red collar. Darwin wondered if the dog was hers. If it was, it had probably been trained to kill naked men on beaches.

Slowly, slowly the sun rose and peeked over the arm of land. Its upper rim was wide and the hidden part would be stunning. There was no fanfare nor clash of cymbals as it came higher.

Then his eyes moved and he saw that she was naked under that gown. It was a nightgown and her body was silhouetted perfectly. He stared, his breathing changed, his body was affected. He was shocked.

How long had it been since he'd noticed a woman's body? Not just since he'd done more than glance to determine to which sex a person belonged, but when had he really looked in order to see a woman?

This one was worth the effort. She was dark haired and her body was perfect. Her legs... Her waist. The gentle curves of her body. She was so different from him. She was made for a man. He was a man.

His body was urgent. He glanced down and frowned at his eager sex. He hadn't given it permission to be that interested. He glanced back to the unknowing woman. She watched the sun.

He watched her.

The dog watched him.

As the morning light bathed her in an iridescent glow, Darwin knew he ought to quietly move away. He was naked. She would be shocked. But he couldn't bring himself to leave.

The dog still monitored the man. Darwin was aware enough to know that. But she continued to watch the sun. Her attitude was one of waiting. She waited for him.

Of course.

She was a witch. In her crystal ball, she'd seen that he would come along that stretch of deserted beach. And she was there to soothe his agitated body and give him peace. Right. But for a price? What? His soul?

She very quietly moved her head as if coming from the trance he'd imagined. Now she would turn, see him and screech, and the dog would attack. Everyone would come clear down from Tallahassee and chase him off to Texas, where people could live strangely and not call attention to themselves no matter what all they did.

He'd take her with him.

She turned her head, then, and looked down the beach.

His gaze followed her direction and he saw his own footprints coming that way.

She turned more, and he stiffened. She would see him.

Instead of running off, he found he was curious about what she would do if she did see a naked man standing, watching her. He waited. Her breast was perfectly outlined by the light in back of her. It was beautifully molded. His hand curled.

She turned more and she saw him. She didn't screech and nothing happened.

She simply looked at him, all of him. He was just about six feet tall. He was over thirty-five, his hair was dark and his eyes were blue. He was a beautifully made man. She asked, "Did you come from the sea?"

And he was aware enough that he knew she wasn't asking if he'd been swimming. She meant did he live in the sea. He nodded.

"Do you speak our tongue?"

She might think he was an alien. But this would be the wrong coast for West Indies aliens. He nodded.

She smiled just the slightest bit and waited.

He wasn't sure what to say or do. And he found he wanted to carry her off. That was shocking to him.

He went slowly to the side of the pier and looked up at her. "Are you afraid?"

She considered that soberly. Then shook her head.

"I would like to carry you off somewhere, but I have no place."

She smiled gently and waited.

"The dog will protect you?"

"I'm not sure."

He looked down and judged the dog. He told the animal, "I have no protection." With the words, he realized he was speaking to her.

She said, "You have come on me at a crossroads in my life. I am susceptible."

His mouth opened with his gasp and his gaze was avid. "Do you mean—?"

Very gently, she clarified, "I want to...I would know you in the biblical sense."

He put his hands to his face and rubbed his eyes. "I'm still asleep. This is a dream."

"Perhaps."

He frowned at her. "Are you sick?"

"No."

"Why would you submit to a man you don't know?"

Her smile widened a trifle as she looked down him. "You have no secrets."

"I could harm you."

"You could have. You didn't."

"I won't?"

"No. I saw you coming along the beach. I knew that you stood and watched me."

"Why are you so careless with yourself? Is the dog that good? How close can I come to you before he attacks?"

"I don't know."

"How was he taught?"

She shrugged and, seeing that, he lost track of the line of questioning.

She explained, "He belongs to the man who is trying to fix my car."

Darwin frowned as he asked, "You don't ride a chariot of fire?"

"No."

"You're mortal?"

"Yes."

"I don't believe you." He put his hands low on his hips and stood with his feet apart. He was beautiful.

She came closer and said, "You aren't mortal. You're disappointed that I am?"

"I'm about as mortal as a man can be. I'm flawed and tempered and hard to please."

She smiled, then she laughed in her throat in a most thrilling manner. "You give a challenge?"

He smiled before he put back his head and laughed aloud. When had he last done that? He looked at her and the sun caught in his eyes in shafts of dancing light. He said, "I have fish from the sea for your breakfast. Come with me."

She took off her thongs and came to the edge of the pier. She stood about three feet above him. She said, "I need help getting down."

He lifted his hands to her waist and by actually touching her he confirmed the impossible. She was real. His hands could almost span her waist. He could feel the coolness of her. He saw the green and yellow flecks in her tan eyes. And he could smell the womanliness of her.

His muscles were eager to show off. He lifted her slowly down until her feet touched the sand. She was shorter than he by six inches. She was wondrously female. His hands moved up her sides and his wrists sneakily touched the sides of her breasts.

He asked, "Don't you want to change?"

"No."

"You can't run around the beach in your night-gown."

"Is that why you're naked? You discarded your pajamas?"

"I was swimming."

She looked out over the water. "I would like to swim in the sea."

"Can you swim?"

"Like a fish."

He admitted cautiously, "I'm a little uncertain about you. I can't believe you would allow me control over you when I'm only a naked man."

"So?" She stepped back and took off her night-gown. The flimsy screen was gone.

She was just as breathtaking as he'd thought. He asked, "Have you been confined or ruined or bank-rupt or divorced?"

And she laughed. "No."

"Then why would you be like this with a stranger? You don't know what might happen to you!"

"All of your questions give me more security. I shock you a little."

"A LOT!"

She laughed again. "Isn't this every man's dream? To come upon a strange woman who is instantly willing?"

"Who's done you harm? What man makes you take this reckless attitude?"

She protested, "Don't back out on me now."

"Do you have a fatal disease?"

"No. And I have protection for you."

He looked off down the beach and shook his head slowly. "While you might be feeling more secure, you're rattling me."

And standing there before him, unclothed, she laughed. Her eyes' glints sparkled and danced, her teeth were white and clean, her breasts jiggled and wiggled . . . and her hand touched his chest.

She had touched him.

The dog still sat there, alert, curious, uninvolved.

Darwin contemplated her hand on his chest. It had been too long since any woman's hand had touched his naked chest and the touch was thrilling to him. His hand made two of hers. His hand covered hers completely. "Do you really want to swim? I've been out for a while and I'm some used up...for swimming."

"Do you want to go back to bed?"

"I don't know how to handle you." He meant it.

"You could kiss me."

His body loved the idea, but he cautioned her seriously, "You scare me."

"I would not hurt you for any reason."

"Isn't that what each man tells a woman?"

"I promise. Come with me." She moved away, but she turned and held out her hand to him.

He suggested, "Why don't I go back to my car and get some clothes on. I'll come back and take you fishing. And we'll have breakfast on the beach."

She put her hands in her hair, and he avidly watched every gesture, every wiggle, every movement as she complained, "You're a virgin."

He laughed in smothered closed-mouth chuckles before he countered, "No."

"Then what's the problem? Does it bother your male thinking because I'm inviting you? Here I have the opportunity to have a...fling. An anonymous fling. No names, no commitments, just go ahead and be reckless...and you are reluctant. I didn't think a man like you would even hesitate. I suppose I mistook you as willing because you run naked. That seems an open invitation, right there."

"I didn't realize how far the current would carry me."

"So you like to privately swim nude?"

"Yeah."

"Ever been bitten by a fish?" She looked down him. "Or a mermaid?"

"Not yet."

"I have two days. I suppose I can gradually work up to getting your consent? If it takes any longer, I don't have the time. I would so like to just say what I want without shocking you so much and do what I want without appalling you. Maybe I should look around. This is an isolated place, but this is where my car broke down."

"I can't believe you're here all alone, on a deserted beach, or that you invite the first naked man who comes along to seduce you."

She demurred, "No, I'm not asking that. I'd do all the work." She was earnest. "I'd be sure you enjoyed yourself."

"You might have noticed that I'm not indifferent."

"That's all that's given me the courage for this assault on you."

He gasped rather too elaborately and put his hands to cover himself as he protested, "An . . . assault?"

She licked her lip and put her teeth into the lower one before she said with lousy earnestness, "You'll love it. After the first time, it isn't too bad."

And he laughed.

She explained, "No names, no personal information. No recriminations. Okay?"

"Do we shake hands?"

"Right."

They did that. Her humor was obvious, and he laughed. So he asked, "What do I call you?"

"Columbine. I'll call you Harlequin."

"I'm sorry that I don't play a banjo."

"It wasn't a banjo, I believe it was a mandolin."

"It looks like half of a gourd."

"There's no romance in your soul."

His eyes were amused. "Are you becoming disillusioned?"

She nodded. "You're almost impossible to seduce. That is shockingly inconsistent with what I thought of men. And you are flawed. Without a soul that holds romance, you'll probably suggest we go to some cheesy motel."

"I believe the word is sleazy."

"Yes." She turned her head and looked around. "You would know the wordage."

"How can you stand here, stark, staring naked in front of a strange man, and say he has no soul?"

She replied studiously, "While I readily agree that you're a strange person, you may very well have a soul—it's romance you lack. I *invited* you inside my dwelling in order to use your body and you declined."

He denied that. "No. I postponed it."

"You're a . . . tease?"

He shook his head slowly as he stated, "I seriously doubt that."

"Then why did you postpone it?"

He ventured cautiously, "Anticipation?"

She dismissed such an evaluation. "I would never believe that a real man would want to do that. It seems to me that men are the sudden type who want sex immediately and again later."

"We're not that crude."

"Sudden." She corrected his word and gave him a side glance that was veiled amusement.

"Who are you?"

She held up her hand and admonished, "No names."

"I mean, are you out for revenge? Are you eager to outwit and conquer me as a revenge on some guy who couldn't appreciate you?"

"Why must you believe that I'm seducing you for a purpose other than it appeals to me to simply—have you."

"Men do that?"

With a marvelous show of exquisite patience, she inquired, "How long were you married?"

Darwin became serious. "You know?"

"I'm not sure. What do I 'know?' "

"I've been married."

She gestured, distracting him with the movements of her body, so that he breathed audibly. Then he shivered. She inquired, "Are you cold?"

"I'm about as hot as a man can get."

"Well, then, why don't we go to my cabin? I can help you."

"I can't believe you're that willing. Do you have a cohort in there to hit me over the head and collect all of my—"

She interrupted with some irony, "You're naked. How could I or any 'cohort' *take* anything from you? Do you have gold fillings? Gold is up."

"What would you get out of it?"

"Instant gratification?" Then she sympathized, "I never realized men had it this tough. I mean, how blatant can I be?"

He assured her, "We get a lot of refusals."

"I thought if *I* was willing, that would do it!" She waited that marvelously pithy second before she added rather sadly, "I overestimated male response."

He groused, "You can't look at me and say that."

She took a studied breath. "I'm disappointed."

"Oh, hell."

She said, "I'll go dress and we'll take the long, *hard* route in this tiresome seduction." She lifted questioning brows. "Would you like a towel?"

"I believe I'd be most comfortable wringing your neck. You have to appreciate my restraint."

That fascinated her. "You are restrained—deliberately? Why? Why don't you simply go with me into my cabin and—"

"I have problems with your remarkable willingness. There's something here that doesn't meet the eye."

She moved a trifle in order to display her nakedness. "What could that possibly be?"

"You baffle me."

With some irony, she suggested, "Maybe you're not too bright."

"You feel that I've blocked you? Now, that must be interesting to a woman like you. Before this, you must have had this same encounter, in which the roles were reversed and you were the defender. Are you feeling befuddled and frustrated?"

"Yes."

He had the gall to say to her, "Now you know how men feel."

But she retorted, "I haven't actually put my hands on you. How would I know how men feel?"

He looked at her as they shared the laugh. He said quite honestly, "If you put your hands on me, I'd explode."

And she said with soft wickedness, "What a waste."

He narrowed his eyes. "Do you have me mixed up with some idiot scion of some fortune? You plan to get pregnant and get your share? You're out of luck. I'm a nobody."

"I can't say that about a body like yours. You really are spectacular."

"I can't believe you're real. Do you realize what you're doing to me? You have eyes, you can see. What's your purpose? You saw me coming along the beach and, yet, you deliberately enticed me. What are you up to? Why me?"

"I saw you yesterday when you came along the beach. You boggled me. I thought you might be back. I watched for you. I was out this morning, restless, and I saw you come ashore. The binoculars are over there by that post. When I saw you coming this way, I became fascinated by the rising sun. I knew where you were every second. I told Ralph to be still or I'd kill him. He takes hints."

"Uhhhhh." He was boggled. "You knew."

"Yep."

"You're something else."

"That's an outmoded saying that dates you."

"What I want to know is, will you date me?"

"Briefly. Two days. I've mentioned this. No names, Harlequin. Instant gratification. You're dragging your heels."

"I have to admit you've proven women don't have it easy. Where did you learn all this? Men aren't this crude. We must have a little finesse. You discourage me a whole lot. Surely we have more feeling?"

"Not that I've noticed."

"Do you know anyone in Minneapolis? Did I make some woman mad when I wasn't sensitive enough? Who set me up for this treatment?"

"No one. You're a ship passing in the night. You have one hell of a guilt trip? What did you do to the female population in Minneapolis?"

A trifle indignant, he responded, "Nothing."

She pronounced, "Never admit to anything where there might be tape recorders."

He was appalled. "You got *tape* recorders here?"

Chapter Two

"Tape recorders?" Columbine chided, "Silly. Of course not. In fact, we're the only two people anywhere around. You ought not swim alone, Harlequin."

"Isn't columbine a flower?"

"Yes. But she was the lover of Harlequin."

"And he played the mandolin for her?"

"Sometimes a flute."

He took a step, but it was done in such a way that he didn't back away nor did he crowd her. She considered that either instinctively or with practice he knew how not to scare or appear to reject a woman.

He said, "I can play a comb with a piece of waxed paper." Then he glanced at her face to see how she would react.

She had to look off over the sea as she considered. "That might do."

"And you? What instrument do you play?"

"I'm learning men."

He went still. "How many have you . . . played?"

"You're my first. I must be clumsy or give the wrong signals or something because it isn't working. By this time we should be recovering."

"That fast?" He was some shocked.

"I've been standing here naked for hours, now, and you don't even look at me."

"I've been looking."

"Why, how sneaky. When did you peek?"

"Constantly."

"You're skilled."

"I wish. I'm not bad, but my wife was tolerant and liked me."

"You were fortunate. Divorced?"

"She was hit by a car that went through a red light. She lived two days."

"Oh, hell." She turned away, bent over and picked up her gown. She shook the sand from it and pulled it over her head.

His lips parted, he frowned, his hands moved, but he didn't know how to stop her and not scare her. He said, "Why'd you do that?"

"I can't compete with a dead woman."

"It's been four years." And it was only then that he looked back and realized four years was a long time. He'd been caught in a vacuum and hadn't noticed. "Who's the president now?"

"Of what?" She was lifting her hair out of the back of her gown.

"Oh, how the mighty have fallen."

"I feel that way. I've had to fight off males since I was twelve. Why can't I catch your attention?" She frowned at him. "Yesterday, I watched you inspect the tools and wondered if you were a thief. But you tidied them. I was impressed. You weren't a looter, you were curious. Those gas pumps fascinated you."

"You watched? Where were you?"

"In the hut with Ralph."

"He didn't bark."

"He was taken from his mother when he was very young and I don't believe he realizes he's a dog. He tries to talk and must be annoyed that he can't."

"We could call him 'dog' for a while. Maybe he'd realize that—"

"He doesn't get out much and he would think it's just another kind of a name. Like calling a man 'boy' or something like that."

"You think I'm immature."

She was unable to stop her quick scan of his adult body.

"—mentally," he added hastily.

"I'm not sure. I can see why men give up. This is a chore and I'm frustrated. I may tear my hair."

So he was helpful. "You're supposed to hold my hand and kiss my wrist and put your arm around me. You're supposed to lure me."

She gasped in surprise, "Oh. You mean saying 'Lie down and let's get to it' isn't enough?"

He shook his head with impatience. "You've been around crass people. I can see I need to help you quite a whole lot. We'll begin. You say, 'You have an especially nice body.' Now how I reply to that is a clue as to how I'm reacting to you. Go ahead.''

''What's your reply?''

''You haven't said the comment yet.''

''Oh.'' She blinked. ''Sorry. Uh—''

He whispered, ''You have an especially nice body.''

''I like yours, too, and—''

''You're supposed to tell *me* that.''

''You have an especially nice body.''

He was disgusted. ''That sounds like a trained parrot. Put a little smoke in it.''

''Yes.'' She moved closer to him and said a husky, ''You have an especially nice body.'' And she slid her hand on his arm.

''You're not supposed to touch me yet. You'll scare me off. You have to be more subtle. Talk about my eyes.''

''Bend down so I can see them.''

He bent down and she put her hand on the back of his head to hold him still so that she could study his eyes. His lashes just about covered them.

He said, ''Your eyes are *tan!* Now that's peculiar. I've never seen anything like that.''

In disgust, she chided, ''Don't say 'peculiar' that way. You'll give me a complex.''

He tried again. ''Odd?''

"Try 'unusual' or—"

"Unique."

"That's okay."

He asked, "What about mine?"

"They're blue."

Moving one hand in small circles, he encouraged her to elaborate. "Sad. Misunderstood. Those of a wanderer."

"What harpies have been feeding you that stuff?"

"Compassionate, earnest women."

She was somewhat hostile. "What did you reply to that junk?"

"I backed off."

"Good. You have good taste."

"Well, what about my eyes? Since you refuse to mention my naked body, we have to begin somewhere. Tell me about my eyes. And my hair. Women are always wanting to put their hands in my hair."

"Why?"

"I honestly don't know."

"Let me see." She put her hands in his hair. "It's thick enough."

He straightened with some indignation. "—enough?"

She giggled. "I've been trying to get some reaction from you. So you're sensitive about your hair?"

He tightened his mouth in mock disgust and put his hands on his hips. He looked at how high the sun had continued its orbit without their control. "I'm hungry."

"Finally!"

He gave her a patient look. "For food."

She was disgusted.

"You're probably one of those women who hasn't the time to get out of bed and eat, so you eat in bed."

"Are there that kind of women?"

"Guys brag."

"Ladies never talk. They never gossip."

"Now wait a minute here—"

She explained, "Men gossip and brag—women exchange information."

"I hadn't realized the nuance."

She echoed thoughtfully, "Nuance."

He was helpful. "A shading of meaning."

She didn't look up, she was still considering. She replied gently, "I know."

He said, "I haven't had breakfast."

"Neither have I."

"Get some clothes on and—" He stopped and his face went blank. He exclaimed, "I've never said that to a woman before now! It's a first! I've never in my life told a woman to put on some clothes." That amazed him.

"Well, hallelujah! I do believe I shall do as you suggest. Maybe clothed I can catch your eye."

He started to turn away, then he asked over his shoulder, "Why me?"

She gestured to the deserted beach. "Of all those available, you stood out."

He looked down his body. "Yeah."

Her laugh was deliciously wicked.

"Columbine?"

She looked back at him.

"It's late. Could I borrow a towel?"

She puffed the word, "Coward."

"I'm just not an exhibitionist."

She looked down his body in an exaggeratedly lascivious manner and observed, "You have every cause to be."

Earnestly he replied, "So—do—you! But I'd rather you didn't."

She protested, "I put my gown back on."

"I mean with other people."

She picked up her binoculars, and they walked through the sand to the shanty hut and he looked around. The dog followed pleasantly.

"Sure you won't come inside?" She gave that a wicked meaning.

"Cut that out. Give me time. You animal." His voice was amused, chiding.

She sighed deliberately and went inside.

With a saucily innocent face, she brought him a hand towel.

He gave her a patient look and waited with his hands on his hips.

She brought back a bigger towel, and he did try that but it wasn't big enough. She brought back a bath sheet. That worked.

He wrapped it around his hips and tied it.

Ralph watched with some interest.

She watched critically and said, "What a shame to cover you up."

"My chest's bare."

She didn't reply.

He told her, "You could go around bare chested."

"Other men . . ." She repeated the two words with more emphasis, "Other men . . . look."

"I never missed a wiggle or a jiggle. I watched."

"You're too subtle."

He bent his head down to observe the obvious bulge pressing against his towel. "I reacted."

"Maybe you're that way normally. How could I tell?"

"I'm not. I know. I'm an expert on me, my reactions, my needs and my libido."

"—and your relentless restraint."

"Have I made you hostile?"

"Irritated."

"You need a back rub."

She straightened and exclaimed, "I'd *love* one."

"I owe you one."

She was disgruntled. "—owe." And she added, "—one."

He was bolstering. "You have to work for them. It's a challenge."

"How do I qualify?"

"I'll surprise you."

With great irony, she guessed, "In fifteen years?"

"Now, don't get impatient. These things need a little time."

She flung out her arms and told the sky. "I had to find the only male who isn't sudden, one who has to plot and plan and be restrained. Who could believe this?"

He comforted her. "When I finally give in, you'll find it was worth the wait."

Her eyes moved as she assimilated his words and she exclaimed, "Women say that!"

"I know."

She narrowed her eyes. "Are you so wicked that you'd pull a reverse on me just because I approached you openly?"

"One does as one must." He put the back of his hand to his forehead.

That's probably what caught her. He was acting. He was being deliberately coy. He was planning a seduction that she would think was her idea.

He told her, "I like your birthday suit."

She scoffed. "This old thing?"

"Young."

She moved so that he could see her better and she replied, "It's all I have."

"Lucky you." Then he said, "I get a kiss."

"Already?"

"You only kiss afterward?"

"Well, if you refused to move the sand with me, why would you take a kiss now?"

"I kiss first."

"Then—?"

He confirmed, "Then I go and catch our breakfast."

"Just fish?"

"Some fruit, hard rolls, coffee."

"Where do I come to you?"

"It isn't far. That way. I've got the whole beach today. If you like, you can bring Ralph. Does he eat fish?"

"He eats everything but humans."

"I'm very glad to hear that he's selective."

She didn't quit. She added, "He's all show, like another male I've met recently."

"Columbine, Columbine, you have so much to learn."

Glumly she supplied, "About fish?"

"About seduction and men."

"And you think you can teach me those things?" She was disgruntled.

"You'll see." He gave her a smug look from under his eyelashes and down his nose.

"As hard as I've tried, you didn't bend an inch."

After he finally quit laughing, he said, "You'll learn. Just be patient." Then he took her into his arms and he kissed her, blowing off the top of her head and making her eyes unfocus, her knees wobble and her heart racket around remarkably.

He propped her against the hut's wall and his hands were a little careless. He asked gently, "You notice the nuances?"

She nodded tiny, little movements.

He sipped another quick kiss. "Come down the beach, I'll be watching for you."

She barely bobbed her head, her face was serious and her eyes were enormous as she watched his face.

He added in a husky voice, "Ladies don't fool around with dynamite. They're careful."

He started away, then he turned back and asked, "You will come to breakfast? You're not a coward."

She never changed expression. She moved her head up and down barely enough to communicate agreement.

He stood sideways and watched her a little longer, then he said, "Hustle up. The fish are eager for the pan."

She watched him out of sight. He turned twice and just looked back, but he went on.

Would she come to him? If she escaped, how would he track her? She had a car that needed repairs and he could trace her license. More cheerful, but glancing back, he washed in a public faucet for drinking water and he put on clean shorts and a shirt and wore a baseball cap.

The night before, he had gathered enough wood for his fire. He started that before he set about catching the fish. It was easy.

His car had a luggage rack around the perimeter of the roof. Harlequin had put rope in holes cut in the woolen blanket tying the loops to the car superstructure. He stretched the blanket out from the car to two strong bamboo poles that could be anchored in the sand. And they had shade.

In that shade, Harlequin put an old army blanket and some pillows that had only ticking on them. He considered it was a lure for the harem's darling.

Columbine arrived as he was filleting the fish. She wore a cotton jacket, an old faded skirt and sneakers. She brought along Ralph.

She watched Harlequin seriously. He smiled at her and was very courteous. He seated her on the old army blanket that was hardy and not especially comfortable. He handed her a tube of sunscreen. He gave her a big kerchief to cover her head. Then he pulled it forward so that it shaded her face.

He fed her bits and pieces of fish from his fingers and his attention was concentrated on her.

He gave her portions of fruit that he'd peeled and sliced and he gave her crusty pieces of hot rolls that had no butter.

He gave her beer. She was dubious about the beer, especially for breakfast. He encouraged, "Just sips. Don't breathe the smell, hold your breath."

She echoed the word as if tasting it. "Smell."

He explained, "Some strange people have to get used to the taste first. You're that type. If they try to taste it while their noses are working, they can get hostile about drinking the stuff."

There was another thoughtful echo from her. "Stuff." Then she considered her Harlequin. "You believe I'm . . . strange?"

Kindly he replied, "You're not normal."

"What's normal?"

"While you do have a point there, any woman who stands outside in her nightgown—and pretends to watch the morning sunrise while some naked ya-hoo that she doesn't know comes up the beach and sees her—is not average."

She looked off into the distance while she digested all that explanation. She said, "I believe you're weird."

He smiled tolerantly, "I'm 'a good influence' for women. I've been told that. Since I can be a good influence to you, in this launching of your adventure of seducing men, I shall be happy to give you my counsel and consideration."

"Glory be."

"The trouble with you, Columbine, is that you're sarcastic and sassy. Those are two traits men can't STAND in women. I'll mention when you're being one or the other, and we can defeat the impulse right away. A woman has to be pliant and respectful to men."

"Am I witnessing a turnabout here?"

"No. It's the real me."

"Perhaps this is why mothers tell their daughters not to get tangled up with men. They're quirky and clever. They can appear shocked to be seduced and then take over the whole game and do it their way."

"More than likely."

"You admit it?" She was indignant.

"You're a rotten seducer," he told her kindly. "No élan, no finesse, no plan. You seized on a likely premise and you botched it. You need a contingent plan."

"You make it sound like a corporate takeover."

He toasted some more roll pieces and agreed, "It's very similar."

Ralph sat watching.

Eventually Columbine inquired, "Aren't you going to give the dog anything?"

"He gets water. Dogs only eat two meals."

"Did dogs figure that out?"

"It's a rule." He gave the dog some water in a battered old pan.

"Isn't that what you cooked the fish in?"

"Yeah. We're through with it—" he pushed it "—for now."

She said, "Well, I'm not going to be here for the next meal."

He was instantly serious. "Did you get your car back?"

"No. I'm after more friendly fish."

"Honey, I can be friendly."

"I hadn't noticed that."

He walked on his knees the several feet that separated them, put aside his cooking utensils, laid her back on that scratchy blanket and he kissed her witless.

Whistling, apparently unaffected by the encounter, he went busily back to tidying up after their meal. He offered her bits and pieces, but she was incapable of doing anything normal like chewing and swallowing food.

Her stunned glances followed him.

After she'd refused any more of anything, he gave her a peppermint candy. He gave her that after she'd been drinking beer. It made the candy taste weird. When she could communicate, she mentioned again, "You're strange."

"No." He looked at her guilelessly. "I'm a new experience." Then he asked, "Where are we going to meet, later, after we get through with our commitments?"

"I'm not sure we should."

"I'm sure. Let's figure out a location. Are you going down the west side of Florida? Or is your business on the east coast?"

"It's none of your business."

He looked at her with some humor. "I'm trying to figure a central meeting place."

"Here."

"I could get tired of having Ralph around and staying in that hut waiting for you to show up."

"Why would you want to see me again?"

He sighed. "There's so much for you to learn. How old are you?"

"That has nothing to do with anything."

"I'm only trying to see how much time we have for kids."

She was shocked. "You have children?"

"No, *our* kids."

"Good grief!"

"Everyone who is anyone always wants a dozen of everything. Handkerchiefs, dish towels, flatware, whatever. Why not kids?"

"This was to be an affair. I have no need for any sort of relationship. At all. I don't want to produce babies for some man who is incapable of having them himself and I don't want any commitment at all. Got that?"

He expressed great surprise. "You just want to roll me around on the sand and get me all sticky and gritty before you discard me."

"Yeah."

He gave her an aloof glance and enunciated, "I'm not that kind of guy."

And she laughed.

He grinned and watched her. "You jiggle when you laugh."

"Nonsense."

He chanted his version of the old nursery rhyme: "Columbine, Lollenbalm, pudding and wine, kissed the boys and made them whine. But when the girls come out to play, Columbine will run away."

She lay back on the blanket, contented and lazy. "You could be very entertaining."

"I'm not even trying to entice you. I know you want some man, right now, for some reason you think is logical. I'm that man. I'm keeping you isolated until you understand why you want...whatever it is you're really seeking.''

''You believe I'm trying to seduce a man for some OTHER reason than just wanting a man?''

''It's obvious.''

''So. You are implying that when men go out and have date sex and leave, that they need something that has nothing to do with sex?''

''Yeah. Mostly those men are insecure.''

She lay back and laughed. Still smiling, she looked at him and said, ''You are entertaining.''

''I'm serious. You have some reason at this particular time to do something completely out of character.''

She got huffy. ''I have only the desire—you do catch the significance of that word?—to experience a man whom I do not know. An impulsive, non-committed encounter. Nothing more, nothing less.''

''You've alibied the impulse in your mind, but there is an underlying reason. What is it?''

''You're wrong.''

''Some man dump you? Some woman taunted you? You're inept? This is a strange encounter for you and you're not sure how to proceed with it. When you make love with me, I want it to be because you want me. Not because you're angry or hurt or feeling insecure.''

''You have a great imagination.''

"Would you tolerate sleeping with me?"

She took a deep breath that fascinated him and she enunciated the words carefully, "That is what I've been trying to do since dawn!"

"No, you wanted to have sex. I want to sleep."

"I think I'll walk down the beach a way. Something else might turn up."

"Well, look around. But I'll be here to distract you when you come back, Columbine, because you aren't going to find anyone nearly as interesting as you find me."

"Hah!"

He stretched tiredly. "I've got to rest up for tonight."

She was standing up but she looked back at him. "What are you doing tonight?"

"I'm going to seduce you." He eased down on the woolen blanket and took two of the pillows for his head. Ralph was willing to share the blanket and Harlequin didn't object to the dog being on it.

She considered the man. "I'll look around. If I come back, you'll understand that I'm anticipating the evening with you only because nobody else is around."

He smiled, his eyes were closed. His smile faded and his breath evened. He was asleep, just like that.

She stood there a long time, silently, looking at him, remembering the things he'd said. Then she looked down the deserted beach and she considered walking anywhere at all. It was not tempting.

His snore bubbled. She knew he was down for the count. He would never know whether she left or not. She might just as well nap while it was cool enough. She moved to the other side of Ralph, nudged him over and lay down, pulling the last pillow out from under the dog.

She settled down, she yawned. She wiggled to get the sand under the blanket just right, then she went to sleep.

Over on the other side of Ralph, Harlequin smiled and then he really did go to sleep.

She wakened and looked at her watch. It was almost two! She'd slept several hours! She turned and looked over Ralph at Harlequin and he still slept. She smiled, eased up carefully and stood up.

He heard her.

She turned Ralph over onto her place to erase her imprint and she stood up, straightened her clothing and licked her lips. She put her hands on her knees and asked, "Still sleeping?"

He stretched and yawned. Then he lounged lazily and asked, "Nobody around?"

"Nope." She sighed hugely in defeat. "You're it."

"Well, darn." He scowled. "I did hope you'd find somebody!"

She put her hands out from her sides. "It's up to you."

He moved tiredly and said faintly, "I probably ought to sleep a little longer."

She said to the world, "This is all there is?"

And from the blanket he said, "Yep. If you will look around you, there isn't anyone else in sight. I have a radio in the car and I heard the last broadcast. The world ended almost an hour ago. We are the last two people on earth. From here on out, it's up to us. You can see the burden on me. Fishing, sleeping, making babies, all that stuff."

"And I?"

"You'll lie around pampered, indolent, breeding." He looked at Ralph. "I wonder if there's a bitch for him anywhere around."

"Are you implying I'm one?"

"You're a lady."

"You are quick."

"No. I'm slow and sensual." Then he said in an aside, "Move, Ralph. You're taking up more than your third." And he pushed the dog over.

Ralph sounded like an elephant that had to kneel down and get up again, but he did move over.

Harlequin pulled Columbine down onto the blanket and said, "I have to see if you got more burn when you were out and about, trying to find a replacement for me. How many did you reject?"

"Actual count?"

"Close. How many?"

"Ohhh, probably five hundred."

He gave an impressed whistle. "How far did you walk?"

"Almost to Louisiana."

"You must be exhausted. Poor girl."

"I'm a woman."

"I noticed that just this morning." He lay beside her, propped on one elbow, and unbuttoned her jacket, commenting: "I just did that left-handed. I'm really a right-handed man, but at times I can appear to be ambidextrous. I'm showing off," he said.

"Now that does surprise me. I didn't think you needed to do that."

He opened the panels of her jacket to reveal no underwear. Her charming and bare chest was exposed. He clicked his tongue once and said, "I remembered just right. Two of them."

She grinned at him.

He leaned over her and saluted each one. Then his tongue went down to be sure there was no lint in her tummy button.

She said, "I didn't bring my protection along."

He lifted his mouth long enough to say, "I have some."

"Oh, really? Why?"

"I took a fast trip into that little town and probably bought their whole supply. The expiration date
is current, even the year."

"Wouldn't it be?"

"It proves how much traffic there is through here
in the spring. No native buys condoms in his own
little town. People would know what he was doing."

"What would he be—doing?"

"Making love with some wily woman who thinks
she isn't eager to try it with him."

"Are you eager?"

"I've been working my tongue to the bone to make
you want me and not to just use me."

She chided, "I wouldn't do that."

He smiled up at her and said, "Not now, you
wouldn't."

"So," she said silkily, her fingers working in his
hair as he saluted her chest. "You believe I want you,
for you, and not for the sex?"

His mouth busy, he just said, "Mmm."

She said, "I like that." And she held his head
against her.

His mouth squeaked a little as he released her.
"All women like that."

"Have you gone around the country, testing that
theory?"

"Guys gossip."

"See? I knew it!"

He elaborated, "They tell what they've heard from other guys."

"So all of your friends are basically innocent?"

"You have to realize I'm thirty-seven and I've been married."

"Well, that does make you an experienced man."

"How old are you?"

"I'll be thirty in a couple of days."

"I remember thirty. It was nice."

"Did you have trouble getting through the birthday?"

"We had a flood that year. We lost about everything and we really struggled, but we all survived. It was an adventure."

"You considered that an . . . adventure?"

"Yeah." He went back to her body, moving her, adjusting her, distracting her.

He heard the cars first and covered her. He sat up. Ralph lumbered to his feet and went out from under the shelter to stand and stare.

The cars had hesitated, but Ralph's stony look decided their move on down the beach quite a distance. Harlequin said, "Good dog."

Ralph replied, "Raf."

Quizzically Harlequin commented, "He can't say the *L* sound."

Chapter Three

Harlequin took off his shoes and then took off Columbine's. He lay back down on his side by her and pulled her close to him. "Kiss me. Make your lips soft and inviting." He kissed her several times. "Want another?"

She moved her knees restlessly and said, "Yes."

He kissed her seriously. He glanced up and around and told the dog. "Guard."

Harlequin was surprised when Ralph got up in one heave and ambled out to sit and look around. He got up and paced and sat in another place, but he always looked out and about and he was "guarding" them!

Harlequin's eyes were filled with humor. "That dog is a guard dog. He is so big and serious looking that he can fake it out! This morning, I thought he might tear me apart. There was never any danger of that."

"Kiss me again."

"So you want another? Are you going to put your arms around me?"

"I'll see."

"What will make up your mind to do that?"

"How you kiss."

He kissed her again, slowly taking the dominant position. His hands moved sensuously and his mouth worked hers wickedly so that it was just fortunate that she was already horizontal.

Her hands crept up his arms and onto his shoulders. She moved her body, squirming under him. She was panting.

He was hot eyed and amused. "Want me?"

"Don't be dense. I've been trying for you all this time. You can't possibly not have noticed."

"—not have noticed."

"It's Pennsylvania grammar."

"Catchy."

Her blouse was again open, her skirt was around her hips and his hands were working her. He was bold and deliberate, and she groaned.

Soon he was sweating rather profusely and he licked his upper lip. "How long's it been?"

She clawed at him and gasped, "Forever."

"For me, too. Not yet. I have to put on the condom."

"Do you remember how?"

"I believe I can do it by myself. Quit that."

"Hurry up."

He did manage and he turned to her eager body and almost immediately sank into her lure. He shuddered and shivered and made hoarse noises.

She strained at him and said, "Don't hurry."

And he laughed helplessly. He braced himself on his elbows and watched her face as he moved gently, swirling just a trifle, pressing deep.

She was swooning, gasping, her hands helpless and pawing at him.

He leaned and kissed her cheek and her forehead and her mouth. He really kissed her. His mouth was skilled and he gave her exquisite kisses as they lay coupled.

She murmured, "Oh." She breathed, "Ah." She said, "Harlequin..." And she questioned, "Now?"

He was fascinated by her response and replied, "Soon."

She moved her thighs along him and curled her hips and pressed her chest up against him. Her mouth sought his and her kisses were deep and hungry, wanting more. She shivered and whispered, "Now?"

And he began to move carefully, skillfully, giving her pleasure. His breathing became harsh. As he moved on her, he would glance around the area. Ralph was watching, turning his head.

Harlequin whispered, "Columbine, what's your real name?"

"Again."

"What?"

"Do that again."

So he did several things, each time asking, "That?"

"No, the other way."

He knew what she wanted, but he thrilled her and himself with his delay. Her hands clutched at him as he withdrew from her. Then he tasted her. He had her wild before he again coupled with her and he took her slowly, deliciously to paradise, to that ultimate rush and on into the void of pleasure.

They were a tangle of sweaty arms and legs and gasping breaths when they again found themselves under that odd shelter and on that tacky, scratchy blanket.

Harlequin smiled down into her eyes, and she closed hers lazily in slow blinks as she smiled back at him. She made sounds of contentment and pleasure.

He asked, "How'd I do?"

She replied, "When you regain your ability, we'll try again. Once can be a fluke."

He decided, "You're a bloodsucker."

"Not blood."

And they stayed entwined for some while. They moved their hands in lazy pettings and they kissed softly. They made sounds that were nothings, but the sounds communicated their contentment.

She said whole words. She said, "Nice." She murmured, "Wonderful," and she whispered, "Amazing."

He replied in kind.

She told him, "I'd never known it could be so nice."

"I'm small, so I don't intrude roughly."

That made her laugh until she got the hiccups.

He said, "Don't breathe while I kiss you and you'll be cured." So he kissed her until she was dizzy. But he did distract her from the hiccups. However, he wouldn't go get another condom from the car.

"Why not?"

"I've promised to seduce this voracious woman tonight and I dare not deplete myself."

"I don't believe you could ever be depleted."

"What a nice thought. However, we can't again. There're people coming down the beach from the other way. Ralph told me."

"How did Ralph . . . 'tell' you."

"He said his name. Without the *L*, of course."

"Don't make me laugh. I can't do anything but lie flat. I'm woozy."

"Oh, that. That's from being perfectly satisfied . . . by me."

"You are really something, Harlequin. I can't believe sex is this nice."

"Who've been your lovers?"

"I've never had any. And I'm going to be thirty!"

"What's so awful about that? You were waiting for me."

"Yes. But now I can understand so much. And a couple of dirty jokes that always baffled me."

"What were they?"

"I can't tell you. You're not a woman."

"I noticed that a long time ago."

"Don't leave me." She clamped her hands around him, holding him to her.

"I must. I have to be sure the condom doesn't slip off." Then he looked aside. "And those people are coming."

"They can't see that far."

"We want to be modest when they come within range of seeing."

"I suppose so." She allowed him to leave her. As she watched him dispose of the condom in the fire, she asked, "How long until dark?"

And he laughed the nicest throat chuckle. He leaned and kissed her gently. "We'll survive until then."

Ralph paced as the group slowly passed them. He was so big and he turned his head and seemed to read their birthmarks and vaccinations as they passed. They went quite far past until the intruders were only dots. And, again, the beach was just theirs.

Lying on his stomach, braced on his elbows, Harlequin mused, "Do you suppose that we could buy Ralph?"

"Why would we do that?"

"He's amazing. All fake, but just amazing. A bluffer. He knows all the tricks."

"So do you."

He looked over at the lax woman lying beside him and he chided, "Back to that, eh?"

She lifted her chest and let it fall, as she then did her hips and finally her knees.

He instructed, "That's undulating. I've never actually witnessed the performance. You're especially good."

"I can't believe I've waited this long."

"It wouldn't have been as nice before this. You had to wait for me to come down the beach and find you."

"Any man would have done."

"But you could have gotten a clumsy or selfish one and you'd have given up on sex without ever knowing me."

She laughed softly. "I do like a modest man."

He amended, "An honest man."

"A lover."

"You have to know how much your own attitude came into play? Your hunger was very stimulating to me."

"It was play. The most delicious kind. I want more."

"Don't get greedy. If I exhausted you now, what would I do tonight?"

"Revive me?"

"Oh, a cold bucket of water pitched on your inert form? Is that sexual foreplay?"

"Hardly." She turned and put her knee over his backside. Her hand went to his hair and she played with disarranging the silken strands.

He growled, "Don't tempt fate."

She was so innocent. "Does my playing with your hair—tempt—you?"

"So does that lascivious knee rubbing my backside."

She raised up and looked down their bodies. She asked her knee, "What are you doing?" Then she lay back as she'd been.

He asked, "What did it reply?"

"What."

"Your knee. What did it say?"

She scoffed, "Knees can't talk."

"How do you make it hold still?"

"I'm not sure."

Since they'd had breakfast rather late, it was after the normal time to have lunch. Harlequin released the canopy from the car and lay that on top of their ground blanket and pillows. The fire circle was smothered with sand and Ralph was told to stand guard. Then Harlequin went to the faucet with the battered pan and brought back water for the dog.

They drove to the tiny town and even in that out-of-the-way place, there was a fast-food place. Harlequin drove into the tidy parking space with the label flower beds and parked. He looked on Columbine and smiled. Then he chuckled. "Your lips are swollen and red. Some man's been kissing you." Then he added, "Your eyes are sleepy and you look like a cream-fed cat. What have you been doing?"

"I don't remember."

He guessed, "You want a demonstration."

"Yes."

"How do you know what I'll demonstrate?"

"You have a trustworthy face, and I am proof that you're skilled."

He considered her and his face was tender. "You stay here. I'll be right back." He got out of the car, but he put his head back in the window and cautioned, "Don't let anybody steal you away." Then he came back and asked, "Besides me, what do you want?"

"I can't organize my thinking. You choose. No fish."

He looked disgusted. "A picky woman. How do you expect to be a beach bum with me and not eat fish?"

Columbine suggested, "There're always citrus fruits. And the popular, ever present fast-food restaurants."

"Anyone as hot as you should know all there is to know about chili."

She yawned and stretched, and he watched that. Then he stood up, rubbed his hand on his chest and said, "Yes."

As Harlequin waited in line he thought about Columbine, the mystery woman. When her car got back, he could riffle her glove compartment and just see who this woman was. She was from or had spent time in Pennsylvania. She would soon be thirty. She could really, really make love and make a man think he was the ultimate.

With a woman who had no other experience at all, that wasn't necessarily an endorsement.

What else did he know? She had humor. Something had rattled her so that she went out seeking an encounter with any man. What had upset her that much? Just being thirty couldn't do that to a woman.

And there he was, Darwin Moore, now called Harlequin, trying to solve a dark-haired woman who intrigued him. A woman who wanted to be anonymous. She was a woman he found he craved and one he wanted to shelter and know. But he was supposed to go down to Jack's and meet some blond woman that would hold still for a setup.

Now, that wasn't very kind of him to be so disgruntled. Jack and Phyllis were good people who had stood by him all this while. He would *have* to show up at their house as scheduled. He couldn't be so rude as to call and cancel. He would go.

But he would have to have Columbine, whoever she was, stashed someplace safe so that he could find her again. Fingerprints. He'd have to get her fingerprints.

He ordered a humongous lunch and carried it back to the car. He put the meals in a padded carrier to keep them warm, and they went back to their beach.

Ralph had kept the place vacant for them and he briefly acknowledged that he knew them.

Harlequin took their blankets and pillows off downwind and shook the sand from them. There was still sand on them but he'd minimized the accumulation. Then he reset their canopy, spread the rough blanket fresh and stacked all the pillows for her.

He smiled at her and said, "Take off your shoes before you get on that magic carpet."

"It's only a ratty army blanket."

"Your attitude needs adjusting." He took her in his arms and kissed her an attitude-adjusting kiss. She became shy and coquettish.

He sat her down and brought the padded carrier with their food intact. It hadn't cooled too much and was so civilized after their makeshift breakfast that it was delicious.

They ate so much that they had to walk along the beach. Again they left Ralph to protect their area from intruders.

Columbine picked up shells. She never looked anywhere but in front of her feet and she picked up every single shell that was whole. It was hard, tedious work, but she persevered. She filled her pockets, his, her hands and his, and she was indignant that he hadn't brought along the padded insulated carrier.

With real curiosity, he asked, "Why do you want them?"

She looked at him annoyed and retorted, "They're there!"

He considered her. She thought her response was logical. She was flawed. He pondered that and decided he could handle a shell collector. He'd keep her away from shelled beaches. But then he thought of other kinds of shells, deadly ones, on other beaches, and he was sobered.

She said kindly, "I'll give them to people and to the day-care centers and gradually I'll hoard only a logical number of shells."

He couldn't think of anything to say that might not annoy her, so he nodded his head once to acknowledge that she had admitted her flaw.

They lugged all those shells back to their oasis. They refilled Ralph's tin pan for him. Then they filled their cups at the nearby faucet and drank deeply. Their sunscreen hadn't worked entirely and their faces were flushed by the sun. They stripped down to their underwear and went swimming.

It was wondrously refreshing after their long walk, the buoyancy of the saltwater was lovely. They laughed in the shallows and played for a long time. Then they dragged themselves up to their shelter and dozed as they talked.

He cleverly slid in information about himself. Soon she knew that he was from Minneapolis, that he was a lawyer in private practice, that he lived in a condo. That showed her that he could afford her.

But it also showed his skill in communication. In bits and pieces, he allowed Columbine to know that his wife had been killed by a woman who'd run a red light. The driver became hysterical over what she'd done and was in treatment for a long time trying to ease her guilt.

He told her of civic strivings in which he'd been involved and he mentioned the names of his close friends and gave their occupations very cleverly by telling of incidents in which what they did for a living was revealed. "For an accountant who sees everything in figures and sums, he can paint like you wouldn't believe. Perry's had two shows and he's sold out both times."

"How many did you buy?"

"One each time. They're big. The walls of the condo can handle them. But Perry learned to make his masterpieces smaller, so the ordinary house could handle them. He's good. I'd like to have your opinion of them."

But he'd told her he knew an artist who was an accountant and the man's name was Perry. If they were separated, she would be able to find him . . . if she wanted to find him. Ahh. That was the rub.

Would she want to? If they were separated, now, would she strive to locate him?

She listened. She didn't caution him again about keeping information to themselves.

He quoted a friend as saying, "Darwin—"

And she heard that because she immediately inquired, "Darwin? Like in evolution?"

"Yeah. We go a long way back."

She'd snorted. "Everyone goes a long way back. How could it be otherwise?"

"No. There were the first experiments that didn't pan out. You can still see some of that same residue. I had an opposing lawyer not long ago who was a real throwback. I almost had to get down to his level.

But I resisted. And one of the jurors said that I was a gentleman. And since I was, my client musta been a lady.

"Was she?"

"Weelllll. Close. But in this particular instance, she was the injured party."

"Do you like law?"

"It's the only way for the world to work. Minding rules that are made by men who don't profit from them."

"No women making rules?"

"Odd you should mention that. But the rules we go by were made long ago before we realized women were good for other things."

She laughed and attacked him! She tussled and squealed and they rolled and laughed. And of course he pinned her, making her forfeit a kiss. He told her she was made for being made love to.

She huffed and puffed and laughed. She ruffled his hair and was trapped partially under him as she watched his eyes and she was soft and sweet.

He could have taken her then, again, but he did not. His kisses were caressing. His hands were gentle. He told her how lovely she was. He talked about her eyes and he asked who were her people?

She mentioned all the nationalities that comprised her background, and they talked about the migrations of tribes long, long ago. They discussed what would happen to the overpopulated world.

Of course, they then discussed where the land was being overused and misused and turned into "deserts" where the topsoil eroded under cattle hooves. And they spoke of the trees that were being destroyed to provide more land.

But they also talked about music they liked and performers they'd witnessed. And so they shared bits of their lives, and he encouraged it because he wanted her to know him. He wanted to know her better. He was beginning to think she was extraordinary. He began to get scared about losing her.

How could he feel that he "had" her attention enough to think he could "lose" her? A man had to be secure in his relationship before he could lose someone. He'd only met her that morning.

How could he feel that she was a part of him?

Only once had he had a one-night stand. It had been a year after Judy had died of her injuries. Exactly a year. His bitterness was so intense he'd picked up a willing acquaintance for that night, to "punish" Judy for leaving him.

He'd been ashamed afterward.

He looked at Columbine, lying on her side, on the ratty blanket. She was so peaceful, looking at the shells, putting her finger gently through them, listening to the particular sounds of them.

It occurred to him that she was a very interesting companion. She didn't particularly bend to his ideas and had opinions she didn't hesitate to express. But she wasn't quarrelsome.

She was willing to walk or swim. Of course, she did have this quirk about seashells. "Do you collect anything else, besides shells?"

Bland faced, she replied, "Pancakes. I have trunks full of them. Some are getting quite strange looking."

He nodded soberly.

She scoffed. "Shells does it."

"Nothing else . . . peculiar?"

"Books. I find it impossible to throw away or give away a book."

"That could be serious."

"I have a friend at the library, and she gently takes those I offer. They probably sell them for twenty-five cents apiece, but I think of the books as being in their vault."

"That's a nice adjustment."

"What do you collect."

"Now how could you know that?"

"Everybody does it, one way or another. As you can see, Frank collects old tools."

"Frank? The guy who runs the station and rents those huts?" Harlequin squinted his eyes. "He must just like to own the tools. He doesn't use them."

"I don't use the shells, either."

"I'm going to make a crown for you so you can be a mermaid and swim in the sea with a crown and here are the tiny seaworm holes that I can use to string your bracelets and necklaces of shells."

"There's this tiny little baby conch shell that would be a lovely ring."

"I'll fix it. Frank probably has an awl that would do just right putting two holes in that. I'll check with him."

"Buy gas there and he'll do anything. He hauled my car away behind his truck to get it fixed."

Harlequin considered, "He's probably in Mexico by now, selling your car to some poor sucker."

"Now you know anyone who raised Ralph wouldn't do anything like that. Frank's a good man. My car will be returned to me all clean and waxed and working."

"Good luck to you."

She turned over on her stomach and rested her chin on her arms. Her eyes were soft and friendly. "When must you leave?"

"The day after tomorrow."

"That soon?"

His heart soared. How could a heart soar? It was encased, connected and committed. It couldn't soar.

She said, "Just some of the day after that. Please?"

And his heart soared again! It did. He was reluctant. "I have to be in—"

"Don't tell me! I don't want to know."

"I must go. Come with me."

"I can't, either. I, too, am committed to a meeting. I was being selfish when I coaxed. I do understand. I'll see you back here at the hut? Would you come back?"

Very seriously he replied, "To the ends of the earth."

She scoffed. "You can declare that so confidently after knowing me less than twenty-four hours?"

"It's weird, but it's true. I want to know more about you. Like, what's your name? While I like Columbine, I'm not at all sure that's how your family calls you."

"They use the telephone."

"Good God, you're one of those?"

She hastened to assure him, "Only occasionally."

He gasped, shook his head one time and said, "I don't know about this. You could just be trying to wiggle out from under such a label. You might do that day and night and drive me right up the wall!"

"I can control impulse."

"Hah! You forget that I witnessed your one track mind in seducing me! What if you're the same way with puns and stuff like that?"

"I could get help."

"From whom?"

"There must be support meetings for this. It's not excessive enough for me, as yet, but I'm sure if the impulse got out of hand, I could find a support group. Don't be alarmed with one slipup."

He lay back and just laughed. "You're amazing! You carried that ball so earnestly."

"I was earnest. I have all sorts of flaws. I'm riddled with flaws."

"Tell me the worst thing you do."

"I read the newspaper back to front, but I hold on to the first section so I get to read it first. It annoys me when someone takes if off my lap and settles down and reads and reads and reads every single damned word!"

"A strong hostility there. Yep. Serious."

She gestured widely, her voice was fast as if to spill out the horrors. "I put the cap back on the toothpaste and I squeeze it from the *bottom*."

He nodded emphatically. "We match...there."

"You do that?"

"Yep."

And they both just lay back and laughed. They looked at each other and continued to chuckle. Then to smile. He leaned over and kissed her soft lips. "I could very possibly become attracted to you."

"Pish and tosh."

"My grandmother said that!"

"So—did—mine! To *everything* she disapproved and she disapproved of—"

He supplied it, "—everything."

"She used to irritate the liver out of me and then she finally died and what happened? *I* started saying it! It's appalling."

"I rather like it. My grandmother was a nicer lady."

"You were probably rarely home. You were out playing some game or having some class or learning to do something strange like how to kiss a willing female and your sisters had to cope with the grandmother."

"She didn't live with us. She had my grandfather to live with and they traveled all over everywhere, eating the food and walking it off. They're still doing it."

"Wonderful."

With some amused satisfaction he added, "They won't leave us kids one cent. They'll spend it all."

"Good for them."

"That's what my dad says and he isn't even kin to them."

"You must have a nice family."

"So did you. You probably miss that old lady who taught you to say 'pish and tosh' so exactly right."

"Oh, yeah. But she was a trial."

"How will you be at the age she was?"

"On my honeymoon. I've found I like being with a man. I won't give it up as long as I'm alive."

"That's all? Just sex? How about my helping you carry all those shells?"

"Handy."

"There you go again. I used my hands to hold your shells and you reply 'handy' in a way that was sneaky and you planned to secretly enjoy your wordage and slip it right by me, didn't you."

"I swear it was an accident!"

"You say that . . . now."

And again they laughed, together, their eyes holding, their hands touching, their humor matching.

They lay lax and contented. He said, "It's a warm day." Then in a minute he added craftily, "Do you have a shower in your hut?"

Columbine said, "Umm."

"Tired?"

"No. Contented. Or I will be later tonight."

"It's getting past suppertime. We need to eat to shore up my strength, so that I can pay my attentions to your voracious demands tonight. I'm nicer if I'm clean. How about a shower at your place? I even have clean clothes and I have a *suit* to wear."

"Glory be."

"You've used that before. Is that another of grandmother's sayings?"

"She always said that with irony. She meant 'How could that actually happen with a dunce like you?'"

He thought about that and replied, "I'll bet she had an inferiority complex and she was astounded that you were so pretty and smart, when she'd never seen any traces of such genes in her family before you."

"I really like the way you think."

"How do you propose to thank me for that instantaneous and expert evaluation?"

"I'll think of something."

"I'll help."

Chapter Four

Harlequin put their gear into his car, taking down the shade blanket and getting rid of the sand on the blanket and pillows.

Then as Columbine watched he coaxed Ralph into leaving his new territory and getting into the car. It was a more limited space for the dog to control, since it was only the back seat. He adjusted.

They drove to the hut, and Frank still hadn't returned with Columbine's car. Harlequin nodded sagely. Then he enunciated, "Mexico," and looked knowing.

She was kind enough to enjoy his different humor.

So they stood there smiling at each other until Ralph said his name, telling them he was going on patrol, but again the dog-vocalized word was without the *L* sound.

Harlequin squatted down and instructed Ralph in the sounding of that letter, but the dog only looked patient as he glanced around. They fed him two cans of dog food and gave him fresh water. Then he left without permission and checked out his real territory.

The hut was very small. The door didn't lock. That surprised Harlequin. "No lock?"

"Who would guess that I was here? That I have new suitcases and clothes that are new?"

He was serious. "This meeting you're attending, are you trying to impress some guy?"

She didn't even look at him. She just replied airily, "Not any more."

He became mush.

But she turned toward her hut. The other hut was filled with strange things like a buggy seat and a plunger washer and old tires that were really no good. That hut had iron bars over the windows and a metal bar lock on the door. Her door didn't even have a key lock.

He followed her inside a pretty decent-looking room, that had a strange mixture of decorator colors, but he was still caught by the lack of locks. "Did you sleep here last night?" He was appalled.

"Ralph was here."

"Hah!"

She bent around Harlequin so that she could see out the doorway. "Shh. You shouldn't hurt his feelings."

"What about you being hurt?"

"I put the chair back under the doorknob."

He was indignant. "You're just lucky you have me with you tonight and tomorrow night."

She flickered with what appeared to be colored lights as she smiled and said, "Yes."

He scolded, "Now don't go getting salacious. I'll probably have to patrol both nights and won't get any sleep at all."

Hastily she assured him, "The chair works great. Really."

"Frank just went off and left you here all by yourself." He couldn't believe that.

"I *told* you that Ralph was here!"

"What good's Ralph?"

Quite enjoying her own words and the tone she used, she mentioned, "This morning at dawn you were very cautious about approaching anywhere near to me while Ralph only watched you."

"Is that what they mean about a watchdog? That's all he does?"

"I believe that sort of response is very close to puns and plays on words."

He scoffed. "Not even close!"

"We'll get an independent opinion."

Sourly he guessed, "Frank."

"He'll be back. I know he will."

"Probably with a slaver and he'll try to sell you to him."

She thought about that with her chin tilted up. "How much do you think I'd bring in gold."

"An ounce, anyway."

She was indignant. "An *ounce?*"

He frowned in thought and said, "Yeah." Then he assured her, "A whole ounce."

She went to the iron bed that had climbing iron flowers on the iron fencelike frame. She pulled back the chenille bed covering and took out a pillow. Then she turned to swing it at him, but he just grabbed her and tumbled her onto the bed with him on top.

With laughter threading her tone, she said, "Had I known your reaction to pillows, I'd have tried this sooner."

Nuzzling her, he explained, "I'm neutralizing you."

"I've never heard it called that."

He moved his face caressingly along her neck as he said softly, "I really like you. It's obvious that I like you."

"That's so sweet."

"We have to go out to eat and we should do it soon so that I can keep my strength up enough to bravely face a whole night in bed with you."

She guessed, "You're getting nervous."

"You'll probably be at my body all night long, and I'll never get any sleep." He was carefully rubbing his whiskers along her throat.

"I like that, too."

"I can't kiss you any more until I've shaved or your face will be all whisker burned."

"I have some lotion."

He turned his shirt collar up protectively. "You have no sensitivity. You think I'm just a sex machine."

"We could find out."

With great, noble forbearance he told her calmly, "I can't stand a woman who makes me laugh when I'm being serious."

She tilted her head down and looked at him from beneath her brows. She didn't say anything but her smile was wicked.

And he laughed.

They showered together. He had to coax her. Although she'd removed her nightgown that morning on the beach, being naked in that confined space with a naked man was somehow different for her.

However, she wanted that, and she blushed and was charmingly reluctant, but she did take off her clothing and she did get into the shower with him.

Whatever else Frank lacked as an innkee—a hutkeeper, he did believe in hot water. Whatever the source was, the hot water was endless. And she was naked and within arm's reach. They had made love that very morning, so his touch, his kisses, his explorations were not all that new.

And she did become curious. She examined him. She was fascinated. So with all that going on, the shower took quite a long time.

She watched him shave. He dabbed shaving cream on her nose and smiled at her tenderly. Then he remembered Judy watching him shave. How long, long ago that had been.

Harlequin did his throat rather carefully. As he put the razor into the water and swished it back and forth, he glanced at Columbine.

Her lips were parted and she was fascinated. Why were women so interested in a man shaving? He didn't mind. He felt along his wet cheeks for any errant bristle and made his face carefully smooth. For her.

Then he said, "Try me."

And she asked, "Where?"

He put his hand to his forehead and said, "I just hope we get some food somehow."

Although they did do some serious exploring and kissing, they did get up off the bed, however reluctantly, and they did go out for dinner. And they remembered to put on clothes.

Along in the evening, he would slide in a casual inquiry. Once, as they waited between courses at dinner, he asked, "—and where did you get your degree?"

"At a university."

"Not a college."

She elaborated, "A college in connection with a university."

"Where was that?"

And she replied a little snootily, "North of here."

Hell, everything but Texas was north of there.

He would ask, "Have you ever seen a play in New York City?"

"No."

"Do they have a civic theater where you live?" A perfectly harmless question.

Her reply was, "Occasionally."

"So. You've moved around. A restless family? Or were your parents in one of the services?"

"On occasion."

"Reservists?"

"I don't recall."

"Or were you one of the tribe of charlatans who went around the country painting driveways with black paint and charging for an asphalt coating?"

"How clever."

"I'll bet your momma danced on the back of the medicine wagon."

"She's never mentioned that. I believe it may have been my grandmother on my daddy's side."

"Why her?"

"She had a way of walking that men's stares would follow her. And she'd give them a haughty look."

"Show me."

"I can't do it. I tried it out in the bathroom mirror—endlessly—but I just never had the knack."

"You stand still and watch the sun rise like no other mortal woman I've ever seen."

"Have you seen any of the goddesses?"

"Only one and that was just this morning."

She gave him a haughty look.

He squinted his eyes and observed, "I think you could walk along and give men sly looks. You just gave me one."

"I did! How'd I do it?"

"You looked sexy and knowing, like you could teach me all kinds of things."

"I could try, but I find you are easily shocked and you gasp and protest."

He looked off to the ceiling corner and mused, "I wonder if I'll be able to stand up anytime soon."

She considered him, sorting his words, but she didn't understand him. Another betrayal of her innocence.

He found a good many indications of how naive she really was. Although she knew some responses or some luring words, she was not practiced.

He said, "So you're a southerner."

"What'd I say?"

He looked down at the plate of succulent bits just placed before him, but he smiled like a cat who knew the canary wouldn't fly away. That showed how naive he was.

But his observation made her more cautious. He didn't get much information from her, so he gave her more about himself. He mentioned Minneapolis again and she chaffed that he was not to be that specific.

However, in spite of her chiding him, the very fact that she protested his saying that would make her remember it.

He told her how lovely she was. He described how it had been for him to come down the beach and see her watching the sun rise. How her gown had been transparent. And she blushed awkwardly.

That surprised him. She hadn't known a transparent gown was revealing? Some women think men see only what the woman wants him to see. That was a truism. Women underestimate men's awareness of them.

But just that morning Columbine had taken her gown off entirely in front of an unknown man. Of course *he* had been naked. And he only then considered that his attention had been so rigidly concentrated on her that he hadn't been as conscious of himself, of the fact that he'd been unclothed. He'd thought only of his attraction. Only of her.

"You were an awesome sight in this morning's sunrise."

"I have no idea how I managed to be so bold. But you came out of the sea like you lived there. You captured my imagination. I only realized you weren't immortal when you were wary of the dog."

"—wary."

"That means careful."

"I'm trying to remember if I've ever heard anyone use the word in conversation."

"It's an exact word. It was what you were. You weren't afraid of Ralph and you didn't back off from him, but you were . . . wary."

"So you were an English major."

"No. I'm a reader."

"What do you read?"

"Selectively."

"Who are your favorites?"

"James Oliver Curwood was my first and Joseph Conrad cannot be beaten."

"You like men's stories?"

She became earnest. "I think, actually, I like men. And with that taste of you, I believe the liking could become addictive."

He was indignant. "You're going around hunting for a fix?"

She got huffy. "I did not say that I was going to go berserk. I said I could become addicted."

He accused, "A hunter."

She was round eyed in shock. "Surely not."

"I shall try to help you in this hour of your need."

She was critical. "You're stingy."

And he laughed.

For dessert they had a swirl of unsweetened whipped cream and chocolate with discreet slivers of sugared crusts placed just so. And they had demitasses with thick coffee as they sat back and smiled at each other.

She asked, "How could I have known what a perfect companion you would be, when all that I saw was a beautifully naked man?"

"You have a superior guardian angel who knew you were in crisis."

"How did you know I was in crisis?"

"You were acting out of character."

She got huffy. "Now how could you know that?"

"No seductress takes off a nightgown over her head that way. She'd muss up her hair."

"How do you know that!"

Ponderously he explained, "I am an observer in the march of time."

And she laughed.

They were in no hurry. They went back to the beach where he removed his shoes and socks and rolled up his trouser legs. He got to watch as she removed her stocking tops from her garter belt and took off her shoes. They locked those discarded things in his car and went off hand in hand in the watching moon, to walk along in the last spreading of the waves' surging reach along the sand.

They didn't talk for a long while. But they looked at each other and they smiled. She flirted. And he stopped them so that he could kiss her improperly.

"You're very careless with your hands."

"I have no control over them. It's a recent problem. I have always been in full command of myself. I have no idea what the trouble is. Do you suppose it's the water?"

"I'll take some of it back to—back with me."

"—to—?"

"Where I live."

"When are you going to realize that we should be together? It is fated. You are the other half of my orange."

She scoffed. "How could you know that this soon?"

"I know."

"I don't."

"Will you take my card and contact me?"

"Perhaps."

He said gently, "I'm trying not to crowd you too much."

She replied, "I do appreciate that. A man finds a willing woman and he does get interested. I am willing. You appear interested in spite of your protests of shock and fright."

He said in dead earnestness. "You scare the hell out of me. I'm afraid you won't give us enough time to really evaluate our relationship."

"There is the chance that if we did have time we wouldn't find this—chance encounter—all that interesting."

He laughed his disbelief. He lifted her and swung her around. She shrieked as the wave broke and he stumbled into it, getting them both wet.

Did she get irritated? No. She pushed him and ran shrieking, looking back. They ended up taking off their clothes and playing in the spending waves. He wouldn't let her go out into the water because he didn't know the currents and he was careful of her because he didn't know her swimming endurance.

So they wore their wet underwear back to the isolated hut. He drove cautiously, obeying all the rules. Ralph met them with serious courtesy and followed them to their door.

They had to shower again to get the salt from their hair and bodies. And their sensual assistance to one another carried them along through the soaping and rinsing and drying and into bed.

They found that there is much to be said in having a bed when two are being seriously sexual. The moves, the turns, the maneuverings are all lovely in sand or gravel or weeds or on boards or cement or rugs, but beds are better.

Was it the long preliminaries that enhanced their mating? Or was it that they now were more familiar beyond that one chance encounter?

Their hands were knowledgeable now and their mouths were surer. There wasn't the hesitancy that had limited their freedom, their impulsiveness. They were languid and certain. They deliberately prolonged their play and several times parted to lie, panting and recovering, before continuing.

She put his hands where she wanted them and her sinuous movements made him shiver with his heat. His mouth was hotter than even his body. His hands were scrubbing and kneading. And he knew all of her.

She was still timid, so he cleverly showed her how to touch him, how to handle him and what to do, but not too much at a time. She was an avid student. She surprised him with her innovation and her eagerness to experiment. He sweat and gasped and shivered. He breathed brokenly and the sounds were loud in the room of that hut.

As they climbed the spiral of delight and ecstasy, he tried to stop them one more time, but she reached under her hip and touched him. He exploded, and she rode him down.

As they lay in a tumbled mess, he whispered, "Next time you do that, warn me."

Her reply was so slow that it took a long time for her to say it. "I don't think I can ever recover enough to try it again. I believe I'll be a sexual zombie for all the rest of my life."

"I'll bet money on the premise that you're misinformed."

"Don't touch me. I'm exhausted. If I went through all that again, I'd expire."

"Expire?"

She moved her lips carefully to say the words, "Fade away."

"Vanish?"

"Umm."

"If you go, I go."

The communication was difficult and she moved her lips with effort. "I believe my fading would be a means of escape . . . from you."

"How cowardly."

"Be quiet. My brain doesn't want to think."

"Kiss me good-night."

"Be very careful."

He touched his lips to hers. "I'll be back in a minute."

Crossly she asked, "You can get up?"

"No. I'm just going to the bathroom." He thought that was funny.

She tried to think what could be humorous and gave up. She began to doze and roused as he gently washed her with a warm wet towel. That touched her heart.

When he came back to bed, she moved and opened her arms. But he arranged her in his embrace. He was too heavy to lie on her arms.

They slept close in that old bed. He went to sleep wondering at the kind of people who would have had such a gaudy bedstead and decided it was from a house of ill repute. No wonder they'd made such innovative love.

In the night he wakened and was riveted to find her there. Fortunately he had his condom supply close by. He made slow and furtive love to her lax body. Again he slept, not sure she'd even wakened, he'd been so sly.

It was dawn when he wakened to find her at his body. He said, "Just who are you?"

"The maid. I'm supposed to make the bed, but since you're in it, I guess I'll just have to make you?"

"Ohh, all right." And he sighed forbearingly.

Then she said, "And since you're one ahead of me, I get this one free."

So she had been aware of his night's invasion. She did it all her way and about drove him out of his mind! And she rolled on the condom. He jerked and cautioned, "That isn't a foot, you know."

She waggled him. "Just about."

When she released him, he took her against him and petted her. He kissed her cheek and rubbed her tummy and admired her. She was lax and indolent. She murmured and nuzzled against him and yawned and stretched.

He watched her and helped her stretch by holding the weights of her breasts. She questioned that and he explained logically. She was unbelieving. So he told her to stretch without his holding help and she agreed it was easier if he helped.

When he claimed that his sex just might fall off, it had been so ill used, she offered to splint it, but he did decline.

"Just trying to zip my trousers would be a problem if it was in a splint."

With some drollness she said, "I would imagine it's hard to zip your pants anyway."

"You're a cheeky woman. Cheeky and sexy and delicious and this is heaven. This is what the peoples of the middle east and the Mediterranean who told of heaven being a place of houris who—"

"Of what?"

"Well, women didn't go to heaven, but the men knew that there would be nubile females to entertain them the way you've entertained me these last twenty-four hours. This is heaven."

"Oh. I thought you were entertaining me."

"Well, yes, but in doing that I am entertained."

"I suppose I don't mind if you enjoy servicing me."

"—servicing."

"Yes, slave."

"Right," he said indulgently.

"Fix my bath."

So he carried her into the shower and bathed her meticulously. She kept saying that was enough, but he was very thorough. She finally said, "STOP IT!"

"Your slave obeys."

"You're a wily man. You agree to anything as long as you get your way."

He was very open about it. "That's how lawyers are trained. But it helps to have that attitude first. It makes the training easier."

He finished drying her and then gently combed her hair as he dried that with her hand-held blow dryer.

She closed her eyes and allowed that and he dried her breasts and all over. She was patient.

She asked, "How did you learn to do hair?"

"I had a horse and its tail was always getting tangled and full of burrs. He was a good horse and I kept him clean and tidy." He combed her hair, showing her that it was free of tangles.

He said, "Your hair is beautiful. It's such a rich black. And your tan eyes are amazing. The green and blue lights in them are like a circus flashlight I had. The bulb was filled with liquid and specks floated in the water if you shook it. The lights danced and twinkled like the colors in your eyes."

"I've never been compared to a circus flashlight in all of my life."

"Men can be remiss."

"Surely there's something besides a circus flash-light that you could compare my eyes to?"

"Stars? I've never seen a tan star with green and blue lights. The only other thing like your eyes are the Christmas candy pellets that are put on cook-ies."

He got to watch her hunt through her suitcase for her underwear. She put on the garter belt first, and braless she leaned around putting on the stockings and attaching them to the belt and she was... fascinating.

She glanced up and caught him. "You're watch-ing."

"You're really interesting. I like that— It's a gar-ter belt. Why don't you wear panty hose?"

"These are cooler."

"A hot woman like you would know to do that."

"Aren't you dressing?"

"I would and I want to, but I can't miss anything you're doing. You're very interesting."

"If you don't hustle up, I'm going to breakfast without you."

He smiled. "I have the car keys."

"Well, rats. I suppose I'll have to dress you."

"My God, woman, you just sent the most sensual thrill through this tired and wrung-out body, you wouldn't believe it."

"Get dressed. I'm hungry for food."

"Yeah. You're like all women. You like to eat before anything else."

"Not necessarily. I'm temporarily depleted and I need food."

"I thought you were going to fade away?"

"I figured it out. I was starving."

"Well, I guess I'd better get dressed. I can't have you walking down the highway to the greasy spoon in that garter belt."

"I'm going to wear a dress."

"Why not slacks and a pullover?"

"I'm trying to make you think I'm a lady, so you won't be uncomfortable with me along."

"Along?" He sat up straight. She was going to travel with him?

Impatiently she elaborated, "To breakfast!"

"Oh." And he was silent and thoughtful as he dressed. He'd wanted her to go along with him to Jack's. And how would that be for the blonde waiting to meet him? She would be uncomfortable.

He looked at Columbine. He would call Jack before they left there and tell him he'd found a woman of his own. He asked, "Have you ever been to Tampa?"

"No, why?"

He smiled. "I'm going to Tampa with you."

"Even I have heard that one."

"But I've never had the chance to use it before. You could have been polite and laughed."

"Ha—ha—ha."

"That didn't sound sincere."

Chapter Five

Frank still wasn't back. Harlequin and Columbine fed Ralph. Again it took two cans of dog food. Ralph made short shrift of both cans, licked his chops and indicated the drawer in the filling-station office. In it were candies. Caramels.

Harlequin inquired of Columbine, "Do you think he gets caramels?"

She shrugged nicely and caught his eye. But she wasn't doing that just to attract Harlequin's attention, she was indicating a fact that was obvious. "He knows where they are."

So they unwrapped one and gave it to him. They watched with offended faces as Ralph drooled and licked and spit it out and lapped it up again. He was messy. He loved the caramels. Plural. They'd given him another.

Harlequin wondered aloud, "How long do you suppose it will be until Ralph realizes he can open that drawer with his teeth?"

"He's a gentleman dog and he would not steal candy from Frank."

Harlequin figured it out. "He can't unwrap the plastic covering."

They went to Tallahassee for breakfast at one of the hotels. They again had a leisurely, well-presented meal.

Then they walked around downtown and looked at the charming preservation of buildings and trees. The capital building was on a hill with wonderful old gnarled trees. It was a charming setting.

And finally they went back to the hut. Frank still wasn't there. They gave Ralph water and talked to him a little. Then the two humans debated giving the watchdog another caramel.

Columbine decided, "I believe it would be a strong indication that we are trying to garner his favor. I do not want a dog. Frank is happy with this creature. We ought not give him another caramel."

"Frank's taking his own sweet time getting your car done." Then he smiled and said, "Smart man. Let's go fishing."

"What do we do about Ralph?"

"He can guard the dump."

"As I recall, he kept people from crowding us."

"By George, Columbine, you are a bright woman."

So the two adults changed into colorful cotton flesh-covering protection. They told Ralph to come along and they went out on the pier and back to the beach.

Harlequin said, "We don't have beaches and salt-water in Minneapolis."

"I should think not." She slanted him a look. "But I understand that the locks that bring ocean-going ships into the Great Lakes have also brought all sorts of parasites that are causing all sorts of problems. Especially some tiger-striped creature that multiplies like crazy and is clogging the water-intake valves for cities."

"Yeah." He sighed. "We tend to do things first and then try to correct our mistakes. Remember that I'm a lawyer and most of my business is making corrections about one thing or another."

"Laws."

"The laws are good." Harlequin was sure. "Don't snort. The basic laws in this country are good. It's the interpretation and bending of those laws that are the problem."

"We should have voted on the Great Lakes locks. Somebody wanted them and just went ahead. Now we have to counter the problems."

"Are we going to talk about the forests next?"

"Or the beaches? Or the public money spent to prevent the natural erosion of private beaches?"

"Let's talk about sex."

"Whose?"

"You have a sassy mouth. Did you realize that?"

"Why, no one has ever before complained about my mouth. What exactly did you find distasteful about it?"

"There you go again. You just can't resist playing around with words."

"Distasteful? How else has my mouth offended you?"

"It's sass."

"You love it."

He put an arm around her and he kissed her sassy mouth. "There, that ought to hold you until I can take care of you improperly."

"How soon?"

"How soon! I'm surprised you can sit down, the way you've been acting with me, you voracious woman."

"Are you complaining?"

"No, I'm looking to see if there are any prowling Peeping Toms, so I can handle your problem."

"A beach encounter? That would be exciting. I've always wanted to experience a beach encounter."

"Why didn't you?"

"Before yesterday, I wasn't that kind of woman."

"What changed you?" And he looked at her to see how she would respond to his question.

"You did."

So he set Ralph to prowling the barricades and he took her under the pier.

"Do you have a condom?" She had hesitated.

"Yes."

"You *expected* me to assault you?"

He nodded as he sighed hugely. "I suspected it wouldn't be until after you caught your first fish and you'd choose that way to celebrate. After your use of me this morning—at the break of dawn—what is it about dawn that turns you on? Just yesterday you accosted me—"

"I did not. I had my back to you. And there you were all excited and upset and needy. What was I to do?"

Quite seriously he urged gently, "What was it that made you so vulnerable?"

"I was rejected. I wouldn't. He wouldn't commit until I did. He angered me."

"He must have been clumsy."

"He was determined. We actually fought."

"How did you win over an earnest man? No woman can."

"I kicked him."

"Oh."

"He was furious."

"Well..."

"You sympathize with him?"

"No. No. I wouldn't want any woman to be forced. I think a better explanation is that he must have hurt."

"He was not gentle with me."

"Ahh. He had it coming. He was a bastard. I wish I'd been there."

"Me, too."

But he had to ask, "Why did you want me?"

"I thought I'd just see what all the fuss was about without any commitment at all. Ships that pass in the dawn?"

"I'm glad it was me."

"You were so careful of me. You made sure I really would. You dragged your feet and evaded, but you obviously really wanted me."

"Naked, that's hard to conceal."

She repeated his word chidingly. "Hard."

He laughed. "I didn't say that deliberately, but it was true."

"I know. You were so gentle. I want you now."

"How clever of me to've brought along this handy blanket. You won't get as gritty."

"Kiss me."

"I'm getting there. Here. Sit right here."

"Why not in the middle?"

"When I get you flat, I don't want your hair in the sand."

"Now, how did you know that calculation?"

"Logic." But he tenderly remembered his honeymoon with Judy and her hair full of sand. He smiled.

"What's funny?"

"That was a tender smile."

She considered him. "Yes. That's what is so wonderful about you. You are tender. Even the way you take care of Ralph. You always wash the sand from his paws."

"Gritty sand is abrasive. I don't want your parts to rub sand and become uncomfortable. I don't want you to hurt."

"So."

"Sit right there."

"Is that better?"

"Soon now."

And he sat beside her and kissed her several sipping kisses. He smiled at her and licked his lips. "You taste so good to me." And he moved his hands on her as he leaned her backward.

She braced her hands and lifted her chest so that he moved her clothing aside to see. Then he nipped at her nipples and gently squeezed the rounds.

She said, "Ummm."

"Me, too."

Her smoky voice gasped, "You, too, what?"

"I like making love to you and when you make those nice sounds it makes me purr inside my body."

She lifted her hands to his fascinating hair and held him to her. Her knees got restless, and he had to find out why, moving his hands and testing.

Ralph snorted his *L*-less sound. And under the pier the lovers lay apart while Ralph watched a couple of people come down the beach. He went forward and the intruders hesitated. The dog went to one side in an obvious gesture that they were to proceed. They did cautiously, with a glance at the indolent couple under the slatted shade of the pier. They carefully climbed over the pier to go on past and quite far the other way, escorted by Ralph.

Having cooled with the interruption, the pair was delighted to begin again and to build their pitch of passion steadily, with their teasing and searching and coupling, until they could resist no longer.

It was a day of love. They swam and flirted and touched their nude bodies without anything but familiarity. They knew each other in sensual delight.

And that evening, after their dinner, they walked the beach in the moonlight followed or preceded by Ralph.

When at last they went back to their hut, her car still hadn't been delivered. Harlequin told Columbine, "Don't worry. If your car doesn't get here, I'll cancel my appointment."

She said sadly, "I can't cancel mine. I promised."

"Then I'll give you my car. I'll go with you."

Her refusal was gentle. "No."

"Well, we can talk about it in the morning."

With all the exercise of one kind or another that they'd had in that day, she was restless and couldn't sleep. He was willing to assuage her restlessness, but she wanted only to be held. So he held her and sang to her. He had a good voice.

Unfortunately Ralph joined in. He was outside their closed door and he howled and varied it, thinking he was singing harmony?

The lovers laughed until tears came. They'd listen, then when all was silent, Harlequin would try again. And sure enough Ralph joined his voice in Harlequin's effort.

How could that be so funny? How could anything be funny when their parting loomed for the next day?

Harlequin asked his Columbine, "Let me know how I can get in touch with you. Let me know your name."

"I'm embarrassed."

"Why would you be embarrassed with me?"

"I've never behaved this way before in all my life."

"I have proof of that."

"But how could you respect me?"

He laughed. "Respect you in the morning?" That old classic. "Honey, I do. You're charming, erudite, beautiful, smart, a swimmer, a remarkable lover. What more could I expect?"

"A lawyer should have a woman who doesn't hole up in a shack with a stranger."

"Why not? I've never been this contented or this happy. The only fly in the ointment is your attitude. You need an attitude adjustment and I know exactly how to do that."

So he did all the adjustments that he could manage and still roll on a condom.

And he slept easily and heavily. He didn't even dream. He held her warm, soft body to his hard, hairy one, and he slept the sleep of a contented man.

When he wakened, she wasn't in their bed. With a strange stillness, he raised up and looked at the bath-stall door. The door was open and there was no sound. Alarm ballooned inside his chest. His breath was harsh. He threw back the sheet and got out of bed.

He saw with that first room scan, but he chose not to believe it. He searched and picked up his suitcase and put it down. But his was all that was there. She was gone. Her clothes, her cosmetics, her shoes, everything was gone. She'd run out on him. How?

He knew. His car. He went desolately over to the window and ran up the shade and—his car was still there! Maybe she was at the bus stop?

He pulled on shorts and went outside barefooted. The only living creature in sight was Ralph who contemplated him in that same watchful way.

As Darwin stood there realizing that she was actually gone, he ceased being Harlequin and he was again just Darwin Moore.

Frank had to be there. She was gone. So her car had been returned. Darwin went to the back of the service station and rattled the door as he called, "Frank!"

In time, Frank opened the door as he buttoned the fly on his time- and oil-stiffened trousers. The man squinted at Darwin and asked, "Who're you?"

"I've been staying in the hut with—" What was her name? "—with the lady. You brought back her car?"

"Yep. Got it fixed, too."

"Where did she go?"

"Darned if I know. She went down the road thataway." And Frank pointed.

"What's her name?"

Frank's wrinkled face went serious. "You don't know?"

"She called herself Columbine but she never gave me a last name."

"You have a squabble?"

"She just . . . left."

"You mean to her?"

"No." Darwin was agitated—how could he get through to the man? Darwin breathed a couple of times, trying to use his reasoning skills and his glance fell on Ralph. He told Frank, "Ralph likes me. I know about the caramels."

"Hell, man, everybody knows about them caramels."

"We took him to the beach, over there, and he guarded it for us."

"That's his beach, anyways."

"I took him in my car."

"Didju now." And Frank thought on that fact.

Darwin watched as Frank slid his tongue on his gums and weighed the evidence. Darwin once had a judge who did just that. He'd finally decided in Darwin's favor, would Frank?

Frank asked, "Where'ya from and whad'ya do?"

Darwin replied at length.

Frank nodded as he stuck out his lower lip in a considering way. "Lawyer, huh."

"A good one. I uphold the constitution."

"We need a coupl'a more a'you."

"What is her real name and where's she from. You must have her license-plate number."

"Weall, I did put down the numbers, but that's only to identify which car. I hardly ever put the state down. It's a low number. Now, where did I put that? Let's see."

Darwin followed Frank into the unlocked station and watched him paw through a drawer of paper slips.

"Did she pay you?"

"Nice girl. 'Course she paid."

"Credit card?"

"Cash."

In the next two hours, Darwin heard about people, about cars, about weather, but he didn't get one grain of help about Columbine.

The time came when he had to call Jack and say he'd be just a little late.

Frank called the operator and said he had a customer that had to make a long-distance call. Would she keep close tabs and let him know immediately how much it was?

She was used to Frank. She said yes.

The phone was a post with a mouthpiece and a holder for a separate earpiece. It was a dial phone with empty circles over the letter groupings. A finger was inserted and turned that circle over to a blocking prong. This dial protested being moved over with a screech and clicked back one slow click at a time.

Darwin got Jack's answering machine. "I'll be a little late and I can't stay long." Then he added, "This is Darwin."

He went back to the only illicit love nest he'd ever experienced and it was a sad, agitated man who showered, dressed and packed his things.

He didn't let Frank put any gas in his car because he wasn't sure the bottom of that hand pumper wasn't oil sludge and his car was too sophisticated to understand or cope with sludge. And he found that Columbine had paid for the hut.

"I done been paid." Frank was gumming tobacco and a little of the juice slid from the edge of his mouth into the grizzled beard that was untended.

Darwin loved Frank. He'd had a great grandfather who had been very similar. He tried to force double payment for the hut.

Frank refused. "It's just one pair of sheets, any way you look at it."

"The water—"

"I got me a well. No sweat."

So Darwin gave Frank ten dollars for Ralph's beach guarding.

All that took time.

Darwin bought a windshield spray and an ice scraper.

Frank screwed up his wrinkles in contemplation and asked, "What'd'ya want one of them things for?"

"I have to go back north."

"You'll change your mind and stay down here. We could use a constitutional lawyer. I could throw a little business your way."

"I'm obliged."

"Find yer woman and come back. You can use the hut 'til you get settled."

They clasped hands.

But when Darwin opened the car door to leave, Ralph got into the back seat and wouldn't budge. Darwin looked helplessly at Frank who shook his head. "My dogs take to certain people. You might as well take him along. He's adopted you."

So they haggled about Ralph's worth. That is, Darwin tried to give Frank some cash for Ralph and Frank refused. "He's just a dog." He pronounced it dawg.

"But he earns his keep. You trained him."

"What's he do? He tells you which drawer has the caramels."

Darwin admitted, "He watches."

"Yeh. He's curious."

"He's a watchdog."

"That's a kind way of putting it. But he doesn't do anything about anybody that comes along and takes things. He just watches them doing it."

Darwin owned the dog that—watched.

Darwin drove south, not even able to watch for a particular car because he wasn't sure what color hers was. Frank was color blind. That explained the variety of decorator paints inside the hut.

Darwin looked for a dark-haired woman and once—trying to see if it was Columbine driving a car—he almost wrecked them both. Rubbernecking on a highway is stupid. That woman had been too old.

As was inevitable, Darwin finally got to Phyllis and Jack's house. They came to the door and opened it even before he could knock.

Distracted, he thrust a bottle of wine in its box at Jack and jammed the rose nosegay against Phyllis's chest as he said, "I can't stay. I have to make a—" He'd looked beyond them, through the entrance door and into the living room. There he saw a woman with a great mushroom bunch of black hair who had a hand on Ralph's head. He said hollowly, "I thought you said she was blond."

Jack shrugged and put out his hands. "Well, the first one was, but she went off with some guy—"

Phyllis put in "—so I called—"

Darwin watched the brunette stand slowly, staring at him. She had on an outsize dress, from which the football shoulder pads had been removed, and her hair was in a frizzled style that was incongruous. She wore no makeup. She was gorgeous. "Columbine?" His voice was hoarse and sound waves sang in his ears.

Phyllis agitated, "No, her name's Karen—"

Moving with effort against those thick sound waves, Darwin pushed forward. He saw that tears had started in Columbine's eyes and she wailed in a whisper, "This dress!"

Never taking his eyes from her face, he soothed, "It's beautiful."

Shocked at Darwin's opinion of that ghastly dress, Phyllis hissed to Jack, "Did you hear that?"

Jack hushed her. "They know each other."

Phyllis scoffed. "He called Karen 'Columbine.'"

Darwin reached Columbine and stopped. "You're here. I've looked—Frank didn't know—I gave Ralph two more caramels." All vital communication.

"Oh, Harlequin, I thought they said his name was Durwood."

Phyllis hissed, "She called him 'Harlequin'!"

Jack was fascinated by the pair confronting each other in his living room. "Shh." He put his arm around his wife.

Karen was saying, "This awful dress...my hair...I didn't want Durwood to like me."

"He would have."

Phyllis whispered, "Who is Durwood?"

Jack replied, "You probably said that on the phone."

Phyllis said, "I remember spelling his name."

Jack grinned. "It no longer matters. Look at them. They're in love. Wonder how they know each other?"

Phyllis guessed, "Probably from school."

The hosts looked at their guests who were completely unaware they were a part of this world. They were alone in the universe.

Harlequin took Columbine into his arms and held her tenderly. "Why did you leave me? How was I to find you?"

Weeping, she explained, "I would have contacted you. I took your driver's license."

That did catch his attention. He reared his head back and asked in some shock, "My *driver's* license?"

"You're a careful driver. You would have been all right."

"You need a keeper." Then he kissed her. It was as if they were glued together like the strands of her hair. He tilted her face so that he could get under the front overhang of that remarkable structure and he kissed her marvelously.

Their audience became sentimental and leaned against each other and smiled and smiled and smiled.

Ralph watched.

As the kiss continued, the hosts left the room. They took Ralph with them and put him into the fenced backyard with their large recently clipped poodle. To Ralph, she looked exotic.

In the living room, the kiss continued so hot that Karen's mushroom hairdo gradually melted and she began to look more like Columbine. And Harlequin searched out the signals that she was really that magical creature. She was. *He* was.

They lived happily ever after. The first several months of that were in the hut. They left it to swim and to find food. The rest of the time was spent as would be expected between Harlequin and Columbine, but he didn't ever play the mandolin or the flute.

Then with summer and a pregnant wife, Darwin took Florida's more particular bar exam.

Eventually he joined a firm that—oddly enough—Frank recommended. And Frank was godfather to their first child.

Jack and Phyllis weren't offended, because they got to godparent the other half of that set.

Sometimes it takes guardian angels hair-raising, inventive, manipulative measures to get the right two people together.

That was one time it all worked out.

* * * * *

SPRING

Lass finds living on our planet at this time a fascinating experience. People are amazing. To be a teller of tales of people, places and things is absolutely marvelous.

This year, Lass is celebrating ten years with Silhouette Books, having had a successful career writing for the Silhouette Desire line. With numerous awards and nominations to her credit, Ms. Small has frequently appeared on the industry's widely regarded bestseller lists. She authored the popular "Lambert Sisters" and the recent "Fabulous Brown Brothers" series.

On the subject of spring, Lass says, "Next to fall, I like spring best. It's so beautifully delicate. To see a barren, somnolent land come back to life is to be witness to a miracle."

Lass Small.

KASEY MICHAELS

Simon Says...

To Melissa Jeglinski,
who made it easy

Chapter One

"Mr. Prescott? I'm terribly sorry to bother you, but—"

Simon Prescott put down the interoffice memo he had been reading and looked at Miriam Lambert. His private secretary had cracked open the office door slightly, poking no more than her head and shoulders through—as though it wouldn't be safe to step completely into the room.

"Yes, Miriam?" he asked politely when it appeared that she wasn't going to say anything more. His tone was noncommittal, but that was no indication of mood. Anyone who had ever heard Simon raise his voice had yet to be discovered. As a matter of fact, neither Miriam nor anyone else at any of the Prescott Hotels could remember seeing their boss lose his temper.

So what was it that Simon Prescott possessed, what sort of mysterious power did he have that instilled in his employees such deep respect and devotion? It was a subject often discussed in Prescott employee lounges.

"Is an escaped orangutan giving birth to quadruplets in the lobby," Simon offered helpfully when she still didn't speak, "or is the building on fire? Miriam, do I alert the talk shows or call the fire department?"

Miriam's pert nose wrinkled as she suppressed a grimace. That was why everyone was so in awe of Simon Prescott, she decided. The man didn't *need* to raise his voice, didn't *need* to rant and rave. He could cut a person off at the knees with his sharp tongue without ever really trying.

But Miriam loved him; all the Prescott Hotels employees loved him, even if none of them could say precisely why.

The secretary laughed nervously at his joke and cleared her throat before continuing. "I know you've specifically asked not to be disturbed while you're looking over the latest legal material on the Cape May property, Mr. Prescott, but your mother is on line one. She's very insistent upon speaking with you, sir."

Miriam cringed slightly as she recalled the woman's sweet, velvet-edged steel demand to have her call put through to her son. "*Very* insistent. I'm so sorry."

Simon's smile dissolved Miriam's apprehension, reducing her once more to her usual status, which, even after five years in his employ, was much like a teenage fan who has just caught a glimpse of her latest idol.

"Don't worry about it, Miriam," he said, reaching toward the telephone that sat on the edge of his desk. "It would take a stronger person than either you or I to say no to Elise. As a matter of fact, Attila the Hun comes most readily to mind."

He hesitated before punching the button labeled Line One and added, "It's nearly noon. Why don't you take an early lunch? I won't be needing you for—" he looked at the elegant gold watch that spanned his strong wrist "—at least two hours."

Miriam, who was to be married in a month and still had a million things to do before the wedding, smiled with appreciation. "Thank you, sir," she said, stepping back as she prepared to close the door, then opened it once more to add, "Good luck with your mother, Mr. Prescott. I think she wants something."

"Miriam, my mother *always* wants something," Simon told her with a smile that displayed his even white teeth to advantage against the golden tan he had acquired while skiing in Aspen with his mother.

The trip was a yearly event, one mother and son had taken since his freshman year in high school. It had been then that Stephen Prescott—his mother's first husband, and now five years deceased—had been given his walking papers.

According to Simon's mother, the annual trips to Aspen were for the express purpose of mother and son "bonding"—a term she had discovered while dating a psychologist who'd had three self-help books make the bestseller list.

"The devil of it all is that no one, including myself, has been able to find a way to say no to her, Miriam," Simon continued. "As a matter of fact, if I can ever find anyone who is immune to my dearest mother's wheedling ways, I'll marry her on the spot!"

"Then it's a good thing I've got Dave, Mr. Prescott," Miriam dared to reply, "because the only other person I'd ever care to marry is you. And I couldn't say no to your mother if she wanted me to shave my head, stick a rose between my teeth and dance the fandango on a table in the main dining room!"

Simon smiled, then waved her out of the office as he punched line one and then put the conversation on the speaker phone. "Elise, hello! How's the rehabilitation going? Have any more therapists run screaming into the cold, Colorado night due to you?"

Elise Prescott Gillian Manchester's girlish laughter tinkled merrily as her voice flowed through the telephone line from her posh convalescent home, filling her son's office. "Oh, Simon, really. How naughty you are. You make me sound like such a perfect beast! Is it my fault that dear Raoul—cruel, sadistic brute of a man that he was—suddenly decided he had been totally mistaken to have considered a lifelong career in physical therapy?''

Simon rolled his eyes, aware that Raoul, an extremely competent man with ten years of experience at the exclusive Colorado facility, had resigned his position and taken up a new post in Florida after being assigned to Elise's case for less than a week.

''Anything you say, darling,'' he responded pleasantly. ''But enough of Raoul. How's your rehabilitation coming along?''

''*Horribly!* Oh, Simon, I'm so wretchedly, terribly bored!''

Simon leaned back in his chair, mentally counting up the weeks since his mother had taken an unfortunate tumble on the ski slopes, breaking her left leg in three places. The date had been January twentieth, nearly eight weeks ago. ''You've only been out of the cast for two weeks, Elise. Physical therapy takes time—''

''For a woman my age,'' Elise interrupted, her voice slightly pettish. ''Go on, Simon, say it. I know I'm old. Too old to be skiing in Aspen with my playboy son. But I *abhor* this place! It's stacked three-deep with *sick* people, Simon, from one end to the other.''

''Hospitals and convalescent homes usually are, Mother,'' Simon replied, tipping his chair forward once more. He picked up a pen and began doodling on a blank sheet of paper, then stopped as he realized that he had begun drawing a hangman's noose. "The people who run them think it works out very well that way."

"Don't be sarcastic, Simon," Elise returned sharply. "You sound just like your father, and heaven only knows I don't need any reminders of that dreadfully oppressive man at this moment—may the good Lord rest his soul. And *don't* call me Mother. You know how I detest it!"

Then her tone softened, so that her son could almost see her smile as she spoke. "Simon, darling, the reason I phoned..."

"Yes, Elise?" Simon asked fatalistically, fully prepared to hear that his mother had decided she "could not possibly *exist*" another day without his presence in Colorado, and likewise prepared to point out that such a trip would be impossible at this time. But she surprised him.

"I want to come home, darling," she said, her tone wistful, like a small child away at summer camp for the first time and laboring under a world-class case of homesickness.

"Home? Well, that's a good one—or at least it's different. And where would 'home' be, Elise? Your condo in Manhattan, your apartment in Paris, or your twenty-room 'cottage' in Connecticut?"

"Connecticut? Oh, my darling boy, I sold that horror last year. Surely you remember? The nicest savings and loan chairman bought it, although I think he might have had to part with it when he went to the slammer. That is what they call it, isn't it, Simon, the 'slammer'? I think I heard it correctly the other night on television. The show had something to do with a robbery, and this man..."

Simon looked owlishly at the speaker phone. Elise had been watching *television?* She *never* watched television. Maybe his mother was right—she'd been locked up too long. The next thing he knew she'd be telephoning him to tell him she'd won five dollars playing bingo at the hospital's social hour. He frowned at the speaker phone, determined to pay strict attention to what his mother was saying.

"...And the police took him away. But, no matter," she trilled airily. "I don't know why I ever purchased that house in the first place. Oh, yes, I do! I never bought it at all. It came as part of my settlement from dear Gillian. I hear he's going to be knighted soon. Just think, I could have been Lady Gillian—if only I could have managed to stay married to such a stick as *Sir* Giles. Or will he be the only one with a title?"

"Do you want me to look it up?" Simon asked, knowing that the way to get his mother to change any subject was to profess an interest in it.

"Heavens, no. They're ancient history, both the cottage and Giles. I summer in Cannes now if you'll remember—after the film festival, and once all the hoi polloi and the tabloid press depart. Manchester gave me the villa as a wedding present. Dear man, I wonder how he's doing now, wed to that silly starlet. If he's lucky, she'll have graduated from nursery school by now."

Simon rested his elbows on the desktop and began rubbing his temples with his fingertips. Keeping his mother's ex-husbands and her residences straight could be a full-time profession, if he had been so inclined. He wasn't, however. "All right, Elise. I give up. Tell me, where *do* you call home these days?"

"Why, Cape May, of course, and the lovely hotel you have there. Silly boy."

Simon abruptly stopped rubbing his temples. It was going to take a lot more than simple massage to alleviate this headache. "Cape May? You're kidding! You haven't stayed at any of my hotels in more than two years, Elise. The last time you were in Cape May was after your—"

"My facelift, darling. Yes, I know. But don't be crude and mention it, because I must tell you, I've quite forgotten it. Before that it was after I had my eyes and chin done—you remember how perfectly *beastly* I looked after that little procedure. You do remember, don't you? You said I looked as if I had just lost a fight with a door. But, now that you've remembered it, I would be extremely pleased if you would forget it again, *forever*. I only brought it up because I look just as unfit for civilization now, even if my face is unaffected.''

"But the cast is gone. And when I spoke with your doctors last week they assured me you had progressed beyond the wheelchair stage.''

"Oh, yes, the wheelchair is gone. But they have me using a *cane* now, Simon. Me! And I look as if my left leg has gone on a strict diet. It's half the size of the other one and I *limp!* I can't possibly be seen in public until I am fully recovered. And don't tell me that I'm odiously vain, because I already know that. I prefer to believe it's part of my charm.''

"So you've taken it into your head that you want to come to Cape May—*now?*" Couldn't she think of another place to recuperate? Couldn't she stay where she was? Simon sighed, wondering why he was wasting time asking himself stupid questions. Oh, no. Elise couldn't do either of those things. They were both too simple.

"Isn't that what I've been saying, darling? I was so sure I had made myself clear. Just consider it. What better place for me to hide myself away than that quiet, backwater town, now, in April, before the tourists arrive. No one I know would even *think* to look for me there.''

Simon gritted his teeth. What did his mother believe happened at the New Jersey shore once summer was done—that the inhabitants rolled up the sidewalks and hibernated? But he wasn't about to explain any of this to Elise, who wouldn't have listened anyway. He'd rather play on her opinion that the town was deserted.

So deciding, he made another stab at discouraging his lovable yet exasperating mother from putting her plan into action. "But, Elise, you couldn't stay in my penthouse by yourself. As you've already said, Cape May is a small town. I'd worry about leaving you there alone."

"Alone? I wouldn't dream of it! Surely you can hire someone respectable and discreet to be my companion, and to help me with my physical therapy. I would like a woman this time, Simon. Raoul was so *brutal*—"

"No, Elise," Simon interrupted. "*You* were brutal. Raoul was in over his head. After all, he'd never had any training in lion taming."

"Oh, Simon, I do love you. You're so droll. But to get back to my new therapist. I'll want a young woman, preferably, and reasonably attractive, as I'll have to look at her every day for at least a month. I can't tell you how depressing it is here, with all these nurses that don't seem to know how to smile. I need youth around me, Simon—youth and vitality! Besides, I miss Jacqueline and Susanne, and they can be with me in Cape May. I've thought it all out, Simon, and this arrangement will suit me perfectly. Absolutely perfectly!''

Simon's chuckle was rueful, to say the least. He had planned on occupying the Cape May penthouse himself for much of the month of April, so that he could be close at hand while he worked on the purchase of some beachfront properties for his newest hotel—a usually straightforward negotiation that was beginning to look as if it had run into a major hitch. The last thing he needed was to have his mother in residence while he was at it.

And Jacqueline and Susanne? Oh, yes. Elise's pair of barking hairballs running around the place would really make for an efficient working environment. Maybe he should hire a few circus acts—a couple of clowns, a sword swallower and a *real* lion tamer— while he was at it.

''Elise, look. I'm flattered that you want to come home, as you call it, but I—''

''No. No, no, *no!*'' his mother interrupted before he could finish. ''I can hear that doomsday tone in your voice, Simon, and I must tell you I have quite made up my mind! I will be arriving in two days, once I find a decent beauty salon here so that I can arrive at the Atlantic City airport without frightening little children. Have you ever thought about children, Simon? I mean, *really* thought about them? I have, quite a bit, actually, since being laid flat on my back. But that will keep. I'll have someone phone with my arrival time. Be there to meet me, dearest, with your young, pretty physical therapist in tow."

"Anything else, Elise?" Simon asked, feeling slightly dizzy. "Or will you be faxing me a detailed list of instructions as to height and hair color?"

"No, I think that's all. Oh, one more thing. She will have to agree to walking Jacqueline and Susanne for me, although I doubt she will mind. You will pay her well, won't you, darling? 'Bye, now. My depressing supper tray is here, but I must eat, mustn't I, to keep up my strength? Kiss, kiss!"

The line went dead before Simon could say another word, which was probably a good thing, because the next word he said wasn't very pretty. It was also very loud, which was, as Miriam and her co-workers knew, totally out of character for their legendarily unflappable boss.

Miranda Tanner checked her small bag of medical supplies one last time in preparation of heading for the Prescott Dunes Hotel, where she would meet her new client.

Well, not her client, precisely, but her client's son, Simon Prescott. *The* Simon Prescott. *Not-So-Simple Simon. Prescott the Pouncer. Smooth. Suave. So-*

phisticated—and in Miranda's admittedly biased opinion—*Sleazy Simon.*

"Aren't you just shaking in your boots, Andi?" her assistant, Bonnie Addams, a petite redhead with an abundance of freckles and an inescapable inclination to plumpness, inquired from her perch on one corner of Miranda's desk.

"You're kidding, right?" Miranda asked, deadpan, snapping the case shut. "I've been on more than three dozen similar assignments before I opted to take over the administrative end of the business. Why on earth should I be nervous?"

"*Why?* For crying out loud, how can you ask that, Andi? You're driving all the way up to Atlantic City alone with the *great man!* What will you do? What will you talk about? I know I wouldn't be able to think of a single thing to say. I mean, Simon Prescott! I hear he's *gorgeous.*"

Miranda turned to look at Bonnie levelly, then ran her hands down over her softly flaring hips, smoothing the crisp white cotton uniform. "I think I'll survive," she said flatly, turning to take her hiplength turquoise cardigan from the back of her chair and slip it on.

"Besides, from what I've read, the *great man* is too busy fighting off models, pseudo actresses, and society debutantes to notice whether or not I have

two heads, much less take time to engage me in polite conversation on the way to the airport.''

She picked up her medical case. ''Not that I
wouldn't like to tell the guy a thing or two,'' she
added under her breath.

But Bonnie had heard her anyway, and quickly
jumped up to put a detaining hand on Miranda's
shoulder. ''Andi, you wouldn't!''

''I wouldn't what, Bonnie?'' Miranda inquired
sweetly, trying to appear innocent, and knowing that
she was failing badly.

''You know exactly what I'm talking about. When
you told me you were going to take this job yourself, you said it was because it might lead to getting
the Prescott Hotels account for all of New Jersey.
You *said,* as I remember, that there are a lot of
openings for temporary medical personnel in hotels
like his that cater to the rich and powerful. That is
what you said, isn't it? I don't remember you saying
anything about giving Simon Prescott a piece of your
mind for trying to buy Mrs. Stein's house and those
other houses for his next hotel.

''As a matter of fact,'' she went on when Miranda didn't answer, ''I think you might even have
promised me that his offer for those three houses had
nothing to do with your decision to take on the job
when we have at least five available temps who have
the nursing qualifications Mr. Prescott required.''

Miranda gave a dismissive toss of her head, setting her mid-length, inky-black hair shimmering in the overhead light, and grinned down at her associate. "Yeah, well, Bonnie, guess what? I *lied!* 'Bye now. I'll call in tomorrow."

Ten minutes later Miranda pulled her compact car into the Prescott Dunes parking lot, checked her lipstick in the rearview mirror, grabbed her medical case, and then headed for the hotel lobby. She knew she looked neat and efficient—except, of course, for the fact that the ocean air always had a tendency to turn her dark mop from smoothly sleek to tousled and softly curling.

As Prescott Dunes was located right off the beach promenade, and the wind was pleasantly brisk, by the time she had reached the glass doors to the foyer she could positively *feel* her hair beginning to curl at her cheeks and nape.

Miranda knew, and her bedroom mirror had more than once confirmed the fact, that her sleekly professional hairstyle might lend credence to her carefully cultivated image of a successful twenty-eight-year-old business owner. However, once the humid ocean air had done its work, that same mirror had also told her that she resembled little more than a curly topped child playing at grown-up.

She pushed a hand through her hair and then blew a swift, impatient breath upward at an errant lock that had swung down to hang in front of her left eye. There were a lot of benefits to be found in living at the New Jersey shore, but harboring much optimism about having many "good hair" days sure wasn't one of them.

"How on earth does Michael Jackson stand having his hair hanging in his eyes?" she asked herself rhetorically as the electric eye built into the door-frame detected her approach and the glass doors opened automatically.

She had taken no more than three steps on the plush mauve carpet—privately wondering how large an army of housekeepers Simon Prescott had to keep on staff to remove beach sand from that carpet—when a man who had been sitting at his ease on one of the natural rattan chairs, stood and headed toward her.

There were several reasons why Miranda knew that the man was Simon Prescott. For one thing, he was the only man in the large, glass-topped, three-story foyer—unless she wanted to count the young man behind the check-in desk. But she didn't for a minute think that Simon Prescott would be caught dead wearing one of his hotel's distinctive crested blazers.

Besides, the man approaching her was doing so at his leisure, as if he had all the time in the world at his disposal.

His visual inspection of her was not quite the sort that she had never become accustomed to the few times Bonnie had talked her into going to a local night spot, but he was definitely evaluating her appearance. His inspection smacked more of an inventory of pluses and minuses, as if he was weighing her against some sort of standard he had already set in his head.

Lastly, and definitely most disconcerting to Miranda, was the fact that the man now standing in front of her was devastatingly handsome. His tawny hair was sun-kissed, which showed well against his to-die-for handsome face. His golden skin, in turn, was set off by sherry-brown eyes beneath winged brows, knee-melting laugh lines that made slashes in his high-boned cheeks, and teeth so white they almost sparkled.

Added to all this perfection of face was a broad-shouldered, slim-hipped, long-legged body clad in casual tan slacks and a mint-green knit shirt opened at the collar to show a discreet glimpse of similarly sun-kissed chest hair. Miranda remembered Bonnie's remarks. *Gorgeous,* Bonnie had said.

Miranda also remembered ruefully that she hadn't been very impressed. At least not then. *Now,* standing face to face with the man, it was another story. Another story entirely.

So this is what all the shouting's been about, she mused, trying not to be too obvious about the fact that she suddenly felt a nearly overwhelming need to take a deep breath. Several deep, steadying breaths. Maybe the swift application of a handy dandy oxygen mask wouldn't come amiss.

Oh, yeah, she thought, carefully keeping her expression blank, *I can see it now.*

And then, just when she was afraid she was about to make a total ass of herself, Simon Prescott opened his mouth and, with his first few words, rescued Miranda from the undoubtedly crowded ranks of Prescott worshipers.

"Ms. Tanner, I presume," Simon said by way of a greeting, his voice suiting him perfectly, for it was neither too low nor too rough, but only faintly drawling and husky, and harbored intriguing traces of an Ivy League education.

None of these attributes, however, served to rob his words of their sting as he held out his hand in greeting. "How good of you to be so prompt. And isn't that a lovely uniform, Ms. Tanner. Tell me, are you perhaps planning to perform open heart surgery this afternoon?"

"Mr. Prescott," Miranda returned crisply, withdrawing her hand from his warm grip as hastily as she could without appearing rude—or frightened by the unexpected, sensual tingle that the touch of his flesh against hers had sent shooting up her arm. "If you're referring to the reason for my uniform, might I remind you that I am a nurse, and that I have been retained by you to take charge of your mother's case."

Simon lifted a hand to his forehead, his eyes closed as he mentally reviewed his telephone conversation with Miranda Tanner of Tanner Temps. *No,* he thought, *I didn't say anything about uniforms. My mistake.*

He opened his eyes once more and, for the second time since the glass doors had opened and Cape May's answer to Florence Nightingale had stepped into the foyer wearing virginal white from her stockings and shoes to her—he admitted only to himself—uniquely flattering cotton uniform, he realized that Miranda Tanner was one extremely beautiful woman.

Her hair was lovely, so soft and touchable, and so in variance with her sterile, hospital-clean uniform. And he liked her eyes. They were as smoky blue and mysterious as the ocean on a cloudy day, and were fringed with an almost obscene amount of long, sooty lashes.

She looked, he decided, like an eminently palatable cross between a young Audrey Hepburn and an even younger Elizabeth Taylor.

And besides being beautiful, Miranda appeared to be intelligent, very human, and a woman more prone to laughter than to tears—although he had a feeling she had a bit of a hot temper.

In short, astutely taking stock of both her soft, dark curls and her stiff-spined posture, she presented a very intriguing bundle of contradictions. Having her in the penthouse with Elise could, to say the least, prove to make his life for the next month extremely interesting.

Unfortunately, Elise would take one look at those same white stockings and demand that the lovely Ms. Miranda Tanner be replaced—immediately. And that, Simon decided, taking one last look into Miranda's smoky blue, faintly belligerent-looking eyes, would be a damn shame.

"Well?" Miranda questioned him when he hadn't said anything. "Is something wrong, Mr. Prescott? Do you wish to leave now, or would you rather discuss the case before we head for the airport?"

Simon's chuckle was soft and intimate, a black velvet laugh hinting of dim lights and secluded rooms. Secluded *bed*rooms. She looked at him quizzically, wondering just what she had said that he had found so amusing. But he didn't give her the chance to say anything else.

He simply took hold of Miranda's elbow and steered her toward the glass doors, which swung open immediately, as if they, like the man behind the desk and the army of housekeepers, were on the Prescott payroll.

"Lesson number one, my dear Ms. Tanner," he said at last, as a man wearing a Prescott blazer and a chauffeur's cap appeared seemingly out of nowhere to open the door to a long silver limousine, "if you value your life, never—never, *ever*—refer to Elise as a *case*. Not unless you have a death wish."

"Oh, really?" Miranda snapped, hating the man more with every passing moment. She was even beginning to dislike his mother, and she hadn't even met the woman yet—although, if she had given birth to Simon, it was doubtful she had any of the gentle, nurturing personality traits of Mother Teresa! "Is there anything else I should know?"

"Plenty, but it'll keep. Now, come along, Ms. Tanner. It's a good thing I decided to engage a Cape May native. Tell Jack here your address and we'll swing by your house and find you something decent to wear. We don't have much time to change you from a depressingly sterile, professional drudge to a sweet young thing."

"Hey, back up a minute! Did I miss something here? *Sweet young thing?*" While Jack stood by, patiently holding open the door, Miranda dug in the heels of her practical, rubber-soled shoes, more angry than she had been in a long time. *If I were to look up the word arrogance in the dictionary,* she deduced wryly, *it would probably say "see Prescott."*

Mentally writing off the Prescott Hotels account, she charged angrily, "What's this about decent clothing? There is nothing *in*decent about my uniform. Or did I misunderstand you on the telephone, Mr. Prescott? I thought you wanted to secure a nurse for your mother, not a playmate."

"Cute, Ms. Tanner, very cute," Simon answered with a smile, making shooing motions with his hands, as if to move her into the back seat of the limousine in the same way she imagined he might herd unsuspecting cattle to the slaughterhouse. "I'll explain everything on the way. Now, chop, chop, Ms. Tanner, if you please. Elise's plane lands in two hours."

Chapter Two

Miranda stood in front of one of a half dozen sets of French doors that led out onto the expansive rooftop deck of the exclusive Prescott Dunes Hotel penthouse. She was watching the sun rise over the ocean on the second day of April and her first full day as Elise Manchester's new nurse, physical therapist, companion, dog walker, and—Miranda had concluded—play toy.

Yesterday had been April first. April Fool's Day. Miranda hadn't realized the date until she was already on the way to the airport, noticing it only by chance as she read the automatic printout on the elaborate entertainment console in Simon Prescott's posh limousine.

The date had been fitting, that was for sure And *she* had ended up being crowned the April fool, hoodwinked into thinking that she could possibly make a success of this job.

Simon Prescott had been the "fooler," if indeed there even was such a word. He, after all, was the one who had telephoned her office to engage "a young, competent nurse with extensive training in physical therapy and rehabilitation." He hadn't said anything about having to walk a pair of snow-white, black-nosed, beady-eyed, yapping little dogs. They hadn't arrived in Cape May yet, but their pictures— yes, photographs!—sat on the top of the grand piano alongside framed snapshots of Elise and Simon.

Although, Miranda considered reasonably as she unlocked one of the doors and stepped out onto the rooftop deck, she didn't really have anything against dogs. Pooper-scoopers maybe, but not dogs. She liked dogs, doggone it!

She did, however, have a lot to say about being told how to dress, and being forced to listen to how much more "alive" she might look if she'd "just do something with her makeup."

The remarks on her clothing had come from none other than Simon Prescott himself, who had waited impatiently in her living room yesterday morning as she had raced upstairs to change into a simple blue cotton skirt and white blouse—and then, once she reappeared, breathless, had pronounced her to look "staid" but "reasonably presentable."

The last bit, the crack about her makeup, had come from Elise Manchester herself once they had all survived the drive back from the Atlantic City airport. Simon Prescott had left almost immediately to return to his hotel in Wildwood, where he was negotiating some deal about which—as Elise had so bluntly stated—neither she nor Miranda "really care a hoot, darling."

Yes, it had been Mrs. Manchester who had made the comment about her makeup.

Pampered Elise Manchester, a woman who thought traveling with less than a dozen large suitcases—one of them stuffed with enough beauty aids to stock the cosmetics counter in any large New York department store—would be tantamount to camping by the side of the highway in a pup tent!

Petite Elise Manchester, who had the ridiculously beautiful blond hair of Zsa Zsa Gabor, the outrageously trim figure of Jane Fonda, the dazzling jewelry collection of Carol Channing, and all the genteel subtlety of General William Tecumseh Sherman marching through Georgia.

Spoiled Elise Manchester, who would probably sleep until noon, or so she had threatened last night when Miranda had suggested a 9:00 a.m. exercise session.

She would then most likely spend the remainder of the day alternately wheedling her way out of her therapy and reminding Miranda—again, as she had done last night—that frowning causes lines and that she, Miranda, seemed "to be in imminent danger of turning into a prune-face, darling."

But, Miranda considered, slipping her hands into the pockets of her teal blue slacks, it could be worse.

Not much, she granted, wincing, but it *could* be worse. Mrs. Manchester had seemed to like her well enough, which was a good thing because, otherwise, Miranda wouldn't have been the least surprised if the woman had ordered "Off with her head!" and expected her son to do the deed for her.

Her son. Miranda squinted toward the sun that had now completely cleared the horizon as she realized that Simon Prescott had been in her mind more than a calm, levelheaded businesswoman should consider prudent.

But she couldn't help it. She would have had to be blind, deaf, and totally prepubescent not to notice that he was one very handsome, desirable male animal. *Maybe even three days dead,* she considered dismally, walking to the railing to look down on the parking lot eighteen stories below her.

And then she saw him. Simon Prescott. Or, as Bonnie had put it, *the* Simon Prescott, who was walking with his already familiar long-legged strides across the nearly empty parking lot. The limousine was nowhere in evidence, but only a few nondescript cars and one low-slung, cherry-red sports car that had probably cost more than her entire small Victorian house—furnished!

It had to be Simon's car. It even looked like him. Sleek, expensive, and—she hated herself for thinking it—disturbingly sexy. Automotive engineers declared that sports cars were designed the way they were, not for any reasons of sexual innuendo, but because it made them "aerodynamically advanced." *Sure they are,* Miranda concluded in disgust, *and, as any woman could tell you, four-inch high heels were designed purely for comfort!*

She leaned over the railing, her eyes following Simon as he approached the entrance to the lobby, noticing that he was once more dressed casually in dark slacks and a dazzlingly white, open-collared cotton shirt, the sleeves rolled up to just below his elbows.

That was all she could see from this distance, and she couldn't even be sure that the shirt was cotton, but Simon Prescott hadn't impressed her as either the silk or polyester type. He might wear leather loafers without socks, but he'd probably install Laundromats in his hotel lobbies before he'd deck himself out in a gold neck chain.

He disappeared under the blue and white striped canvas canopy, his tawny hair glinting in the early morning sunlight, and Miranda came out of her musings with a start. He was coming upstairs, up here—to find that his Tanner Temps hireling was lolling around on the rooftop deck sunning herself instead of working.

Miranda headed back into the enormous living room, which was decorated in traditional mahogany furniture, with artfully scattered Oriental carpets all but covering a lovely parquet floor. She looked around wildly for something she could do that would make her look as if she actually *was* doing something productive.

She had just reached the kitchen area when she heard the soft whisper of the elevator door sliding open in the foyer off the living room.

Quickly picking up her half-empty coffee cup from the counter where she had left it earlier, she strolled leisurely into the dining room, doing her best impression of a person who had no idea she was not alone.

"Oh," she said in a surprised tone, blinking furiously before realizing that it was pretty silly to pretend as if she believed herself to be the sole living organism in the penthouse, considering that Mrs. Manchester and the housekeeper, Mrs. Haggerty, were also in residence. It wouldn't do to play *too* surprised to see someone else in the room. After all, she was supposed to be competent.

So why don't I feel competent? she asked herself silently. "Good morning, Mr. Prescott. We weren't expecting you today, were we?"

"We? Is there someone behind you, Ms. Tanner?" Simon asked, leisurely advancing into the living room and seating himself on his favorite chair. Miranda Tanner looked very nice this morning. *Very* nice. Late last night, when he had been kept awake for hours by the memory of her smoky-blue eyes, he had decided on his course of action. Now, he was glad he had.

"Or am I to deduce, Ms. Tanner," he continued, "regretfully, I might add, that you subscribe to that depressing medical habit of referring to yourself and your patient at one and the same time, as if you spoke for both?"

"Elise sure didn't find you hiding in some cabbage patch," Miranda muttered under her breath, realizing that a total lack of physical resemblance wasn't enough to keep anyone from immediately recognizing that Simon Prescott was Elise Manchester's son. They both had the ability to make her seriously consider committing mayhem every time they opened their mouths.

Simon picked up the neatly folded morning newspaper that was on the table next to him. The corners of his mouth trembled slightly as he attempted to conceal his appreciation for the comment his mother's nurse had most definitely not wanted him to overhear.

But a keen sense of hearing was a Prescott trait— *one* of the Prescott traits. There were others, and he decided to demonstrate one of his better ones by generously ignoring Miranda Tanner's inspired insubordination.

He spread the half-open newspaper on his lap, pretended to scan the headlines for a few moments, and then looked at Miranda. He liked the way her dark hair seemed as though it couldn't make up its mind whether it wanted to hug her shapely head like a sleek cap or go its own way, curling lovingly against her cheeks and nape. "How are things going so far, Ms. Tanner? Is Elise behaving?"

Miranda deposited the coffee cup on the dining-room table and walked completely into the living room area, to sit on the Sheraton-style couch across from Simon's chair. She may have been Elise Manchester's nurse for less than twenty-four hours, but it didn't take long to assess a patient, and she had come to some conclusions—some disappointing conclusions.

"That would depend upon your definition of the proper behavior for a woman recovering from a very serious injury," she said, doing her best to control her temper. "If you were to inquire as to whether or not your mother is getting adequate rest and not overtaxing herself, then I would say that she is being a model patient."

"Really?" Simon's left eyebrow rose a fraction, as he was faintly surprised by this praise of his mother. "Please, go on."

"I had every intention of continuing, Mr. Prescott," Miranda said, purposely taking on her "professional" no-nonsense tone. "However, if you are wondering if she is ever going to make any progress if she insists upon being the one who is calling the shots in her rehabilitation, then I would have to say that, so far, I believe I'd have less problems motivating a potted plant."

Simon threw back his head and laughed out loud. "Ah, Ms. Tanner, I suspected as much. That's one of the reasons why I drove back down here this morning. Elise is a power unto herself, I'm afraid, and from the way she spoke yesterday, I got the idea that she plans to milk this broken leg business for all it's worth."

"Meaning?" Miranda asked, wishing the skin around his sherry-brown eyes didn't crinkle so intriguingly when he smiled.

"Meaning, Ms. Tanner," he said, rising to look out through one of the French doors, "that Elise is between husbands right now. And if there's one thing my mother cannot stand, it's being without male companionship. If she can't be in Paris, or London, or Monaco—which she feels she can't be, at least not until she can throw away that cane she hates so much—being fawned over by half a dozen adoring supplicants, she will just make do with the one man she knows she can always depend on—me."

"*You?*" Miranda couldn't keep the astonishment out of her voice, and spoke before she could guard her tongue. "That's funny. You sure don't look like a mama's boy."

Simon inclined his head in her direction, as if bowing. "Thank you, Ms. Tanner. It's true. I severed the apron strings in my early teens, I believe, when Elise became Mrs. Gillian."

"Her second husband," Miranda said, remembering the virtual laundry list of surnames she had read on Elise's engraved luggage tags when she had helped the housekeeper unpack the woman's suitcases late last night.

"Number two, yes," Simon continued. "Elise attempted to retie those apron strings a few years ago, when Manchester became ancient history, but I eluded her, choosing instead to introduce her to Count Ivors, who was staying in one of my hotels. The arrangement worked beautifully for all three of us. You'll no doubt see her collection of opals while you're here. They come from the count, who has also faded into the pages of Elise's personal history. But don't get me wrong, Ms. Tanner. I do love my mother, in my own way, as she does me—in her own way—and I will always be there for her."

"Which is why you're here now," Miranda concluded, sighing. "But if you're going to be here and the housekeeper is going to be here, why do you need me? Mrs. Manchester can do her rehabilitation as an outpatient at the hospital."

As soon as she said the words, Miranda regretted them. *Oh, that's good, Andi, real smart!* What was she trying to do, for crying out loud, talk Tanner Temps out of a job?

"Because I would much prefer that Elise's rehabilitation be monitored here, in the penthouse," Simon said, and Miranda closed her eyes momentarily in relief.

"And," she heard him say, "it's not as if you won't be kept busy—at least not once Elise figures out that spring is here and she's wasting time playing the invalid while she could be queening it on the Riviera. The minute she tires of having all of us at her beck and call—you, me, Mrs. Haggerty—she'll make your life a living hell, trying to complete her rehabilitation in a single week."

Miranda could feel her blood beginning a slow boil. She might want the Prescott Hotels account so bad she could taste it, but she'd be darned if she was going to waste her time and talent baby-sitting a spoiled middle-aged woman whose favorite occupation, it seemed, was to watch everyone around her jump through hoops.

"Now, look, Mr. Prescott—" she began, only to have him cut her off.

"Simon, Ms. Tanner," he corrected, his smile once more doing something strange to her equilibrium, "or should I say, Miranda? I'm afraid we're going to get to know each other fairly well over the next month or so. As I've already told you, I've thought about our situation last night, and again as I drove down here this morning, and I can see no other way to go about this. We're just going to have to humor Elise until she makes up her mind to get better. There's no other way."

Miranda hopped to her feet, her fists jammed hard against her waist. "Wrong, *Mr.* Prescott. There most certainly is another way—and it doesn't have a single thing to do with treating your mother as if she were made of priceless crystal or some such nonsense."

Simon leaned his shoulder against the doorjamb and eyed Miranda with open appreciation. He didn't know whether he was more impressed by the fact that she was standing up to him or the notion that she might be considering standing up to Elise—which was much like trying to bail out the *Queen Elizabeth II* with a thimble. "Oh, really, Miranda. And, pray tell, what would that way be?"

Miranda opened her mouth to speak, then closed it again, spreading her hands in mingled confusion and exasperation. "I—I don't know," she said in self-disgust, then just as quickly rallied. "Not yet. But I'll figure out a way if it's the last thing I do. Mrs. Manchester is going to get my help whether she wants it or not. And, furthermore, she's going to *like* it!"

"Very interesting," Simon said, pushing himself away from the doorjamb. "You will keep me posted, won't you? I believe I'd like to sell tickets to that particular showdown."

He began walking toward the short hallway that led to the elevator, then stopped, turning to face her. "Oh, by the way, have you had breakfast?"

"Just coffee," Miranda answered absently, still trying to figure out how she would motivate Elise without having to resort to actually building a bonfire under the woman. "Mrs. Haggerty offered to make me something earlier, but I'm not used to being waited on, I suppose."

"Really? Even by waitresses? What a pity. I was about to suggest that—as Mrs. Haggerty is here in case Elise wakes earlier than her usual hour of noon—you join me downstairs for breakfast. That way we could discuss our living arrangements for the next month, among other matters. But," he added, shrugging, "if you think you wouldn't be comfortable—"

Miranda rolled her eyes, wondering yet again how she had come to be trapped in the middle of this circus. "Which is it, Mr. Prescott?" she asked, running a hand through her hair without a thought to her appearance. "Are you inviting me to breakfast, or trying to score points off me? Either way, you're sure not going out of your way to make a better second impression.''

''Second impression, Miranda? I don't believe I understand.''

''Yes, you do. You blew your first chance at making a good impression yesterday. *Staid!* Who uses the word *staid* anymore?'' She hesitated, then added, ''But, then, you probably don't care what sort of impression you make on people. You probably even think it's a part of your charm.''

Simon inclined his head as if acknowledging a direct hit by her verbal dart. ''Are you trying to get yourself fired, Miranda?'' he asked silkily. ''I wonder if you're just opting for the easy way out, rather than attempting to look at Elise's case as a challenge to your professional training?'' He shrugged. ''Either that or—perish the thought—you really don't like me.''

''I'm not a quitter!'' Miranda was stung into replying. ''As to whether or not I find you irresistible, Mr. Prescott—if that's what you're hinting at—I very much doubt whether my opinion bothers you either way.''

''That's where you'd be wrong, Miranda. And it's *Simon*. If you're going to insult me, at least call me Simon.'' He walked over to take her arm and lead her toward the elevator. ''Now, come along. We've got a lot to discuss, and I've discovered that I don't like arguing on an empty stomach.''

"Earlier you said that concern for Mrs. Manchester's care was one of the reasons you came down here this morning, Simon," Miranda said as they lingered over a second cup of coffee now that the breakfast dishes had been removed. "What are the other reasons? That is, if you don't mind telling me about them?"

She hoped the question sounded innocent. They had survived breakfast without coming to blows, filling the time between ordering the food and eating it with talk about Elise's case. Miranda had been favorably impressed with not only Simon's extensive knowledge of orthopedics—he had admitted to a bit of independent study since Elise Manchester's skiing accident—but also his genuine concern for his mother.

They had even progressed to the point where she felt at ease addressing him by his first name. It was a whole lot further than she had ever expected to get—especially when he sat there staring at her as she spoke, his intelligent brown eyes and the full, masculine shape of his mouth reminding her that, when it came to looks, his would have to be measured in the Greek god category.

But now it was time to get on to other subjects, and more than time to pull her wayward thoughts back to saner things. Besides, she was pretty sure she already knew the answer to her question. In fact, she was convinced of it.

She only hoped she could keep from reaching across the table and strangling him when he voiced it and exploded her new image of him as being a nice, likable—and, yes, *desirable*—guy who took care of his mother. She lowered her head, avoiding eye contact as she waited for him to speak.

"No, I don't mind discussing it, Miranda," he answered, wondering why she suddenly seemed so ill at ease. It was as if he had a bit of food stuck between his front teeth or something, and she didn't quite know how to tell him about it. "It's no great secret. I'd already planned to be in town at least three or four times a week. As you may have already read in the local newspapers, I'm negotiating the purchase of some properties for a new hotel farther down the beach."

"Another hotel? Really? Gee, I must have missed that. Well, I've been busy lately with tax preparation at Tanner Temps."

Miranda winced, knowing her voice had come out in a small squeak as she had suppressed an urge to scream. Why couldn't she ever bend the truth without feeling like a neon sign had just appeared on her forehead, flashing Liar, Liar, Pants On Fire! She cleared her throat and tried again. "How interesting. Will it, um, will it be a *big* hotel?"

Simon laid down his napkin and placed a five dollar bill on the table for the waitress. He didn't pay for his meals since he owned the restaurant along with the rest of the hotel, but he always made sure to generously tip the staff.

"Look," he said, knowing the waitress probably wanted to clear the table—and that he'd like to be alone with Miranda. "It's warm enough for you to go outside without heading back upstairs first to get a sweater. How about we walk off our breakfast with a short stroll along the promenade? We can talk about the new hotel, and I can show you where it will be built. That is, if that's all right with you?"

"I suppose so," Miranda answered carefully, sliding out of the booth before he could rise. She couldn't believe she had struck pay dirt so quickly. Yet, now that she had him on the subject of the new hotel, she wasn't quite sure she wanted to talk about it.

"But I must be back upstairs soon to begin earning my keep," she temporized, "whether your mother is awake yet or not. I want to work out an exercise schedule. And although you have a good exercise room in the penthouse already, there are a few more pieces of equipment I need to get from the local surgical supply rental facility if I'm to follow the instructions laid out by her doctors in Colorado."

"Ah, a schedule," Simon said, escorting her through the foyer and out onto the decorative covered walkway that led to the street. "Just the sort of thing to make Elise pull out all the stops trying to avoid following orders. She hates any sort of regulation or restraint."

"Now there's a surprise," Miranda countered sarcastically, shaking her head. "I'm awfully glad I charged you my top rate, Simon, because I believe I'm going to earn every penny of it."

"Miranda," Simon told her as they approached the street, "if you get Elise back on her feet in anything less than six weeks, I'd say your rate would be cheap at twice the price."

They crossed Beach Street which was nearly devoid of traffic at this early hour, climbed a short flight of steps to the promenade, and headed south toward Decatur Street, Miranda lost in thought as sea gulls screeched above their heads.

She smiled absently at passersby, residents of Cape May who celebrated any fine day of any season by taking a stroll on the low promenade or the beach itself, before saying, "I think I've got it now. I'll have to make a game of it, won't I?"

Simon, who had believed he could almost hear the gears working in Miranda's brain as she processed what he had said about Elise's dislike of scheduled activity, smiled at her deduction. "Just as if she were a willful two-year-old, Miranda," he agreed affably, nodding to an elderly couple who were strolling by arm in arm.

Miranda looked up at him, for he was more than a full head taller than she, and grinned in appreciation. "Perhaps if I offered her a lollipop each time she completes a set of exercises?"

"A diamond tennis bracelet would probably work better," Simon suggested in mock seriousness before catching Miranda's hand to help her avoid being hit by an approaching bicycle. It was being ridden by a middle-aged woman whose wide, slightly frightened eyes made him think she might have recently begun her own exercise program and was now considering bike riding a debatable project.

Miranda's mouth opened slightly as she felt the unexpected contact of his flesh against hers and she acknowledged that the tingle that had immediately run up her arm hadn't been present the last time she'd held hands with a man.

As a matter of fact, she couldn't ever remember being so struck by a simply physical touch. So why did her senses—which had obviously not had any recent conversations with her brain—decide to pick

Simon Prescott to react to like some love-struck teenager on her first date?

Once the woman and her wobbling bicycle had passed them by, Miranda tried—not very hard she admitted—to remove her hand from Simon's disconcerting grasp, then resigned herself to leaving it where it was.

She wasn't looking for trouble, but she was intelligent enough to know that she liked Simon's light, yet faintly possessive touch, liked the impression that they were together on this stroll, a "couple."

She didn't like *him*—of course, she didn't—but it was spring, for crying out loud, and she enjoyed being seen strolling the promenade with such a handsome man.

And if that made her a silly female, well, what of it? It was only a walk. It wasn't as if anything would come of it. Especially once they got farther down the beach and she was reminded of how much she disliked the man.

Simon shortened his usual long strides as Miranda suddenly seemed inclined to walk more slowly, wondering what she would do if he were to slip his arm around her waist the way the obviously honeymooning couple were walking in front of them, but then decided that he might be pushing things if he were to make such an obvious move.

Yet, Miranda attracted him.

Not that that should be so surprising, even though it had been unexpected. It certainly wasn't as if he hadn't felt attraction to a woman in the past. It also most certainly wasn't because he had been bowled over by her beauty or charm.

He had dated dozens of beautiful women, women whose faces and forms had graced many a stage, screen, and magazine cover; women he had worn on his arm like magnificent ornaments; sleek, expensive women who laughed at his jokes whether they understood them or not, knew all the right people, made love with him without messing either their hair or their makeup, and picked at their food like discriminating canaries.

Plastic, nearly interchangeable women, fawning over him, praising him, wanting something from him.

Miranda Tanner didn't seem to be the least bit impressed with him, or his money and position. And, unless he was wrong—which he usually wasn't—she didn't particularly like him, either.

Miranda Tanner, he felt sure, not only wouldn't laugh at his humor if she didn't understand his point, but possessed the quick understanding to match him word for word in a battle of wits. In other words, she wouldn't be boring.

Miranda Tanner wasn't the sort who sought out the "right" people. She smiled a greeting to everyone who passed by, and didn't seem to measure friendship by the bottom line of a financial statement. She wasn't "plastic."

He already knew that she didn't starve herself in order to insert a pencil-slim figure into the latest French fashions. Her form was not heavy or thin, but pleasantly shaped—womanly, touchable—without protruding hip bones or sunken cheeks. Besides, she had eaten every last bite of her substantial breakfast without once saying, "Oh, dear, I really *shouldn't—*"

All that was left was to imagine how Miranda Tanner would make love.

Simon sneaked a look at her as she pushed her free hand through her hair that was curling every which way around her face in the breeze off the ocean, then gave a dismissive toss of her head as if to say "the devil with it!" Her nearly makeup-free face glowed with health and the effects of the spring sun, which had left a random sprinkling of freckles across the bridge of her nose and on her cheeks.

Did she have any idea how wonderful she looked? How tempting?

The light of a sharp intelligence lit her lovely blue eyes and, as he had already learned, she had a quick humor and a considerable temper. Even yesterday, when he had first seen her walking so confidently into the hotel foyer dressed in that ridiculously prim nurse's uniform, he hadn't been unaware of the fires burning so closely beneath the surface.

No, Miranda Tanner wouldn't be the sort who made love and discussed the latest Broadway play at the same time, allowing him the use of her body in much the way she would allow a dress designer to drape her figure with his latest original.

Miranda Tanner would give her all, and to hell with anything but the moment, the experience. She would immerse herself in an intensity of feeling he himself couldn't remember having since his early college days. Then, making love had been an innocent rite of passage that had more to do with delightful shared investigation than sex.

Of course, he realized ruefully, there was something else that differentiated Miranda Tanner from the women he had known for these past ten years or more. Miranda would only give herself to a man she loved, totally, unconditionally—and then only to a man who loved her just as much in return. She wasn't the interchangeable sort.

Which left him... where?

Nowhere, he told himself, wincing at the direction his thoughts had taken, had been taking, ever since he had met Miranda Tanner. She was a nurse, companion to his mother, and destined to be a completely transitory female in his orbit.

He smiled ruefully, wondering if Elise would be cooperative and thwart Miranda at every turn, dragging out her recovery. Miranda might only be in his life temporarily, but it was spring, after all, and a little romance with a real, touchable woman couldn't hurt.

Besides, it might prove to be extremely enlightening.

Chapter Three

"There it is," Simon said with some satisfaction, pointing to a large vacant stretch of land lying across Beach Street and beyond the end of the snaking length of the promenade.

Nearly vacant anyway. Aside from the remnants of the foundations of several old buildings and a few asphalt parking lots, stood three homes too new and nondescript to be considered historically important, yet too small to serve as anything more than private residences.

These particular houses, these particular blocks, did not figure in the famous wagon or horse-and-buggy tours of the lovely Cape May Victorian houses that sported fanciful turrets and the occasional widow's walk that helped make the area a popular tourist stop.

Technically, this particular stretch of land was not exactly "in" Cape May at all, which was one reason it was so prime for new development. There were no strict rules to follow to keep any building historically correct.

In short, the entire area had been ripe for the plucking.

The three houses had once been located directly in the center of the faintly rundown jumble of stores and small restaurants now gone—the properties purchased and subsequently leveled by Prescott Hotels. But these three stumbling blocks to his plans still stood, side by side by side, facing Beach Street—still very much inhabited.

"There *what* is, Simon?" Miranda asked, shielding her eyes with her hand, and peering down the curve of the beach to where Helen Stein was busily hanging out blazingly white bed sheets in her small backyard.

Miranda shook her head. Even after suffering a broken hip due to a slip on the ice last winter, seventy-year-old Helen doggedly refused to allow her daughter to help with the housework.

Stubbornly independent, Helen had solved the problem of having her married daughter "do" for her by rising before dawn each day and completing the chores long before the young woman could drive into town from her suburban home.

Simon laughed as he looked at her. "You'll have to do more than squint, Miranda, if you want to see it as I see it. You'll have to help yourself to a first-class dose of imagination, as well."

He indicated the land with a sweep of one hand. "Picture this, Miranda. A single building, shaped as sort of a wide-open U—so that each veranda faces the ocean—five stories high, with the bottom floor devoted to exclusive shops—and a rooftop restaurant, of course. The view will be magnificent.''

"And are you planning to paint the whole place pink?" Miranda snapped, looking at the same land and still seeing Helen Stein struggling with her laundry basket. "Oh, yes—I can visualize it now. Pink stucco, white wrought-iron railings loaded with curlicues—and maybe a plastic flamingo or two beside the kidney-shaped pool. Lovely."

She wasn't being fair and she knew it. She could accuse Simon Prescott of a lot of things, but bad taste was not one of them. His Prescott Dunes Hotel was a model of understated elegance.

"You like pink stucco, Miranda?" Simon questioned her, tearing his gaze away from his mental image of his newest venture to look at her quizzically. Something was wrong here. They had been getting along well until a moment ago. Why was she attacking him? "I had you pegged for more of a traditional person, rather like your Victorian cottage. You even had a wicker bird cage in your living room."

She avoided his eyes, turning about swiftly on her heels to head back down the promenade with or without him. "Yeah, well, what I like isn't the question here, is it? I mean, I *like* those three houses your demolition crews have left standing over there as if they were the sole survivors of some sort of blitz. Where do they figure in your plans, Simon?''

He stood still, looking after her for a moment in mounting confusion, then sprinted to catch up with her, falling into step alongside as he said incisively. ''Let me take a wild stab at something, okay? You were lying to me before, weren't you, Miranda? You did know about my project. You knew about it and, to take this thing to its next logical step, you don't much care for it. Do you?''

Miranda halted so quickly that she nearly stumbled. ''No, Simon. I don't like it. As a matter of fact, on a scale of one to ten, it's a big zero.''

She was beginning to get very angry, which she knew wasn't smart, but the sight of Helen Stein doggedly maintaining her last shreds of independence had really made her blood boil. She wanted to say more, much more, but clamped her jaws shut tightly, unable to decide where to start.

Simon waited patiently for a few moments, admiring the flush that had invaded Miranda's cheeks, then said pleasantly, ''Will I have to go down on my knees on the promenade and beg—which might prove moderately embarrassing for at least one of us—or are you going to tell me what's on your mind? I know you're waiting for some signal from me. I just don't know what it is.''

"I don't want to talk about it," Miranda mumbled, beginning to walk once more. "I never should have said anything in the first place. I have a big mouth. Bonnie, my assistant at Tanner Temps, says so. Everybody says so. I'm surprised it isn't posted on billboards on the way in to town. To Whom It May Concern; Andi Tanner Has A Big Mouth!"

"Andi?" Simon repeated consideringly as he matched her stride for stride, the two of them passing by other, less energetic walkers making their way along the promenade. "Is that what your friends call you? I like it."

"Well, bully for you," Miranda countered, looking down the beach, mentally measuring off the distance from where she was to the Prescott Dunes, the tallest, the most prominent feature on Beach Street. "*I* like Miranda." She shot him a look that, by rights, should have sent him reeling down onto the sandy beach, mortally wounded. "And I happen to like Ms. Tanner even better!"

Simon wasn't about to be deflected by her broad hint that they return to their first, formal footing. "All right, Miranda," he said reasonably. "We'll settle for the middle ground. Now, to get back to this abrupt change of mood. I fail to see your problem, unless you're one of those people who simply dislike change for its own sake. What's wrong with building another hotel in Cape May?"

"Nothing's *wrong* with building a hotel, Simon," Miranda answered, forced to smile as one of her former clients walked by and waved to her. She hadn't wanted to smile. It broke into her bad mood—and just when she was beginning to enjoy it, too. She was also rather enjoying the fact that Simon Prescott—*the* Simon Prescott—was chasing after her down the promenade like a friendly puppy, trying to get her attention.

"Ah-ha!" Simon exclaimed, slipping his arm across her shoulders, then sliding it down so that it rode her waist as they walked along. "So it isn't the hotel itself that bothers you. We're making progress. Not much, I'll admit, but some. All right, if it isn't the hotel, it has to be something to *do* with the hotel. What could it be, what could it be? Let's see...is it animal, vegetable, or mineral?"

"We're not playing twenty questions here, Simon," Miranda shot at him, mentally packing her bags for her ignominious departure from the penthouse suite.

She had done nothing but open her mouth and insert her foot since she had met Simon Prescott. He might be acting as if her continual outbursts were amusing, but they had to be wearing thin by now. God knew she herself was rapidly becoming pretty bored with these unaccustomed mood swings.

"No, we're not, are we?" Simon replied, holding her back by the simple means of the pressure of his hand against her waist as they waited to cross the street. In just the short time they had been out walking, traffic on the street had doubled.

"What is it, Miranda? What have I done to upset you? I'm being serious now, I promise. I want to know what has been bothering you ever since we met."

She looked up at him quickly, frowning. "You noticed?"

He smiled, making her long to hit him—either that or bury her head against his chest. "Oh, yes, Miranda. I've noticed. You don't want to like me. Every once in a while your animosity slips a notch or two—like over breakfast this morning—but for the most part you look at me as if you're examining me for hidden flaws."

"You're imagining things," Miranda said, her voice once again slightly squeaky, revealing her lie to both of them.

"Don't interrupt, please, Miranda," Simon countered, his own voice maintaining its usual, calm tone. "I'm trying to make a point here. Now, as I see it, this zeal to make me into a villain has something to do with my latest project."

"Oh, really?" Miranda snapped. "You figured that out, did you? What did you do, look inside my head with your X-ray eyes?"

Simon grinned at her. "It won't work, you know. I never get angry, no matter how many verbal pins you might try to stick in me. It's part of my winning Prescott charm."

"Some charm," Miranda groused, blowing at a stray curl that had slipped onto her forehead. "But I give up. Go ahead, talk."

"Thank you. Having already seen your house, I know you don't live in any of the three houses that are all that's holding back construction, so I can only believe that someone you know lives in one of them. Or am I wrong, and you had a half share in the ice cream parlor we demolished last week?"

Miranda bowed her head, ashamed of herself. "I didn't own a share in any of the businesses. If I did, I'd be a charter member of your fan club. I've heard you've paid top dollar for all of the properties your company has purchased so far."

"Which leads us straight back to the three houses," Simon concluded, nodding to the bellboy who had called a greeting as the glass doors opened automatically. "My lawyers have promised me that the negotiations were all but concluded, but we've hit a slight snag in the past week. None of the people who live in the houses will talk to anyone anymore.

My lawyers think someone's gotten to them, organized them, so to speak. They haven't thought up this hold-out on their own.''

He was getting too close for comfort; both to her and to the truth. Miranda walked swiftly, determinedly, toward the discreetly located private elevator that led up to the penthouse.

"Not just *people,* Simon," she informed him, looking for the button that would summon the elevator. She couldn't get upstairs fast enough, pack her bags, and get out of there, away from this maddening man. But she couldn't resist correcting him. "They have names. Helen Stein, Bridget O'Shaughnessy, and Angelo Pantoni."

"Stein, O'Shaughnessy, and Pantoni," Simon repeated, extracting a key from his pocket and inserting it into a slot Miranda now remembered having seen yesterday, accessing the elevator. "Sounds rather like an ecumenical law firm, doesn't it? Which one of them is related to you?"

The doors whispered open and Miranda rushed inside, then turned to face front, hoping the usual unwritten rules of elevator etiquette would keep Simon silent while the two of them watched the numbers above the door illuminate one by one as the car climbed to the penthouse.

The elevator had risen no more than three floors when Simon stepped forward and hit the Stop button, bringing the car to an immediate halt. He wasn't about to let Miranda get away from him yet—not when he felt he was getting very close to some answers.

He might, he considered to himself as he admired Miranda's attractive form, even learn something about the three houses.

Miranda cast her eyes frantically around the walnut-lined cubicle, as if looking for visual evidence of its sudden lack of motion. "We've stopped!" she exclaimed, some small part of her mind acknowledging that she had just pointed out the obvious.

Then she jammed her fists onto her hips and glared at Simon, who, she decided, was looking entirely too pleased with himself. "Just what the *hell* do you think you're doing?"

He ignored her outburst. "Let me repeat my question, Miranda. Which one of the three is related to you? That is what's bothering you, isn't it? You don't want Aunt or Uncle Whomever to sell the family homestead to the nasty millionaire who probably isn't giving him or her half of what the property is worth. How much are you telling the Terrible Trio to hold out for, hmm?"

Miranda looked at him in complete astonishment. "Money? Do you really think this is about *money?* Heavens, Simon, but you're dense!"

She turned once more, then added, "And I'm not related to any of those dear people, although I'd be proud to have any one of them as part of my family. *Honored!* Now start this elevator, if you please. I want to get out of here."

Simon couldn't believe it. By telling him the names of the owners, Miranda had just as good as admitted that she had made herself a part of his problem.

His lawyers had told him that the last three properties had been as good as in the bag until a few days ago when, as if from left field, a letter had come in, declining "your generous offer."

And now, without a single hint to warn him in advance, he was standing face to face with the person who had succeeded in throwing a monkey wrench into his plans.

She had to be the one—nothing else made any sense.

Both he and his legal staff had decided that it had been nothing more than a ploy to up the price, this sudden refusal to sell, especially when they considered the fact that the three properties stood directly in the middle of the acreage and it would be impossible to build without them.

Simon had entertained the notion that some ambitious lawyer had gotten hold of the three owners and told them they could get triple their asking cost for the properties now that construction had already begun, which was why Simon had decided to bring himself, and his not inconsiderable charm and powers of persuasion, to Cape May in the first place.

He was willing to up the offers. He was willing to add perks, such as helping the owners to relocate, paying their moving costs—but he had not been prepared to deal with an interfering crusader, which was what he now had the sinking feeling he was going to have to do.

But it wasn't all bad, he acknowledged with what he knew was probably a typical male, sexist reaction that he should have dismissed as beneath him. Yet it was true—if he was going to have to negotiate with an idealistic crusader, at least Miranda Tanner was a *beautiful* idealistic crusader.

Simon leaned against the corner of the elevator compartment, carefully blocking the small control panel, just in case Miranda decided to take matters into her own hands and attempt to restart the elevator. In her present mood, he wouldn't be surprised if she hit the emergency button, setting off the alarm and bringing everyone in the hotel to the rescue.

"You wrote that letter, didn't you, Miranda?" he asked at last. "The so polite, so proper letter signed by the Terrible Trio. You know, when I read it for the first time I got the impression that I should have been reading between the lines. Proper as it was it seemed to be permeated with veiled sarcasm, all directed at me. But you know I ignored the impression. I thought I was just overreacting."

He smiled, shaking his head. "However, now that I've had the great pleasure of listening to you live and in person, I think I'll fish the letter out of my briefcase and read it again. You misspelled 'rescind,' by the way. According to the documents already in my possession, the word you were striving for is correctly spelled r-e-n-e-g-e."

That got a reaction from her and she swung around to face him, fire in her eyes. "Renege? Nobody's *reneging* on anything here, Simon. They never signed anything final—only a preliminary agreement. Nothing binding. And they only signed those because they felt they had no other choice."

"Really."

"Yes, *really*. Simon, those people are old. They've lived there for most of their lives. They don't have any place to go if you tear down their houses. You're taking their lives away in exchange for another hotel."

Simon rubbed at his forehead, doing his best to understand, and failing badly. "That's ridiculous, Miranda. With the prices I've offered them, they could go anywhere in the world that their hearts desire—*twice*."

Miranda backed away from him, slowly shaking her head and not stopping until she ran out of room, her back pressed against the paneled wall.

"You really don't have the faintest idea what I'm talking about, do you, Simon?" she asked, more disappointed by his total lack of comprehension than she would have believed possible.

"Not even a clue," Simon admitted openly. "I'm a businessman, Miranda. I'm in the business of building and running hotels. I saw a need for another hotel in Cape May. I had my people locate a prime location for that hotel. I had my legal department make offers on the properties involved. The current owners accepted my offers and construction is about to begin. That's how business is done."

He lifted his right hand, rubbing the back of his neck. "At least, that's how it's usually done. But this time we didn't wait to break ground until we'd dotted every *i* and crossed every *t*."

Miranda pounced on his admission, sensing at least one small victory. The cost to her heart, her newly vulnerable, susceptible heart, would have to be calculated later, once she was away from this man whose nearness was beginning to do strange things to her equilibrium.

"Ah-ha! Then you admit it. The negotiations with Mrs. O'Shaughnessy and the others *aren't* binding! End of story, Simon. The Terrible Trio, one—Prescott Hotels, zippo! Now hit that button, and let's get the hell out of here."

"Eventually, Miranda, eventually," Simon said, pushing himself away from the wall while still careful to keep his body between Miranda and the control panel. "First, tell me why you decided to get involved with the Terrible Trio."

"Stop calling them that!" Miranda exploded, forgetting that she had used the same term only a few moments ago herself. She noted the distance between herself and the control panel and quickly realized that she wasn't going anywhere until Simon Prescott said so.

Simon Says, she thought in disgust. She'd *never* been very good at that particular children's game.

She spread her hands, giving in. She'd get nowhere until she told him everything he wanted to know. "Should I do this in words of no more than two syllables, Simon?" she asked in frustration. "I mean, a man who calls his own mother by her first name and admits that she can be bribed with a diamond tennis bracelet can't possibly have much understanding of *real* people."

"Now you're getting personal, Miranda," Simon pointed out reasonably, "which is never a good idea in business discussions. However, as this elevator is a rather unique boardroom, I suppose we can bend the rules a little." Miranda whipped her head around to glare at him, making her curls bounce. "You know your hair looks incredibly soft and touchable," Simon found himself saying.

His intent had been to deflect her anger, but within a heartbeat of uttering the words he knew he had taken a figurative strike two in this particular "at bat" with Miranda Tanner.

"Not that you'll ever know," she shot back at him, then continued, "Let's keep this professional, shall we? I'll apologize for my personal remark if you'll apologize for yours."

Simon shrugged, as if indifferent. "If you want me to say your hair doesn't look touchable, fine. I won't allow another compliment to escape my lips for the duration of our discussion."

And afterward? Miranda longed to ask, but held her tongue. *Aren't you ever going to say anything nice to me again?*

Beating down her traitorous thoughts, Miranda clapped her hands once, as if calling this impromptu class in human understanding to order, then folded them together.

"Let's start with Mrs. O'Shaughnessy, shall we?" she began, starting to pace the corner of the elevator she had begun to consider as her territory. "Bridget is around eighty, give or take five years, for she refuses to tell anyone her exact age. She's lived in that

house on Beach Street for nearly half a century—
about the same amount of time as the rest of them."

She paused, wondering if it was fair—or even
smart—to continue. On the one hand, she was revealing this personal information about her friends
in the hope of making them seem more real to Simon. On the other hand, she could be giving him
some important ammunition that he might be able to
use against the very people she was trying to help.

"Bridget O'Shaughnessy," Simon prompted her.
"Over twenty-one and a long-time resident of Cape
May. What else?"

Miranda bit her lip, about to refuse to say anything more, then decided to trust Simon's integrity.
He wouldn't use the information she was about to
give him to hurt anybody and, remembering how
understanding he was with his own rather difficult
mother, she thought she might even be able to soften
his heart a degree or two.

"Bridget's husband died over twenty years ago,"
she continued rapidly. "She has no children, only a
niece who lives in Kansas. Her niece visits Bridget for
a month every summer and she's offered her a
home—which is very nice of her. But Bridget has
spent the best part of her life living close to the
ocean.

"Simon, the first sound Bridget O'Shaughnessy
hears when she wakes in the morning and the same

sound that lulls her to sleep at night is the pounding of the waves against the shore. She can't imagine herself in Kansas, halfway between two oceans—and neither can I, frankly—but Bridget feels she can't in good conscience spend any of the money she'd get from you on herself, as she'd always planned to leave her house to her niece.''

Simon didn't bother pointing out that, whether Bridget purchased a new house in Cape May or moved to Kansas, the niece would get all of the money eventually. This discussion wasn't about money, which had been obvious ever since Miranda had begun speaking. And it wasn't about fields of waving wheat as opposed to the white-tipped waves of the Atlantic Ocean.

This was about *people,* people he hadn't given a thought to when he'd planned to displace them, believing that a healthy profit overrode any other considerations. Suddenly, unexpectedly, he felt Miranda might have good reason to dislike him.

''And Mr. Pantoni?'' he prodded gently when Miranda fell silent. ''What's his story?''

A small smile played about the corners of Miranda's mouth as she thought of Angelo Pantoni, a squat, round man with a bald spot on his head and a booming voice.

''Mr. Pantoni is an opera buff, Simon,'' she explained, remembering the last time she had visited the man and had to pound on the door for nearly five minutes before he heard her knock over the strains of Mozart's *The Marriage of Figaro*.

"He not only sings it, but he plays it on his ancient record player. Plays it very *loudly* on his record player—with his dog, Puccini, accompanying him. Angelo is very good, and Puccini makes up for his own lack of vocal ability with sheer noise. Nobody ever complained, you understand, because the owner of the pizza shop to the right of his house was also an opera lover, and Helen Stein, whose house is located on the other side, is almost stone deaf. Mr. Pantoni is sure he'll never again be able to find such a comfortable arrangement."

"An opera buff with dog accompaniment. This gets better and better. And how about Helen Stein? What's her reason for refusing my offer?"

Miranda opened her mouth to answer, but he held out a hand, forestalling her. "No. Let me guess. The nearly stone deaf Helen gives piano lessons to *tone* deaf students and is afraid she'll lose her clientele if she relocates somewhere else in Cape May. Or, better yet, she's sentimentally attached to her banister and can't bear to have it torn down."

"I could really learn to hate you, Simon Prescott," Miranda said, leaning against the paneled wall once more. "Helen Stein, for your information, is a perfectly lovely old lady who became one of my clients when she broke her hip early last winter. She's been doggedly maintaining her independence for years, which isn't easy when her daughter keeps insisting she sell the house and move in with her, her husband, and their five children—all under the age of ten, I might add. Your offer made her feel as if she had no other choice but to give in."

"Until you got to her," Simon concluded for her. "Until you got to all of them." He spread his hands in disgust. "Miranda, you're sticking your nose where it has no business being. You do know that, don't you? I'm offering them money. Cold, hard cash, with which they can control their own lives. All you're offering them is a delaying tactic. In the end all three of them will have to give in, either because of their health or because their families will prevail. And, in the meantime—"

"In the meantime," she interrupted rather smugly, "I'm holding up the construction of your hotel, and most probably costing you a ton of money. Don't expect me to believe that you really care for these people, because I'm not buying it!"

Then she remembered that her feelings were not important, and her voice softened as she continued. "You weren't there when I visited with Helen and Angelo and Bridget a few weeks ago and Helen broke down—that proud, proud woman broke down and *cried* because her daughter had just told her that she couldn't bring her four-poster bed with her when she moved because it was simply too big. Helen and her husband slept in that bed for all of their married life, Simon. She can't give it up!"

Simon saw the sheen of tears in Miranda's smoky-blue eyes and discarded his idea of raising his offer for the three properties. Some things just couldn't be measured in dollars and cents—and obviously this was one of them.

Damn his legal department! Why hadn't they told him about these three people? All the other buildings had held businesses, businesses whose owners had welcomed either the chance to relocate and build fine new establishments or the option of retiring on their profit.

Now he was faced with the unappealing picture of himself as a dispossessor of nice, cuddly old people who had never really wanted to go anywhere in the first place. The thought didn't please him. He was Simon Prescott—not Simon Legree, damn it, about to toss Little Eva out onto an ice floe!

He pushed himself away from the wall, taking two carefully measured steps in Miranda's direction. "Can we call a truce here, Andi?" he asked, laying a hand on her arm.

Miranda looked at Simon's hand as it lay on her arm, then gazed up into his face, trying to decide whether or not he was about to tell her that, although he was touched—"really touched"—by her story, he was about to order his lawyers to pull out all the stops in trying to jam through the sale of the three houses and wanted her out of the line of fire first. "A truce? What sort of truce? What do you want?"

Simon smiled at her obvious confusion. "Wrong question, Miranda," he said, stroking her soft skin with his fingertips. "You might not like the answer. What you should be asking right now is what am I willing to settle for, considering that I've already acknowledged that I'd only be wasting my time negotiating with the Terrible Trio. You're the one calling the shots, aren't you, Miranda?"

She averted her eyes. "Don't be ridiculous, Simon. I only offered my assistance in composing the letter to your lawyers. They felt they had no one else to turn to. And please stop calling them the Terrible Trio. It's insulting."

"It's a whole hell of a lot shorter than reeling off the names Stein, O'Shaughnessy, and Pantoni every few minutes," Simon pointed out reasonably, idly moving his fingers up to her elbow, then skimming them along the sensitive skin on the underside of her upper arm.

"But to get back to the point," he continued as he noticed that she was becoming flushed once more, and this time he was fairly sure it wasn't from anger.

"You began this thing from the sidelines, content to stand back, lob in a grenade, and then watch the explosion. However, thanks to Elise's skiing accident, you've been thrust smack in the middle of the battle, face to face with the enemy."

"So?" Miranda was finding it difficult to breathe, let alone think. Did he have to stand this close to her? Did he have to touch her? Did she have to like it all so much?

"So," Simon continued, moving slightly so that he stood directly in front of her. "I suggest we join forces, look for a compromise that will satisfy all parties. I'm sure we can do it if we just put our heads together."

Miranda stuck out the tip of her tongue, to moisten her suddenly dry lips. "Put...put our heads together?" she echoed his last words, her overactive mind giving them a whole new meaning that had very little to do with business. "Then you still want me to be your mother's nurse? You aren't going to dismiss me?"

He tucked the index finger of his free hand under her chin and lifted her face so that he could look directly into her eyes. "Miranda Tanner, I haven't been able to *dismiss* you ever since you walked into the foyer of this hotel yesterday."

"Oh." Miranda's voice was barely audible. "Really."

Simon began lowering his head, his destination firm in his mind. "Yes, Andi, really," he drawled, stepping even closer, so that their bodies were melted together from knee to hip. Her touch inflamed him, sending all thoughts of the Terrible Trio and Prescott Hotels out of his head.

Miranda's eyes fluttered closed as Simon's lips met hers, and a tingling awareness shot straight through her, all the way down to the tips of her toes. She felt his arms slip around her waist and shoulders, drawing her close against him, and she put out her own hands for a moment before clinging to him tightly.

The explosion of passion between them was as sudden and as intense as their clash of words had been earlier, and when Simon moved to deepen the kiss, Miranda willingly opened to him.

Simon reveled in her surrender...but gradually realized that, while the privacy of the elevator might have worked reasonably for their discussion, it was a remarkably poor choice to begin a seduction.

Visions of his king-size bed in the penthouse danced in his head even while he told himself he was definitely moving too fast. Simon maneuvered Miranda around so that he could reach the control panel.

Miranda stirred slightly in his arms as he opened one eye and pushed the button for the penthouse. His attention returned to the matter at hand as he slid his fingers into the soft short hair curling at the nape of her neck, his eyes closing once more.

And the matter at hand was keeping Miranda's mind on nothing but him until the elevator doors opened and they could adjourn to more comfortable surroundings.

He moved his mouth on hers, gently biting at her full bottom lip, then slanted his own lips over hers, delving into her mouth once more. He was aroused by the slightly tangy taste of sea salt on her skin.

His hands curved against either side of her small waist and he had to remind himself to go slow, no matter how eagerly she might be responding to him. He hadn't forgotten his first impression of Miranda's character. If he went too quickly, pressed this unlooked-for advantage too far, he might end by losing everything he had gained.

Besides, he was in no real rush. He wasn't orchestrating a quick conquest. As a matter of fact, he really wasn't sure exactly what he was planning. Right now, with Miranda in his arms, he didn't want to think beyond the next moment.

Somewhere in the back of his mind he felt the elevator glide to a halt and heard the faint whisper of the doors sliding open on the penthouse floor.

But before he could bear to release his hold on Miranda long enough to escort her out of the elevator, he also heard Elise trill from somewhere behind him, "Why, good morning, darling. Is that my new nurse you have clasped to your chest? My goodness, Simon—and it's not even noon yet, is it?"

Chapter Four

Miranda pushed herself away from Simon so roughly that she nearly fell, then quickly turned her back to both the foyer and Elise Manchester, who was already heading back into the living room, leaning rather dramatically on the cane she had sworn she hated.

Miranda was appalled at her abandoned behavior of a few moments ago. Groping in an elevator with a man she had barely met! How could she be so stupid—so easily taken in?

"Oh, God," she groaned under her breath. "You're a smart one all right, Tanner—a real Einstein! If this is what the man can accomplish in a few minutes in a stopped elevator, what do you think he'll do if he ever invites you in to see his etchings? First two guesses don't count."

"Do you always talk to yourself, or is this a recent aberration?" Simon asked quietly. Then he added, "And don't overreact. Just follow my lead. There's no real harm done, Miranda. Elise is a real sucker for romance."

"Romance!" Miranda shot back at him, then lowered her voice and repeated in an agonized whisper, "Romance! Are you out of your tiny mind? What we were doing in this elevator had nothing to do with romance."

"Really?" Simon was doing his best to keep a straight face, and failing badly. He didn't know which he was enjoying more, Miranda's kisses, or her determination to beat herself over the head with what she'd done.

Either way, neither her innocence nor his attraction to her could be denied. He held open the elevator door by leaning his long frame against it, then crossed his arms in front of him, grinning at her. "Well, I give up—if it wasn't romance, Miranda, what was it? Because *something* sure as hell was going on between us in this elevator a few moments ago."

"Don't even say it! You know perfectly well what was going on," Miranda gritted out from between tightly clenched teeth, glaring at him. She was trying to understand why, even now—embarrassed and disgusted with herself as she was—she still felt as if her feet were hovering several inches off the floor. "We were both upset—and we just . . . we just . . ."

"Of course we did, Miranda," Simon said, rescuing her as she backed away from saying anything more. "Although, personally, I'd rather blame it on the spring air."

"Spring air? Oh, give me a break, Simon!" Miranda sighed in exasperation, completely forgetting that earlier she'd given herself that same excuse for being affected by Simon's charms. "You've *got* to be kidding."

Simon, tired of serving as a human doorstop, took her hand and led her out of the elevator, which she had shown no signs of ever leaving on her own. "I'm being serious here, Miranda. Have you taken a good look around lately? The birds are building nests, the bees are buzzing, flowers are pushing up through the ground. You can't take three steps in any direction without running into Mother Nature busting out all over. And you know what they say about spring, don't you? How does it go? In spring a young man's fancy turns to thoughts of—"

"Never mind the recital, Simon," Miranda said, pulling her hand free as she cut him off just as he was really beginning to enjoy himself. "I know *exactly* where a young man's fancy turns to, thank you. Besides, your mother is waiting for us in the living room. Now, *you* follow *my* lead, and pretend nothing has happened. Heaven knows precious little did, now that I think about it."

"Thank you so much for that sterling endorsement of my romantic prowess, Miranda. There's no chance of me getting a swelled head with you around, is there?" Simon replied undaunted, then followed after her as she strode across the foyer and into the living room to where his mother was sitting at her ease in a brocade side chair, her back to the pair of them.

"Mrs. Manchester," Miranda began bracingly, hoping for the best, "how good it is to see you up and about so early." *Brother,* she thought, wincing, *and is that ever an understatement!* "You're beginning to get around like a real pro with that cane," she continued quickly. "Did Mrs. Haggerty help you dress? Have you eaten breakfast?"

Elise Manchester looked up at the two of them, her impish gaze hinting that, although the older woman knew full well what she had seen, she would not so much as utter a single *word* about it again if Miranda and Simon preferred to pretend that nothing out of the ordinary had happened.

Besides, as Simon could have told Miranda if only she'd asked, he knew his mother well enough to know that Elise saw the whole elevator incident in her own terms—those terms most probably including the word "blackmail."

He had already decided that within the next few minutes, she would play on what she'd seen in order to get both herself out of today's physical therapy session and somehow try to worm something out of her son for good measure.

And when Elise spoke, she demonstrated that Simon hadn't become too rusty at reading his mother's mind.

"I've nibbled on some strawberries and cream, yes," Elise informed Miranda, then smiled as she added, "but if you think I'm going to do any of those *boring* exercises today with that ridiculous instrument of torture the therapists call a rubber band, you are sadly mistaken. Simon is here, and I wish to spend every moment with him. He visits his poor, decrepit old mother seldom enough. Heaven only knows how much more time I'll have to be with my only child. Did you bring me something, darling?"

"Not unless you want some of the sand in my shoes, Elise." Simon stepped in front of Miranda and took hold of his mother's delicately outstretched hand. "Now, what is this about not doing your therapy? Are you planning on taking a stab at playing *Camille* today?" he asked, bending to kiss her smooth cheek. "I have to tell you, it will be a real stretch of your acting talents, for you look entirely too beautiful to convince anyone that you're dying."

Miranda, immediately recognizing that Simon and his mother were conversing on two levels—one she could hear and another more personal one she couldn't understand—prudently retreated to a nearby chair to watch two masters in action from somewhere safely out of the line of fire.

Besides, she didn't need the openly teasing look Simon shot her out of the corner of his gorgeous sherry-brown eyes to convince her that she should have kept her mouth shut in the first place and, as he had said, followed his lead.

Elise Manchester *wasn't* going to say a single word about finding her son and her nurse kissing in the elevator. She wasn't going to reprimand Miranda, or fire her, or even make snide jokes about working people who dared to kiss the king. Nope. She was just going to dig in her heels and refuse to do her therapy—daring Miranda to challenge her when they both knew that Elise now held the upper hand.

And Simon! Ah, there was another master of the silken tongue. He played Elise like a fish, reeling out just enough line to make his mother think she could get away at any time, then pulling her in close once more to remind her who was in charge. A too-beautiful-to-die Camille, indeed! Miranda rolled her eyes. It was getting so deep in here she'd soon have to roll up the hems on her slacks!

Miranda was brought back to attention by the sound of Elise's dainty laugh, tinkling like ice cubes sliding into a crystal glass. "Oh, darling, you are such an outrageous liar," she told her son, lifting a hand to pat his cheek. "You know how terrible I look. After all, I'm fifty now. I'm positively *ancient!*"

Simon propped himself on the arm of the chair and winked at Miranda. "Fifty, Elise? Let me think about that a moment, all right? That would mean you were sixteen when you had me, wouldn't it? Five years ago you had been twenty, and last year you told me you weren't a day over eighteen at the time. You know, if you keep this up, either I'm going to have to start lying about my age or we're soon going to have to explain how you gave birth at the age of ten."

Elise's full bottom lip came out in a pout. "I *was* a child bride, you know. Besides, darling, age is only relative—whatever that means."

"Relative?" Simon repeated thoughtfully. "Now there's a thought. Maybe you should start telling everyone that I'm your brother?"

Elise almost frowned—almost, because frowning caused lines and she was very careful about such things—and considered what Simon had suggested. Oh, he was teasing her, of course. Simon existed to tease her. But he had a point. He was thirty-four now, and had even begun to gray a bit at the temples. It would take some doing, but it *might* be possible to convince people that...

"Elise," Simon said, rising to his feet, "I can hear the wheels turning in your head, but you can forget it. I wasn't being serious. Now, what do you say you and Miranda get started on that therapy? I have some work to do here in town, so I'll be out of earshot if you feel it necessary to moan and groan. And if you're very good, I may have a present for you when I join you for dinner.''

"And luncheon, darling?" Elise questioned him, clearly not about to let him get away so easily. "Surely you and Miranda can't bear to be parted from now until six o'clock?"

Miranda nearly had to forcibly restrain herself from sinking completely into the chair cushions—or throwing one of them at Simon's back. So much for their unspoken agreement. Obviously Elise wasn't the slightest bit shy about changing the rules of war when she felt herself to be losing a particular battle.

Simon turned to smile at Miranda, a heart-stopping grin that made her forget the cushion and instead long to pick up the vase sitting on the table next to her and bring it down on his head—repeatedly, until it had served to wipe that smug, satisfied look off his face.

"It will be terribly difficult, Elise, I agree," he said solemnly, then added, "but I believe I have some extensive research to do concerning the firm of Stein, O'Shaughnessy, and Pantoni. Isn't that right, Miranda?"

Miranda's eyes widened, partly in shock and partly because he had actually remembered her friends' names. "Simon," she asked nervously, thinking how bowled over at least Mrs. O'Shaughnessy and Mrs. Stein would be at the sight of the hotel magnate, "what are you planning to do?"

"Do? Why, I'm really not quite sure yet, Miranda," he answered honestly. "However, I think I'll start by searching out a store and buying two bouquets of spring flowers, a Pavarotti album, and a box of dog biscuits. That seems like a fair place to begin, don't you agree?"

Miranda leaped to her feet, her anger making her forget that she was speaking to her employer—and with his mother in the room. "Simon Prescott, if you go turning your charm on those poor old people to get what you want, I'll—I'll . . ."

"You'll what, Miranda?" Simon asked, then shook his head. "No, don't tell me. I'm sure I'll find it much more fascinating to guess. For now, I'll just comfort myself with the thought that you find me charming."

And then, before she could think of anything else to say, he leaned down and kissed her firmly on the mouth before heading for the elevator.

"If he thinks he can bring me a silly bouquet of flowers and make everything right again, well, I tell you, Miranda, that man has another think coming!" Elise exclaimed, picking up the cane that had been resting against the chair and thumping its end down hard against the parquet floor.

"And don't you settle for flowers, either," she continued instructively, "unless there are more than three dozen of them—all red roses. Now, what was this business about record albums and dog biscuits?"

Miranda, who had been touching her fingertips to her lips as she looked toward the foyer, caught between feeling smug and wondering if she should be running for her life, turned to Elise questioningly. "Pardon me, Mrs. Manchester? Did you say something?"

Elise rolled her eyes in mock dismay. "Uh-oh," she said, shaking her head, "as I remember hearing somewhere... and another one bites the dust! Well, I won't fib and say I didn't see it coming the first moment I saw the two of you together. Fascinating creature, isn't he, my dear?"

"Fascinating? I suppose so," Miranda said firmly, returning to stand in front of Elise's chair, "but then, I've been told, so are snakes." She dropped to her knees and removed the woman's left shoe with hands that, to her surprise, were remarkably steady. "Now, we'll begin with a few basic foot flexes while you're still in the chair."

"Simon's got more women than Hollywood has parking lot attendants, you know. And like those parking lot attendants, they're all just hanging around, hoping against hope to be discovered as the next big movie star. But I don't want that for him. Really I don't. I want Simon to have a real woman, not one who is anything like me. It's time."

Miranda, who had taken hold of Elise's foot and begun moving through a series of range-of-motion exercises, looked up in confusion. "Are you talking about Simon—and *me?*"

Elise smiled. "No, my dear, I'm talking about two people neither of us know. *Of course* I'm talking about you and Simon. One of the reasons I insisted he engage a young, attractive female as my therapist was because I get so tickled watching him make his conquests. As a matter of fact, I have wagered Mrs. Haggerty her afternoon off against my pearl pin that he'd have you wrapped around his thumb in less than a week. Poor Mrs. Haggerty—and she works so hard, too. But I had another reason. It's time Simon settles down, and you've been a happy surprise. I thought I would have to go through at least a half dozen nurses until I found the right one."

Miranda still held onto Elise's silk stocking clad foot, but she had stopped working on strengthening the muscles around the woman's ankles. "It was just a kiss, Mrs. Manchester," she said reasonably, "not some sort of cosmic explosion. And I am *not* wrapped around Simon's little finger, so don't go making any announcements to the newspapers. As a matter of fact, I'm not even sure I *like* your son.''

Or you, either, she added silently, returning to her task. Elise Manchester's left calf, visible below her flowered skirt, was noticeably thinner than her right calf, showing Miranda that there was a good reason for her therapy. But the woman certainly wasn't in any real danger.

Miranda was a trained nurse—actually over-trained for the job she was doing. And if she had a single brain cell left functioning in her head, she'd get the heck out of here—now!

Nothing else made sense. Elise Manchester saw her as little more than a toy for her son and a pawn in a game she delighted in playing. Miranda couldn't believe the woman was serious about using her injury as an excuse to find a wife for her son. She just couldn't be!

And Simon...well, Miranda still wasn't quite sure what sort of game he was playing.

She deposited Elise's foot back onto the floor and stood up, looking straight into the woman's eyes. ''Mrs. Manchester, I—''

''Elise, my dear,'' Simon's mother interrupted quickly. ''If you're going to be watching me in the throes of agony while you push and pull at me, I believe it is only fair that you call me Elise. Now, if you'll get that ridiculous rubber band from my bedroom, I'll show you how well I can stretch it. I'm actually quite accomplished with the thing, you know. After all, I can't spend the rest of my life with this silly cane. It doesn't even have a gold knob.''

''You *want* to exercise?'' Miranda asked, torn between wanting to run as fast and far from the Prescott penthouse as her common sense could take her and wanting to do the job for which she and Tanner Temps had been hired.

Elise's look of confusion was so patently innocent that it was nearly laughable. ''Was there any question that I did?'' she inquired sweetly. And then she smiled, and Miranda knew she had been beaten by one of the best. ''Besides, I don't believe you're the sort to run away just because a man has kissed you. Or am I wrong?''

Miranda ran a hand through her hair, for that same errant lock had fallen into her face again. ''No, Elise, as a matter of fact, you're right. If I left here it wouldn't be because your playboy son kissed me— or even because, idiot that I am, I kissed him back. And I wouldn't leave here because you plan to prove to Simon that it's time he got married.''

Miranda shook her head as if to clear it. ''*Married!* Heavens, I can't believe this. I can't believe any of this! If I left here, Elise, it would be because I have a healthy dislike for being used the way both you and your son used me this morning. And I *will* leave if I ever get that feeling again. Now, do we have a deal?''

Elise grinned—not a small, careful smile as she had done so often, but a full, face-splitting grin. ''Oh, indeed, yes, Miranda. We have a deal. I'll do my exercises and you'll stay. I'll even call off my bet with Mrs. Haggerty. Anything, my dear. I'll do most anything and everything to be able to watch my darling Simon come up against a woman whom he has kissed senseless in the private elevator leading up to the penthouse suite of one of his fabulous hotels— and she still can't be sure she *likes* him!''

Miranda left the penthouse just before five, refusing as politely and as firmly as she could Elise's invitation to dinner, saying she had to go out for a while to check in at Tanner Temps.

It had been a bald-faced lie, of course, but Miranda knew she had to get out of the place before Simon came back. She had to visit with her friends, to make sure they hadn't fallen under Simon's spell and given him their properties outright. She also had to spend some time alone, talking herself out of the growing fascination she had for Simon Prescott.

The man was a menace to her peace of mind. He had the face and body of a dream, the cultured speech of the best Ivy League colleges, and the winning ways of a politician kissing babies at a church social.

"I wonder how fast and far he'd run if he knew his mother was indulging herself in a little off-the-wall matchmaking?" she mused out loud as she walked along the beach. She had changed into more casual attire and her sneakers were filled with sand, but the beach was still too cold in the April evening for her to go barefoot.

She had stopped off for a fast-food dinner of a hamburger and French fries, then visited with Helen Stein, who had told her about Simon's visit that afternoon.

So far, according to Helen, Simon had done nothing more than apologize for not realizing that the three neighbors had "certain special needs" that his lawyers had not addressed in their offers for the properties.

"And he gave me these lovely daffodils and tulips, Miranda," Helen had added, blushing like a young girl. "I haven't had anyone give me flowers since my Sid died, Lord rest his soul. Bridget got daisies—her favorite, although how he knew that I can't understand—and Angelo's Puccini took to the young fellow straight off. Dogs and kids," Helen had whispered insightfully, "*they* know. If dogs and kids like you, you can't be anything but nice."

But, Miranda had decided as she waved goodbye to Helen Stein and turned to walk back up the beach, like a politician out for votes, Simon Prescott hadn't really delivered anything more than flowers, dog biscuits, and vague promises to "look into things."

Miranda bent to pick up a small, perfect shell that was winking in the setting sun, then tossed it back into the ocean. She wished she could trust Simon, but she barely knew him. *You barely know him, but that didn't keep you from clinging to him like sand to a wet bathing suit when he kissed you,* she reminded herself.

"Hello, Miranda. Nice evening to be outside, isn't it? Have you ever driven down to Cape May Point, and watched the sun set over the Delaware Bay? It's quite a sight."

Miranda kept on walking as Simon fell into step beside her, not bothering to look up, for she had recognized him by the sound of his voice. Besides, she was happy to know that he had come looking for her, and she was afraid that might show in her eyes. She was already in deep enough without giving him more ammunition.

"No, or at least not this early in the year, anyway," she answered, bending to pick up another seashell and tossing it in the same direction as the first one. "But it is a lovely evening, isn't it?"

"I missed you at dinner tonight, Miranda," was his only response.

She wet her lips and swallowed down hard on the lie she had prepared to explain her absence, the same one she had used on his mother earlier. Yet, why should she bother? He'd been able to see straight through her ever since they'd met. Why should she waste her time with a fib? "I thought I needed some time on my own, to think," she answered honestly.

"About me?" Simon asked, slipping one arm around her waist as if he had every right to do so. "Elise, who, by the way, has begun calling you 'that darling Miranda', told me that you're not sure you like me. Might I ask why?"

Miranda sidestepped, eluding his light grasp. "That's one reason," she said pointedly as she resumed walking, suddenly chilled, as if his close proximity had been keeping her warm. "You might be used to moving this fast, but I'm just a small-town girl. I'm not up to such sophisticated games—neither yours nor your mother's."

"My mother's?" Simon looked at her intensely. "Elise has nothing to do with this. What are you talking about?"

"Trust me, Simon, you don't want to know. Just take my word for it. Besides, I—I don't want to get hurt."

Simon sighed, shaking his head at her honesty, and at the fact that it had hit home. He had been coming on a bit strong, he supposed. But he was used to seeing what he wanted and then taking it. "Is that what you think that kiss was about, Miranda?" he asked, imitating her by picking up a mussel shell and skimming it over an incoming wave. "Did you think I kissed you as part of some sort of *game* I'm playing?"

"That thought had occurred to me, yes," Miranda answered, deliberately watching two sea gulls squabble over something on the beach rather than look at Simon. "Back there, in the penthouse, it's like you and Elise live in your own world, speaking your own language. This morning I felt like a blindfolded spectator at a tennis match."

"What you're trying to say is that my relationship with Elise is unusual," Simon said, taking hold of Miranda's arm and guiding her out of the way of an incoming wave.

Miranda smiled at this understatement. "Bordering on peculiar, actually," she told him. "She acts like a flirting teenager—a particularly willful teenager—and you indulge her while at the same time leading her just where you want her to go."

"I couldn't have said it better," Simon told her, watching the way the evening breeze off the ocean was doing a dance in Miranda's hair and longing to join it, pushing his fingers through the errant curls as he drew her close and kissed her.

But first he'd have to settle this business about Elise. "My mother is the original Peter Pan—and never mind pointing out that Peter Pan was a boy. She never grew up, mostly because she never had to. She has been petted and pampered all of her life. For a while, in my crusading years while I was in college, I tried to point this out to her, but I gave it up as hopeless when she told me she knew perfectly well what she was and was happy with her life. It's pretty hard to fight that kind of logic, Miranda," he ended on a smile, "so I decided to go with the flow. Besides, it's kind of neat having Auntie Mame as my mother."

"Auntie Mame," Miranda repeated, shaking her head. "A little of Peter Pan, some Auntie Mame, and maybe some of Gypsy Rose Lee's mother all wrapped up into one. But you're right, Simon, she is something else—and I do like her. She worked like a dog today on her exercises."

"For which I have to thank you," Simon pointed out as they neared a small outcropping of rock. He motioned for Miranda to seat herself. "I know Elise has agreed to exercise because she doesn't want you to leave, depriving her of amusement while I chase you and you run the other way, but at least we'll end up with the desired results."

"Which are?" Miranda asked as he sat down beside her, the two of them looking out over the ocean as the gray twilight slowly turned to darkness. She looked at him curiously, wondering if he knew all about Elise's ridiculous suggestion that she, Miranda, might be the woman who could become her daughter-in-law, then dismissed the idea. Even Simon, for all his intelligence, couldn't possibly have figured that one out.

Simon turned to Miranda and smiled, a smile that made him look so endearingly boyish that she couldn't help but return it, even knowing what she knew. "Simon? You didn't answer me. What is it that you want?"

"Elise's recovery, of course," he said quickly, taking her hand and, in an old-fashioned manner that thrilled her to her toes, lifted it to his lips, only to turn her hand over at the last moment and press his mouth against her palm.

"That," he said, looking deeply into her eyes as he retained his hold on her hand, "and more time for us to discover if the small-town girl and the playboy have anything more in common than a nearly overwhelming need to touch each other, be with each other, kiss each other...."

His voice trailed off as he took both her hands in his and lifted them onto his shoulders, then pulled her close against him. His mouth descended to capture hers before she could remember that she should, at this very moment, be hopping down off this rock and running away from Simon, from the temptations he offered her, from his slightly nutty, lovable mother, just as fast as she could.

But, the thought registered somewhere in the back of her brain, there was no place to run to, no escape from Simon Prescott, even when he wasn't anywhere around her.

In the short span that she'd known him, she'd memorized the look of the laugh lines around his sherry-brown eyes. She'd learned to recognize his confident, almost arrogant, long-legged gait even at a distance. And she'd come to appreciate the way his soft, well-modulated voice and elegant way of speaking caressed her ears each time he spoke.

She had already acknowledged the way his nearness made it difficult for her to breathe. To think. To remember her mother's warnings about smooth-talking handsome men who came to Cape May, romanced some local girl for a week, a month, a summer, and then left, never looking back.

She might not be an impressionable young girl any more and this might not be summer. But, as Simon had already pointed out, it was spring. And in spring a young man's fancy still turned to...*oh, Lord, but his mouth tasted good!*

Miranda allowed her mind to go blank and surrendered once more to Simon's kiss. She felt his arms pulling her close against him, and reveled in the way he moved one hand to the back of her head as if he couldn't get enough of running his fingers through her hair.

And as she kissed him back, not caring if all the citizens of Cape May were suddenly to appear on the beach and see just what she was doing, Miranda knew that her mother's lessons had meant nothing.

Common sense couldn't win against the yearnings of her heart, the excitement of Simon's touch, the sure knowledge that this man—this strong yet gentle man whom she barely knew yet had recognized at first sight—held the key to her happiness.

She allowed her arms the luxury of clinging to him.

She gave her fingertips the gift of touching the smooth warm skin of his face and throat.

She permitted her body the earth-exploding rapture of yielding to his caresses as he slipped a hand beneath the hem of her blouse and captured one of her breasts.

And she granted herself permission to softly moan deep in her throat in response to the pleasure that rippled through her as his thumb glided smoothly over her nipple.

None of these things might have been the smartest moves she had made in her life, but she no longer cared.

Simon felt Miranda's surrender and gloried in it even as he knew he might be taking liberties she hadn't planned on granting. Once again—after promising himself that he wouldn't give in to his recently formed yet extremely insistent desires—he was holding her, kissing her, taking yet another forward step in a direction he had never traveled before meeting Miranda Tanner.

Her mouth was so sweet, her skin like silk above the lacy edge of her bra, her first tentative response to his lovemaking so exquisitely shattering.

His hands slipping back down to her waist, he moved to stand up, taking her with him, so that they could cling together all along the length of their bodies, straining to be closer, ever closer.

His lips left hers and he whispered into her ear. "We do pick our places, don't we, Miranda? First an elevator, and now a not-so-deserted beach. I'd suggest we adjourn to my penthouse, but we both know Elise is waiting for us, eager to watch what happens next as if we were the leading characters in her own private play."

Miranda shook herself back to sanity. "And why would I want to go to your penthouse, Simon?" she asked, avoiding his eyes.

Then she realized that she could hardly play the innocent at this point. After all, she knew her lips were probably swollen from his kisses, her chin was tingling from its close contact with his early evening beard. Her blouse was partially unbuttoned, its hem nearly completely free of her slacks.

Miranda stepped away from him, quickly rebuttoning her blouse, and added, "Never mind. Dumb question. Forget I asked."

Simon gave her a moment to compose herself, then took her hand, leading her across the beach to the promenade, still faintly visible in the darkness thanks to the lights lining Beach Street.

"I have a present for you, Miranda," he said conversationally as they walked along. "Elise was thrilled with the cane I bought her, but I had to give a lot of thought to selecting my gift to you. It had to show not only my gratitude for helping me with my mother and my business project, but serve as a token of my affection, as well."

Miranda looked up at him, shaking her head. "I didn't ask for a present, Simon," she told him, not liking the idea of being bought. "I'm not your mother, you know."

He let go of her hand and pulled her against his side, his arm around her waist. "Don't I know it! If you were anything like my mother, anything like any of the women I've dated over the past dozen or more years, I'd be in Atlantic City right now and you and the Terrible Trio would still be dealing with my legal department. Besides, I wanted to buy you a present. Aren't you the least bit curious to know what it is?''

Miranda allowed herself to luxuriate in his closeness. His admission that he found her company enjoyable was more soothing to her mind than his kisses had been. She didn't want him to merely want her. Suddenly, without bothering to stop to think why, she knew she wanted him to like her. Maybe even love her. It could happen, couldn't it? Stranger things had, hadn't they?

"Well?" Simon prodded when, lost in her daydream, Miranda didn't answer him. "Aren't you curious?"

She smiled up at him, suddenly feeling completely at ease in his presence. "Should I lie, and say I couldn't care less?"

"I don't think so. Not if you want to be believed," Simon said. They stopped just inside a soft puddle of light cast by a nearby street lamp and he reached into his pocket, withdrawing a small jeweler's box that he placed in her hand.

Miranda was immediately angry, all her rose-colored thoughts of a few moments ago shattered into a million pieces. A present was one thing—some small token of appreciation for helping him with his mother—but she wasn't about to accept a piece of expensive jewelry from the man. It was too personal, and that sort of gift could logically be seen as one that came with strings firmly attached.

"Well? Are you going to open it?" Simon pressed her as she stopped just at the curb across the street from Prescott Dunes. "I put a lot of thought into this gift, Miranda, and I'd be very disappointed if you didn't at least look at it."

"Oh, sure, *embarrass* me into it, why not," Miranda shot back, lifting the lid with trembling fingers, her eyes closed as she prayed that, whatever it was, it at least didn't look as if it had cost the earth. Then, opening her eyes once more, she took a deep breath and looked down at the small objects settled in the middle of the bed of blue velvet.

And then she laughed.

"I thought them suitable, considering the fact that I've already had the pleasure of hearing Puccini howl along with the female lead in *Carmen*. You are planning to see Mr. Pantoni again, aren't you?"

"Of course." Miranda closed the lid on the pair of pink latex ear plugs. She stood on tiptoe to kiss him on the cheek and, for the first time since meeting him, lied outright without feeling the least bit guilty, her words a wild understatement of her actual feelings. "You'd better be careful, Simon Prescott," she warned, "because I believe I actually could begin to like you."

"Of course," Simon echoed, grinning.

Then, before she could move away, he took advantage of Miranda's closeness by pulling her against him and sealing her mouth with a searing kiss that lasted through one and one-half changes of the stop light before he let her go.

On the other side of Beach Street, high above them in the penthouse, the vertical blinds that had been propped open by a slim, gold-topped cane slid closed and Elise Manchester smiled in satisfaction. Just as she already knew—nobody could withstand Simon's charms, no matter how they protested. After all, he was *her* son!

Chapter Five

"I like you, Elise," Miranda said more than a week later as she and Simon's mother sat across the dining-room table from each other, eating lunch.

"That's nice, darling," Elise answered placidly, toying with a chef's salad. "You already know how very much I enjoy your company. We should visit Palm Springs together, you know. You could do with a California tan, and I—"

Miranda pointed her fork in the other woman's direction. "Don't interrupt, please," she said in her most professional, nurselike voice, having learned that the only way to get anywhere with Elise was to take the upper hand and then hold on for dear life.

Elise sighed. "So like Simon," she said tragically. "A bully to the core. Yet, like my dear son, you say you like me. I can't imagine why."

"Don't push your luck, Elise," Miranda warned jokingly. "You're not the easiest patient I've ever had, you know, and you only work hard when you want to, but I repeat, I *do* like you. However," she pressed on, raising her voice to cover the yapping of the two white balls of fur that were running around the table in ever-increasingly quick circles, "I will not—repeat, *will not*—have anything to do with the care and feeding of either Jacqueline or Susanne.''

Jacqueline and Susanne, the pedigree dogs that had arrived only that morning from Elise's condo in Manhattan, had made their presence felt immediately, disrupting the first therapy session of the day as they danced around their mistress, seemingly delirious with happiness at being reunited with her again.

Simon was nowhere to be found, of course, as he had taken himself back to Atlantic City the same night he had given her the ear plugs, having to respond to some sort of management crisis—or at least that's what he had told Elise. Miranda hadn't even spoken to him on the telephone, as Mrs. Haggerty always answered it and he always asked to speak with his mother.

Miranda had her own idea about why Simon had gone, and it had nothing to do with the management of Prescott Hotels. She believed he had deliberately put some space between himself and her before things went any further between them.

She couldn't blame him.

Their ride up to the penthouse that last night had been a steamy one, to say the least. He had backed her up against the paneled wall the moment the doors had slid closed and they had kissed furiously until the elevator had reached the top floor.

She had felt as if she was his first ice cream sundae after a month on a diet, and he was going to devour her in two bites—not that she had complained. She had understood his need, for she had felt the same way, as if she couldn't get enough of him.

If he had pushed the Stop button again, as he had done earlier in the day, there was no telling what would have happened. But he hadn't. She had been vaguely disappointed at the time, but now that he was gone, Miranda could only be grateful he hadn't taken advantage of her unexpected response.

Miranda had only popped her head into the living room for a moment, murmuring a quick good-night to Elise before escaping to her own room, hoping against hope that the older woman hadn't noticed that all her lipstick was gone and there was a slight rosy spot on her chin from Simon's evening beard.

And in the morning, after hiding in her room until nine, she had emerged only to learn from Mrs. Haggerty that Simon had left for Atlantic City just before midnight.

Later that morning she had been surprised to see that the housekeeper had placed a vase of long-stemmed white roses in her room. She still had the card, even though the roses had wilted and she'd had to remove them last night, all except for one that she had pressed between the pages of a nursing book she had brought with her. The card, written in a bold, slashing hand, read simply, "Think of me...Simon."

Coward, she had thought at the time, and *coward* was what she was thinking now. Her head was beginning to ring as Jacqueline and Susanne's high-pitched yips and yaps threatened to make her believe that, in comparison, listening to Mr. Pantoni's dog yodeling along with an operatic soprano was to be treated to a treasured moment in music history.

"You don't like my little darlings?" Elise asked now, pouting as if Miranda had insulted her personally.

"I'm not planning to leave them anything in my will, no," Miranda answered as Jacqueline—or was it Susanne?—tried to jump into her lap. "I thought I could look at it as just another part of my job, Elise, but there's no way I can walk these dogs in public. Not if they're going to wear those ridiculous rhinestone collars!"

"Rhinestone? Darling, I'd never allow rhinestones on my dogs."

Miranda knew her eyes were just about bugging out of her head as she picked up the dog and examined the jewel-encrusted, sky-blue leather collar. "You mean these aren't rhinestones?" she asked, unable to believe anyone, even Elise, could be so outrageous as to outfit a dog in diamonds.

"Cubic zirconiums," Elise corrected, patting the corners of her lips with her linen napkin before rising, leaving her cane propped against the table. "After all, Jacqueline and Susanne live in Manhattan, Miranda," she added, smiling as if to show that she knew she was being illogical, "and I wouldn't think of taking a chance on having them mugged, now would I?"

Miranda abandoned her own lunch and, depositing the dog on the floor once more, followed her patient into the living room. As she walked behind her, she noted the absence of the cane with satisfaction. "Okay, so who does walk the dogs?"

Elise settled herself into her favorite chair with a small sigh. It wasn't easy getting around without the security of her cane, but she had received a cable from her friend Countess Leidy this morning, reminding her of a party at her villa in Capri that began the first of May. If Simon refused to be cooperative and come back to Cape May so that she could watch him struggle with the throes of what any fool could see was a serious attraction to her pretty young nurse, then there was nothing else to keep her here, was there?

"I've been thinking, dear," Elise said as she watched Miranda seat herself on the couch.

"Uh-oh," Miranda said, pretending to suppress a shiver of apprehension. "I don't like the sound of that. The last time you were 'thinking' you had my associate Bonnie scouring all the local stores for a whole afternoon, trying to locate some solid chocolate truffles.''

"And they were delicious, weren't they?'' Elise declared firmly. "Now, please listen to me. My therapy is coming along swimmingly—you said so yourself—but I believe there is more to this business of building up my leg muscles than what I've been doing so far. Isn't it time to step up my sessions?''

Miranda looked at her skeptically, sensing trouble. Simon had warned her that his mother only moved when she had something specific in mind. "What's the rush, Elise? Or are you planning to enter a marathon?''

"Me? Don't be silly, Miranda. Personally, I can't imagine why anyone would want to perspire in public,'' Elise answered, patting her knee so that one of the dogs jumped up into her lap. "It's just that, since you've failed to snare Simon and make my stay interesting, I think it's time I get back to my own life.''

Miranda sat up straight, nearly choking on her indignation, sputtering, "Now that I've *failed to snare Simon!* For crying out loud, Elise, I never even baited the trap!'' Then she subsided against the back of the couch, adding quietly, "Besides, Simon's been in Atlantic City for the past week.''

"Yes, he has, hasn't he," Elise remarked, scratching the ecstatically lolling dog behind its ears. "Did I happen to mention that he asks about you constantly whenever he telephones? I always tell him that you're out, or otherwise engaged, so that he can't speak to you."

"What? Why?" Miranda couldn't believe what she was hearing.

"Ah-ah! As you said earlier, Miranda, don't interrupt," Elise cautioned, then continued gleefully. "He seethes, absolutely *seethes* through the wires whenever I say that—especially in the evenings. But I've instructed Mrs. Haggerty to give the telephone to me whenever Simon calls, even when he expressly asks for you. Have you given any more thought to trying my new peach blush? Simon should be here anytime now, and you'll want to look your best."

A thousand thoughts tumbled through Miranda's mind, the most prominent being Jackie Gleason's words as his character in the old television show, *The Honeymooners,* Ralph Kramden, warned his wife, "One of these days, Alice! One of these days—bang! Zoom! Right to the moon!"

But she didn't give in to the temptation. She hadn't been in Elise's company for the past week and more without learning anything. What Elise lived for was excitement, and the thrill of seeing her nurse-therapist react as she wanted was one satisfaction she wasn't going to give her.

"Really?" was all Miranda commented when she could find her voice. "You know something, Elise, you and I really should go on *The Oprah Winfrey Show.*"

"Who is she?" Elise answered blankly.

"Oprah has a daily show in which she interviews interesting people. You could appear with a group of women just like you. I would imagine Oprah could call that show 'Women who stick their noses in where they don't belong, and the nurses who strangle them.'"

Elise looked shocked for a few moments, her hand stilling on the dog's fluffy fur, then laughed her tinkling laugh. "Oh, you don't mean that, darling girl, do you? I'm not an interfering sort of mother, am I?"

Miranda directed a long, dispassionate stare at the woman, saying nothing.

Elise rolled her eyes. "Oh, all right. So I am. What of it? I'm fifty-six years old, Miranda—and if you tell anyone that I swear I will deny it with my dying breath—and it's time I had some grandchildren. Do you really think I want Simon to marry one of those flighty actresses or one of those bean-pole models he dates? Of course, I don't. They wouldn't give him children, they'd give him ulcers!"

"So you picked me," Miranda said, still trying to understand how the woman could have made such a choice.

"Not really, Miranda," Elise answered honestly. "As I told you before, you were only to be the first of many 'real' women I hoped to bring into Simon's orbit. Watching the nurses while I was in the hospital, and then in the convalescent home, I decided that a nurse would be perfect for Simon. So marvelously dedicated, so caring."

"Uh-huh," Miranda commented wryly, not feeling at all "marvelously dedicated and caring" at the moment.

"You see, when I was injured—as I lay day after day in my hospital bed after the operation to set my broken bones—I realized that I'm not getting any younger, even if I find that notion difficult to believe. I don't want to wake up an old woman one morning and not have any grandchildren to spoil."

"So you hatched this plan to have Simon and me fall in love with each other? That was playing a real long shot, Elise," Miranda pointed out reasonably.

"Oh, I know that. I hadn't hoped to be first time lucky. I came here fully prepared to launch a siege on this penthouse until I found the right woman. But, as luck would have it, I struck gold the first time."

"Well, *eureka* for you," Miranda answered dully. "Elise—much as I like you—has anyone ever told you that sometimes you seem as if your mind is just a half of a bubble off center?"

"I'm sorry, dear," Elise answered, gently dislodging the dog from her lap. "I'm afraid I don't understand that term. The center of what? Oh, never mind. It's enough that you stand up to me. I admire that in you, Miranda, I truly do. But, to get back to what I was saying, shouldn't I be doing more therapy? I refuse to wear slacks in public, you know, they aren't the least flattering, but I cannot show these legs in Capri."

"Capri?" Now Miranda was beginning to understand. Elise was bored with her new game, and about to hoist anchor and move on. Well, so much for her matchmaking, thank goodness, because, no matter how much his mother might say she wanted Simon to marry, Miranda doubted that Simon was about to walk down the aisle on Elise's orders.

"You could walk Jacqueline and Susanne, I suppose," Miranda suggested, feeling inspired. "It would do you good to get out in the fresh air more than you do by lounging on the rooftop patio. Besides, walking barefoot in the sand would do wonders for your calf muscles."

Elise gave a delicate shudder. "Barefoot? Must I? Well, I suppose, if you insist."

"Ms. Tanner?" Both Elise and Miranda turned to see Mrs. Haggerty entering the living room, carrying a portable telephone. "There's a call for you. Would you like to take it in here?"

Miranda shot Elise a triumphant look. So much for Elise's screening of her calls from Simon! "Yes, I'll take it in here, Mrs. Haggerty, thank you," she said, more than ready to gloat when she heard Simon's voice on the other end of the line.

But of course it wasn't Simon. It was Bonnie, and she had phoned to say that Helen Stein wanted to see Miranda as soon as possible, adding that Mrs. Stein sounded fairly agitated. After quickly consulting her watch, Miranda told Bonnie to say that she'd leave right away, then hung up, her eyes narrowed, her lips drawn into a thin white line.

"Is something wrong, my dear?" Elise asked, noticing that Miranda's freckles were standing out very clearly on her pale cheeks. "You look as if you're expecting something dreadful to happen at any moment."

Miranda blinked once, then looked at Elise. "That would depend on what Simon's done," she told her. "Mrs. Haggerty," she said, smiling up at the housekeeper, "would you be kind enough to find the dog's leashes for me, please? It's such a nice day that Mrs. Manchester and I are going to take Jacqueline and Susanne for a walk along the beach."

"We are?" Elise squeaked, realizing she had not seen such purpose in anyone's eyes since Simon had forbidden her to go hang gliding in Rio last year. "Where are we going?"

"Where?" Miranda smiled. "Why, we're going to go pay a little visit to the *real* world, Elise. I think it's more than time you saw it!"

Simon drove into Cape May shortly after three o'clock, still swearing under his breath at the stupidity of the people in his legal department. He encouraged his people to use their own initiative, but there was a difference between acting independently and jumping in with both feet without first checking with the boss to make sure the pool had been filled, damn it!

A week's work—exploded in a moment by a premature, incomplete announcement! Not only that, but Miranda already knew about it, or else she would have been at the apartment with his mother when he'd phoned.

Mrs. Haggerty had assured him that Miranda hadn't packed her bags and left, which had been Simon's first question. But she had told Simon that both Miranda and his mother—God! she'd taken Elise with her!—had gone out for a stroll on the beach just after Miranda had received what had seemed to be a "disturbing" phone call.

Simon slapped the palm of his hand against the steering wheel. Miranda hadn't been around for any of *his* calls, why did she have to be on hand to take the one call he had hoped against hope she wouldn't have been there to receive?

Not that he wouldn't be able to explain everything. Once Miranda and the Terrible Trio had heard his explanation, everything would be all right. Hell, he'd be a hero!

He pulled into a parking space directly in front of Mr. Pantoni's house and stopped, unhooked his seat belt, and jackknifed his long frame out of the low-slung seat to stand on the sidewalk. Sure. He'd be a hero all right. If Miranda let him *live* he'd be a hero.

Simon knocked first on Mr. Pantoni's door, but there was no answer. "Strike one," Simon muttered, retracing his steps to the sidewalk and heading for Mrs. Stein's porch. "Strike two," he said after ringing the doorbell several times. Though he knew for a fact that Mrs. Stein was deaf as a post, she would have had to have heard him by now.

"Third time's the charm," he said, looking toward Mrs. O'Shaughnessy's house with some satisfaction. At least they were being cooperative by all being in one spot, so that he'd only have to tell his story once.

He climbed the steps to Mrs. O'Shaughnessy's front porch slowly, deliberately, feeling that he should think about what he would say, and how he would say it. He'd much rather say nothing at all, but simply walk into the house unannounced, take Miranda into his arms and kiss her senseless—just to remind her that, while she might avoid his telephone calls, she couldn't deny the attraction between them.

But he wouldn't do that. Simon was a man who held onto his emotions with a tight rein, a man who refused to let anything or anyone get under his skin. Or at least he had been until a week ago, when a beautiful angel in a stiffly starched white uniform had walked into his hotel lobby and knocked him for a loop.

He had been physically attracted to women before Miranda. Plenty of times. But never before in his life had he found himself thinking of any of those women when they were not around.

Miranda was a different story. He thought of her day and night, even once back in Atlantic City and surrounded by beautiful, desirable women. He thought about her compassion when she spoke of the Terrible Trio, her willingness to go toe-to-toe with the powerful Prescott Hotels in order to defend her friends. He remembered with mingled humor and respect the way she managed Elise, for Mrs. Haggerty had reported daily on his mother's progress with her therapy.

But mostly, he thought about Miranda's dark curls blowing in the breeze off the ocean and the mysterious depths to her smoky-blue eyes when he caught her looking at him. He recalled her smile of simple pleasure when he'd given her the ear plugs. He contemplated the taste of her mouth as she surrendered against him, the feel of her breasts as he cupped them in his hands.

Simon loosened the tie at his neck slightly, trying to collect his thoughts. He'd been working constantly since his return to Atlantic City. He'd been trying to settle the Terrible Trio and clear his desk of any pressing business so that he could return to Cape May to help rehabilitate his mother to her former jet-setting self. He wanted her happily out of the picture so that he could romance Miranda Tanner as she'd never been romanced before!

His desk was now clear, and Elise ought to be able to carry on with her therapy without twenty-four-hour assistance. But with this legal department screw-up throwing a stop sign up in front of his plans, breaking through the Terrible Trio roadblock might not prove as easy as he had hoped.

"Well, Prescott," he reminded himself quietly as he stood at the edge of the porch, "nobody ever got anywhere standing still," and walked purposefully to the door, knocking twice on the heavy oak.

Immediately, the barking he had not heard at Mr. Pantoni's broke out, joined by the high-pitched yapping of—Simon realized with a sinking heart—Jacqueline and Susanne. "Oh, this is going to be a real joy, from beginning to end," he said, rolling his eyes heavenward as if for divine assistance.

A moment later the door opened and he was face-to-face with Miranda, whose lack of expression told him how she was feeling more than he would have learned if she had greeted him with an exasperated "You!" while aiming a large cast-iron frying pan at his head.

"Simon," she said quietly, standing back to allow him entry. "We've been waiting for you. An attorney named Jackson phoned about an hour ago saying you were on your way."

"Did he now?" Simon answered, stepping into the living room, for the house was small and there was no foyer. "I'll have to remember to thank him—reward him in some way for this second good deed in less than a day. It's too bad we don't have a hotel in beautiful downtown Baghdad. He'd really enjoy being a bellboy there."

"Well, there you are, Simon. It took you long enough, darling. What did you do, slither here on your belly? You should have, after what you've done to these perfectly *darling* people."

"I love you, too, Elise," Simon said smoothly, inclining his head in his mother's direction and seeing that she was sitting at her ease on a rather frayed and faded tapestry chair, looking as regal as if she were holding court from her throne. Jacqueline, Susanne, and Puccini had stopped barking and were now lying on the floor beside the chair, Elise's loyal, adoring, and thankfully silent subjects.

"Mr. Pantoni, Mrs. Stein," he continued, politely acknowledging the presence of these two people who were sitting side by side on the couch. "Where's Mrs. O'Shaughnessy, out in the kitchen putting the finishing touches on the tar and feathers? Or are you willing to hear what I have to say before you run me out of town on a rail?"

Helen Stein put one cupped hand to her ear and leaned closer to Mr. Pantoni. "What did he say, Tony? He got some leather stuck on a nail? I don't think he's wearing any leather, not that I can see. Tony?"

Mr. Pantoni patted Helen's hand, shaking his head. "Turn up your hearing aid another notch, Helen," he all but yelled into the woman's ear. "Mrs. Manchester promised not to talk so much once Mr. Prescott got here."

Miranda hid a smile behind her hand as Simon looked to her inquiringly. "Elise has been telling everyone about her safari in Kenya, Simon," she explained, wishing she didn't have to say anything to him but somewhat touched to see that he had bothered to come to Cape May to speak to her friends personally. "Helen wasn't too pleased to hear about the wounded lion that charged the encampment one night. To Helen, a cat is a cat, and she can't bear to hear of one of them dying—"

"Which it didn't do," Elise broke in. "Our guide merely tranquilized the beast, tended to its wounds, and then took it a safe distance away, all of which Helen would have learned if she hadn't turned down the volume on her hearing aid. You know it was a photographic safari, Simon. I couldn't bear to actually shoot anything."

"I don't know about that, Elise," Simon said, looking at Miranda. "You've succeeded in shooting me down all week. I had a rather long and extremely informative conversation with Mrs. Haggerty on my car phone as I was driving down here, and she told me that you've been intercepting my calls to Miranda."

Elise dismissed his words with a flip of one hand— the hand that bore a ring holding a Tiffany-cut diamond large enough to have Helen Stein remark loudly, in what she clearly thought was a whisper, "Did you ever see anything like it in your entire life, Tony? Stick that thing in her navel and she could be a belly dancer! Dressed to the nines in the middle of the afternoon! Duked out like Astor's pet horse—or so my mother would have said."

Now it was Simon's turn to cough discreetly into his hand in order to cover a laugh at his mother's expense.

But Elise didn't seem to be in the least insulted. She only smiled as Mrs. O'Shaughnessy came in from the kitchen, carrying a large plastic tray heaped with homemade peanut butter cookies. "Bridget!" Elise exclaimed as she took hold of the tray, smiling just as if she wasn't more accustomed to delicate petit-fours served on doily lined silver platters. "They look delicious. Simply delicious."

She turned to Simon after Mrs. O'Shaughnessy had said hello and then begun passing the tray of cookies around the room. "Simon, darling, did you know that Bridget has at least twenty nieces and nephews? And grand-nieces and grand-nephews? And Helen has shown me pictures of all her grand-children."

"Really?" Simon responded, wondering what any of Elise's information had to do with the point. He watched as Miranda slipped into a nearby chair, then went to stand behind her, a hand on her shoulder, as if to anchor himself. It was as if he had walked on-stage during the second act of a play already in progress and didn't know either the plot or any of his lines. "I didn't know you liked children, Elise."

"Didn't like children? Why, Simon, I had you, didn't I? I positively *adore* the little darlings. I had hoped that you'd be one of a half a dozen or more, but it wasn't to be. Now I long for grandchildren, so that I might take them with me when I travel, opening whole new worlds to them as I did to you when you were young.''

''Like Auntie Mame, Miranda, although I have to admit that grandchildren bit is new. She's full of surprises today,'' Simon whispered as he leaned down close beside Miranda's left ear.

''In spades,'' Miranda answered just as quietly. ''Only these nonexistent grandchildren will have to call her Elise, you understand, so that no one will get the idea she's old enough to be a grandmother. She's been expounding on the subject for the past ten minutes. I was beginning to wish you'd show up, even if you're only going to tell these poor people what they already know—which is that you've found a way to kick them out into the street.''

Simon looked past Miranda to see that Elise had the Terrible Trio enthralled with the beginnings of a story about Princess Di's wedding—a tale he knew would take at least an hour in the telling. ''Look,'' he said softly, ''do you think we could go somewhere and talk?''

''You're kidding, right?'' Miranda stiffened in her chair, even though the feel of Simon's warm breath against her ear was enough to want to make her slide to the floor at his feet and agree to anything. ''I think you should talk to these people first. Your attorney, Jackson—in his first phone call to each of them this morning—said that they only have ten days to pack up and get out of their homes before you bring in the wrecking ball.''

She swiveled around in the chair, nearly coming nose to nose with him. "Oh, Simon, how could you do this! They're devastated!''

He looked into her eyes, seeing her pain, and didn't know whether he still wanted to kiss her—or strangle her. How could she believe he'd be a party to anything that cruel? His legendarily unflappable temper went off like a rocket.

"That tears it!" he announced, standing up straight and looking around the room, glaring at each person in turn. "I've had enough! Mrs. O'Shaughnessy, Mrs. Stein, Mr. Pantoni—Puccini—listen up! Elise—shut up!''

"Simon! I don't believe this. How dare you speak to your mother that way?'' Miranda was also on her feet, unable to connect what she was hearing to the man she had thought she knew. Where was the finesse? The suave sophistication? The cool, collected man of the world who moved in and took charge without ever raising his voice?

Raise his voice? Miranda sniffed at this glaring understatement, shaking her head. He hadn't just raised his voice—he had *yelled!* Helen Stein would have heard every word without even turning on her hearing aid. Hell, they'd probably heard him in Atlantic City.

But Elise, who had just been describing the royal coach, only smiled, looking up at her son. "Finally, Simon. Congratulations! I was beginning to wonder if you had ice water in your veins, just like those paper dolls you've been dating ever since I can remember. Well, good for you, and my best wishes to Miranda! I can't tell you how much happier your life will be now that you've discovered *le grande passion.* Goodness knows it has done wonders for me!"

"Mother—" Simon gritted from between clenched teeth, knowing that his use of the term she disdained would get her attention, then turned back to the Terrible Trio, mentally taking in the fact that Helen Stein was leaning forward on her seat, madly trying to adjust her hearing aid.

"I don't have time to explain right now," he said, trying to maintain some lingering shreds of composure, "but suffice it to say at this moment that a member of my legal department did discover that you are legally bound to the commitment to sell your properties to Prescott Hotels. We begin demolition in ten days."

"Oh, Simon," Miranda said on a sigh, turning away from him.

He grabbed onto her hand, so that she couldn't leave. "However—and this is a big however," he continued, "Jackson did not bother to confer with me before making his calls to you. That's why I'm here today—to tell you that everything is going to be all right.''

"You have a plan, don't you, my darling boy?" Elise asked, beaming at him adoringly before turning to Mr. Pantoni. "Simon's a genius, you know. Not quite smart enough to run his own life, you understand, but simply *brilliant* with business matters.''

"Simon, what—" Miranda began, only to be cut off when Simon silenced her with a look. He turned to address the Terrible Trio once more.

"I'll be back in an hour to explain everything to you. I promise, you'll be very pleased. But for now,'' he looked at Miranda once more and, his tone softening slightly, ended, "for now, ladies and sir, I've got something else to do. Come on, Miranda.''

She dug in her heels. "I don't think so," she told him, suddenly apprehensive. She had never seen Simon in this mood and she wasn't quite sure she trusted herself to be alone with him right now.

"I think I'd rather have you explain what you meant by saying everything is going to be all right. It doesn't quite hold water when you've already said that you're going to be tearing down these houses in less than two weeks.''

"Oh, go with him, Miranda," Helen Stein chided, giving a dismissive wave of her hand. "We want to hear about Princess Di's wedding. We'll be here when you get back.''

Miranda shook her head in utter amazement. ''I don't believe this! Aren't you worried about losing your homes? I mean, all this talk about Kansas, and beds that don't fit, and...and Puccini's arias, for crying out loud! Aren't you even the least bit interested in what Simon has got planned for you?''

''Nope,'' Mrs. O'Shaughnessy said, smiling. ''We're much more interested in what he's got planned for *you,* my dear. You will come back and tell us, won't you? I have a fresh apple pie in the kitchen.''

''Apple pie,'' Miranda echoed dully as Simon started for the door, his hand still holding tightly to hers so that she had no other choice but to follow him or refuse to budge and make a scene that would be embarrassing to everyone. Well, maybe not to *everyone.* Everyone except for herself was smiling as if something wonderful was happening.

''Oh, I give up!'' she exclaimed in exasperation, and allowed herself to be led out of the house.

She refused to speak while they stood at the curb, waiting for a break in the traffic. Not that Simon said anything, either. He just stood there, looking rather amazed with himself—and too smugly satisfied to suit her—then unceremoniously dragged her across the street and onto the beach.

"We'll walk south," Simon announced, tugging at her hand once more.

"Why?" Miranda pulled back, sick of being told what to do. When had she lost control of her own life? *Simon says,* her mind teased her, *you must do as Simon says. Well, not this time!* Simon always told her what to do, even when he didn't say a word—and Elise had darn near planned her entire life for her. It was time she made at least one decision on her own.

"Do you really need a reason? All right. There's less people down the beach."

"Good point," she said, then added firmly, "so we'll walk north."

"Why?" Simon threw her own question back at her, his grin youthful as the breeze ruffled his hair. Losing his temper seemed to have done wonders for his mood.

"Simple. Because there are *more* people up the beach."

He looked down at their clasped hands, then smiled at her. "I guess we could compromise and walk east. How good are you at treading water?"

Miranda gave up the argument and began heading south. What difference did it make, anyway? She just wanted Simon to tell her what he'd done. Then she could go some place private and let her heart break.

But Simon wasn't talking. He was just walking along, still holding her hand, and looking handsome, if slightly out of place, in his tailored business suit, sand undoubtedly pouring into his dress shoes with each step they took. As if realizing that he wasn't quite dressed for the beach, he pulled his tie loose, slipped it from underneath his collar, and stuffed it into the pocket of his jacket.

If he had looked handsome in his suit, he looked even more handsome now, with his white shirt opened at the neck. "Simon," she asked, breaking the silence when she thought if someone didn't say something soon she might scream, "why didn't you try harder to talk to me when you telephoned the penthouse?"

The moment the words were out of her mouth she regretted them, knowing that she was admitting that she had missed him.

He let go of her hand for a moment to strip off his suit jacket, then, hooking it on one finger, he flipped it back over his right shoulder. He looked at his ease, in control of his emotions once more, and totally, devastatingly, irresistible.

"Good question, Miranda," he said, gently directing her hand behind him, then sliding his own hand lightly around her waist, so that they were walking arm in arm—just as if there were no unsolved problems between them.

"Thanks." Miranda rushed into speech in an effort to make the question sound less personal. "Now, how about a good answer? I mean, you didn't even try to learn whether or not Elise was coming along well with her therapy. It was as if you'd lost interest," she ended, then winced as she realized she'd said too much.

"Mrs. Haggerty kept me up to date on Elise," Simon told her. "Besides, I have the greatest confidence in your abilities. You didn't even have to resort to lollipops—or diamond tennis bracelets."

No, Miranda thought glumly, *all I had to do was to look like good wife material for Elise's son.* Not that she was going to tell him that! One display of his supposedly nonexistent temper was more than enough for one day.

"Anyway," Simon went on when she said nothing, "I was too busy trying to settle the Terrible Trio and clearing my desk of any other problems so that I could devote myself full time to thinking up ways to get you back in my elevator."

Miranda pulled slightly away from him and looked up into his face. "Oh, really?"

He pulled her against his side once more, guiding her toward the street. "Yes, really, Miranda. And don't pretend you didn't know that I've been thinking of you night and day ever since I left. You're not easy to forget."

"Unforgettable, huh? Gee, I've always wanted to be unforgettable." A small smile played around the corners of Miranda's mouth. This was beginning to be fun. They could talk about the Terrible Trio later. Right now she wanted to hear what he thought about *her.* "Tell me more, Simon," she teased, gaining confidence with every step they took. "And give me the long version—I think I deserve it after what you've put me through this past week."

"Later, Andi." He bent down and kissed the top of her wind-tossed curls, knowing that if he took her in his arms now, here on the beach, he couldn't be responsible for what happened. "For now, what do you think of the view?"

Miranda shook herself out of the very pleasant daydream she was having—the one that had a lot to do with the powers of spring, buzzing bees, tales of love at first sight, and Elise's plans for her future— and looked in the direction Simon had indicated with a nod of his head. The block of modern condominiums on Beach Street was nothing out of the ordinary. "What? I don't see anything."

"No?" Simon questioned, beginning to feel very satisfied with himself. "Not even that Sold sign on the gray condo? The condo with three single-story units—each with two bedrooms, modern kitchen, combination living and dining rooms, laundry facilities and other amenities too numerous to mention—all designed with the retiree in mind? You don't see all of that, Miranda? Shame on you.''

Miranda took three quick steps forward, standing clear of Simon, to stare across the street at the large gray building. Her heart began to pound rapidly in her chest as she realized what Simon was saying. It *was* a perfect building—absolutely perfect!

She turned back to Simon, tears stinging at her eyes. ''Simon?'' She longed to say more, but all she could do was slowly shake her head and repeat, ''Simon?''

He slid his jacket off his shoulder and folded it neatly over one arm, then propped his fists against his hips. ''Mr. Pantoni gets the middle unit, since Mrs. O'Shaughnessy told me when I visited her last week that she doesn't mind Puccini's howling, and we already know that Mrs. Stein couldn't care less as long as she remembers to turn down her hearing aid before the opera starts.''

''I—I can't believe it!''

''You should. You started it all. Anyway, I've arranged to have all their belongings packed and moved this weekend. Oh—and the purchase price for their current homes remains the same. The condos are my way of saying I'm sorry, and I've learned my lesson. Next time I'll think of the people, too, and not just the progress or the project. I have you to thank for that, Miranda.''

"Me? I just wrote a letter," Miranda protested, but only halfheartedly. She had made a difference. And it felt good. It felt very good.

"Don't be modest, Miranda," Simon warned, taking a single step in her direction. "As a matter of fact, I have to thank you for a lot of things. Do you think fifty or sixty years of thanks will be enough...if you'll have me? Remember, it's a package deal. You, me—and Elise's half dozen grandchildren."

Miranda's bottom lip began to quiver as she gave way to happy tears. *"Oh, Simon,"* she wailed, her voice breaking as she launched herself into his arms.

Epilogue

"Good evening, Mr. Prescott, Mrs. Prescott. Lovely evening, isn't it?"

"Definitely, Jack," Simon answered, his hand at Miranda's waist as he guided her across the lobby of the Prescott Dunes and toward the private elevator leading to the penthouse floor.

"Mr. Prescott?"

Simon frowned for a moment, then turned to look toward the concierge's desk and the young woman just rising from behind it to approach, an envelope in her hand. "I'm sorry to bother you, sir, but this cable just arrived a little while ago. I was going to have it sent up to your room, but..."

"But now I'm here, so you can give it to me, instead," Simon finished for her, taking the offered envelope. "Thank you, Jennifer. Good night."

Miranda seconded Simon's farewell, giving Jennifer a wave. The two women had grown up together and Miranda knew Jennifer well. As a matter of fact, they had already made spur of the moment plans to go shopping together tomorrow.

Simon would be busy himself inspecting the construction on the newest Prescott hotel. It was the reason they had come to Cape May today in the first place, only a week after returning from their honeymoon in Paris to Simon's apartment in Atlantic City.

Bonnie, who now ran Tanner Temps while Miranda remained a silent partner, would probably go with Miranda and Jennifer, which meant they'd spend half the afternoon talking rather than shopping. It would be just like the old days, only *these* days—these three months, one week and six days, to be precise—Miranda was a happily married woman!

"Is it anything important, darling?" she asked now, nodding to indicate the envelope.

"I don't know. It's from Greece. Do we know anybody in Greece, Andi?" Simon opened the cable envelope and withdrew a single sheet of paper. "Well, I'll be damned," he said a moment later, then chuckled softly.

"Probably," Miranda answered smoothly, vainly trying to pull the cable from his fingers, "or at least you will be if you don't let me see that."

Simon deliberately held the paper out of her reach as he inserted his key to access the elevator. He motioned for Miranda to precede him before entering it himself and pushing the button that would take them to the top floor. They had only arrived in Cape May a few hours ago, and hadn't gotten farther than the lobby, having dropped off their luggage there and then immediately gone out to visit the Terrible Trio in their new homes.

Miranda snatched the cable before the doors had completely closed and began reading. "Why, it's from Elise!" she exclaimed, smiling as she remembered that her mother-in-law had written them a note a few weeks earlier that mentioned something about possibly going on a private cruise with "a few titles, a few rich commoners, and no other female under the age of forty—for I'm no fool, darlings."

"Yes. I had already figured that out. Keep going, Andi." While Miranda resumed reading the few lines, Simon smiled secretly, then pressed the Stop button before leaning one shoulder against the paneled wall of the elevator.

"Married?" Miranda exclaimed as she read Elise's cable. "I don't believe this. Elise has gotten married?"

"Again," Simon added, shaking his head. "Elise is married *again*. I think I'm beginning to spot a trend, Miranda. Do you think she's going to try for the *Guinness Book of World Records,* or will four marriages be enough? This one's got a title, though. If I remember correctly, she had a bee in her bonnet about a title just after her skiing accident. So, now she's Lady Elise Whittington. More power to her, I suppose."

"I suppose," Miranda said consideringly, "as long as she's happy. But, Simon...it says here that she's considering sending Jacqueline and Susanne to us again until she and her nobleman come to New York for Christmas."

Simon pushed himself away from the wall. "She says what? I didn't read that far."

"She also asks why she hasn't heard anything about her first grandchild yet," Miranda told him before folding the cable and handing it back to him. "Simon?" she questioned, looking up at the illuminated numbers that showed that they hadn't gone higher than the fifteenth floor. "I think we've stopped, darling."

"Yes—how about that?" His grin was devilish. There was no other word for it. "Miranda, have you noticed anything different about this elevator since we were last here?"

"Different?" Miranda looked at the closed doors, then began a slow turn, to look behind her. "No, I don't think so—*Simon!* I don't believe it! There's a *couch* in here!"

He came up behind her, sliding his arms around her waist as he buried his head in her hair. Her wind-tousled curls smelled of sweet salt air and the perfume he'd bought for her in Paris, the perfume that reminded him of spring flowers. "Yes, I know. I called this morning and had it put in here."

Miranda leaned back against him, so that he could kiss the side of her throat. "You phoned with that order?" she questioned, closing her eyes as a delighted shiver ran down her spine. "So Jennifer, Jack—*everyone* knows about this?"

"Probably," Simon answered reasonably, releasing her only long enough to guide her toward the couch. "Do you care?"

She sat down gingerly, feeling stupid yet slightly decadent. "I don't know. I mean, the last time you pushed the Stop button in this elevator, the day you proposed to me—"

"Was an exercise in frustration that gave birth to a small fantasy I became determined to live out the *next* time I got you alone in this stopped elevator," Simon finished for her. He joined her on the couch, gently lying her back against the cushions, his body pressed against hers. "So, what do you say, Mrs. Prescott?"

What *could* she say? Miranda looked up at him as he leaned over her, then slipped her arms up and around his neck, pulling him down to within a heartbeat of her smiling mouth. "I thought the game was *Simon Says.*"

"There's been a slight change of the rules," Simon told her, beginning to nibble at the side of her chin. "Now the game is *Andi Says.*"

He moved slightly, carefully insinuating himself even closer to her, then went about persuading her by kissing her fully on the mouth, a long, drugging kiss that left them both breathless. "Well?" he asked long moments later, looking deeply into her eyes.

Miranda's smile hinted at the success of his plan, and her words confirmed it. "I think I like this new game, Simon," she said, beginning to loosen his tie. "Repeat after me, darling. *Andi Says...* Lady Elise deserves a grandchild."

Simon's grin faded even as his sherry-brown eyes began to twinkle. "I love you, Miranda Prescott," he said solemnly. "I love you with all my heart."

"And I love you. You're crazy, but I love you."

Some glorious minutes later, the first of five heirs to the Prescott hotels empire became more than just a twinkle in his father's eye—right there, on a comfortable couch, somewhere between the fifteenth and sixteenth floors of the Prescott Dunes Hotel in Cape May, New Jersey.

*   *   *   *   *

> "A little Madness in the Spring
> Is wholesome even for the King."
> Emily Dickinson

SPRING

The onset of spring has certainly brought on its share of "Madness" in the male beast, but to learn that this reaction is "wholesome" is rather comforting isn't it?

Could the guy who spent the winter lying prone on the couch, watching one hundred and twelve hours of sports on the tube every weekend, really be the same guy who brought you a bouquet of daisies last Wednesday for no good reason?

Could the man in your life, who thinks the dollar movie and a bag of popcorn is a big deal, be the same man who announced that he's taking a week off—and the two of you are going to spend that week lying under a romantic moon on some Caribbean island?

Could the fella who tells you he wants "to see the world" before he settles down be the same fella who stops at every baby carriage as you walk together through the park, just so he can make inane *goo-goo* talk to each drooling, giggling infant?

Yes, he could. If it's spring.

For the spring is the season of rebirth, of budding, of nesting.

And billing and cooing. For heaven's sake—don't forget the billing and cooing!

What seems impossible during those long, drab months of winter, too energetic for words as he drags himself through the dog days of summer, and left too late as the leaves begin to fall in autumn, all seems perfectly logical to the male in this wonderful season of spring.

Even if you see spring as the time to pack away your

woolies and break out the lawn food and sheer curtains, remember that the male in your life sees spring in an *entirely* different way. So put those mundane chores on the back burner and pull out your prettiest clothes, your most alluring perfume—and maybe even your dancing shoes. The land is coming to life, the juices are beginning to flow again and that fantastic guy, that special man, that terrific fella—that usually elusive, yet wonderful ''King of Beasts''—is out for a little ''wholesome madness.''

Now just *fancy* that!

Kasey Michaels